A Dance Macabre

NAOMI LOUD

A Dance Macabre Copyright © 2024 by Naomi Loud

All rights reserved.

No part of this book may be used or reproduced in any manner whatsoever without written permission except in the case of brief quotations embodies in critical articles or reviews and certain noncommercial use permitted by copyright law.

This book is a work of fiction. Names, characters, businesses, organizations, places, events, and incidents either are the product of the author's imagination or are used fictitiously. Any resemblance to actual persons, living or dead, events, or locales is entirely coincidental.

FIRST EDITION

Cover Design: Cat at TRC Designs

Editing: Louise Johnson, Literary Maiden Editing

Proofreading: @shanireads

www.naomiloud.com

AUTHOR'S NOTE

WARNING: These characters are **extremely morally black**. They do not have a single redeemable bone in their bodies (yes even the FMC, she's kind of the worst one of the bunch if we're being honest). These characters will act in heinous ways toward innocent people throughout this book and STILL get their happy ending. Even if you have loved my books in the past: Please be warned that **this is by far my darkest book**. This story is fiction and I do not condone in any way shape or form my characters' actions and behaviors throughout this story. If you do not enjoy seeing the villains win, I implore you to turn around now. But if you're still here reading this, and excited to meet the villainous pair, then buckle up baby, and welcome to the Perverse City series.

This is a **dark romance**. It deals with heavy subject matter and may contain triggering situations such as gore, maiming, cremation, dismemberment, decapitation, cheeky non-con drugs (trust me they'll be happy about it in the end), oppressive ruling body, hunting humans for sport, ritual sacrifice, public defilement of a corpse (non-sexual), public executions, murder, blood (lots of it), attempted drowning, dubious consent, reverse glory hole, impact play, blood play, knife play, exhibitionism, anonymous sex, bondage.

To my teenage self.
The one who didn't think she was going to make it ...
I'm so happy that you chose to fight instead.
Because look at us now.

The only pain in pleasure is the pleasure of pain.

— ANNE RICE

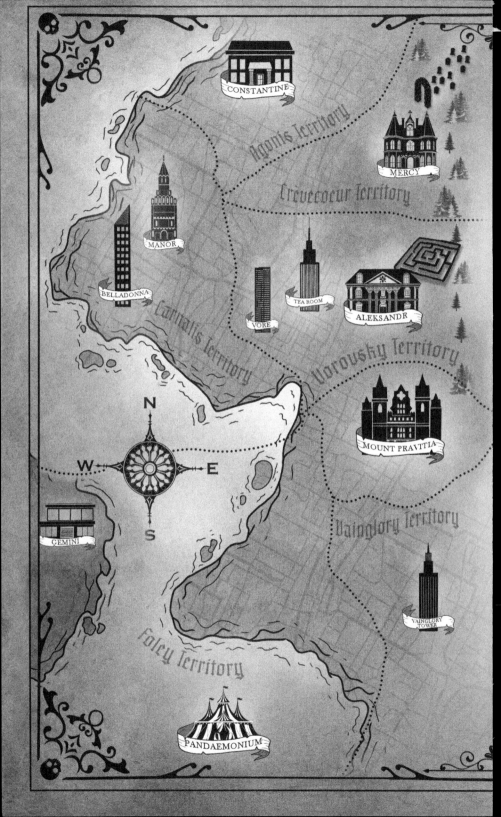

Vainglory

Vane-glor-ee

OMNIA VANITAS

All is vanity

Crèvecoeur

Krev-kur

MORS MIHI LUCRUM

Death is my reward

Vorovsky

Pravitia

Pra-vit-tee-a

Vor-ov-skee

MELIUS NIMIUM QUAM NON SATIS

Better too much than not enough

Foley

Folee

MUNDUS FALLI VULT SIC FALLATUR

The world wants to be deceived, so let it be deceived

Agonis

A-gaw-nis

CAEDES EST UBIQUE

There is slaughter everywhere

Carnalis

Kar-na-lis

SINE LIBIDINE NON EST VITA

Without lust there is no life

1

MERCY

*T*he first death I ever experienced was my own.

Ripped out of my mother's womb by sterile gloved hands and forced to take my first breath into this vile, repulsive world.

I've been dying ever since.

We all have.

Because what is life, if not just a series of small deaths until the inevitable end?

No one ever sees it coming.

This one laying before me certainly didn't.

"*Gods be damned*," I mumble under my breath.

Blood is dripping by my heels. I take a small step to my right, avoiding the growing puddle slowly leaking onto the onyx marble floors.

I peevishly eye the body thrown over the metal gurney.

It was a man before it became a lifeless corpse. Now it's just a worthless amalgamation of skin, muscles, and sinews—soon to become pulverized bones and ashes.

That'll teach him to try to break into *my* Grounds and dare to touch *my* things.

Death, the great teacher.

I wonder if he sensed it.

I wonder if he felt the air shift, the *swish* of life's pendulum taking its last majestic swing before my dagger found its home between his ribs. If I were one for whimsy, I'd keep jars full of all the dying breaths I've ever had the pleasure to bear witness to. I'm certain they would create a morbidly beautiful symphony, like seeking the sounds of the ocean inside a seashell.

With a sigh, I walk over and turn on the cremator.

The giant stainless steel cube was an eye-sore until I had a custom carved stone covering made for it. Now it matches the muted tones of the room, the dark space, vast in size, but hidden underground.

I value my privacy.

Walking back to the gurney, my eye snags on the flickering candlelight reflecting on the dead man's signet ring. The sound of my heels echoes as I speed up to reach for his cold hand. The sigil engraved into the gold is a symbol I recognize immediately: A hand, palm facing down, with strings tied and hanging from the tips of the fingers.

I groan out loud, pinching the bridge of my nose.

This is the last thing I need.

I clench my fists, stiletto nails digging into my palm, bristling at the thought of who must be behind this. With impatient jerks, I try to tug the ring off of the man's pinky finger but it's stuck. Huffing under my breath, I stalk to the drawer full of surgical instruments and pull out an autopsy bone saw, then press the blade to his skin just below the ring, cutting through the bone. Placing the finger to the side, I wheel the body into the cremator, the flames catching onto the clothes in seconds.

I usually take pleasure in watching them burn. I savor death with pride and reverence.

But today, I barely glance at the flames. My mind seethes

with irritation as I throw the severed finger into my purse and exit the room, texting Jeremial, my valet, to ready the town car.

THE CITY OF PRAVITIA IS BUSTLING WITH GLIMMERS OF LIFE, THE stars above overshadowed by a plethora of artificial lights. Thankfully, the town car windows are tinted and soundproof, otherwise I'd also hear the *relentless* existence of life. Loud, grating, and never ceasing to aggravate me. I'd kill every Pravitian to cross my path if it meant I could seek out a single moment of peace in this damnable city.

From beneath my large fringe-rimmed hat, I barely glance at the passing landscape. I know the curves and corners of every building, every street corner.

This city is my birthright, every death within it belongs to me, and I have no doubt Pravitia will also bear witness to my death.

The vehicle finally stops in front of Vainglory Tower and I roll my eyes, my temper spiking now that we've arrived. The building is as gaudy as the man himself. With its gold-trimmed facade, it pierces into the dark sky, flourished with garish statues of long-dead ancestors flanking the entrance.

The car door opens, and Jeremial appears. I've never seen him out of a black suit, blond curls framing his face. He offers his hand, assisting me onto the dirty streets. With a defeated sigh, I smooth out my black sheath dress and readjust my leather gloves up my elbows before taking my first step toward the building.

The guards spring up when they see me enter. I don't bother announcing myself and they know better than to stop me. As I cut through the expansive lobby, with its imposing chandelier hanging above me and elaborate murals depicting the Vainglory family history, I pass a trickle of his most devoted followers exiting the building. My lip lifts in a disdainful snarl.

Peasants.

Thankfully, this must mean I've missed the last of their adoration.

And it means I know exactly where to find the vile creature.

If I had the patience for beauty, I'd describe the Vainglory bathhouse as breathtaking. Rows of Corinthian columns on either side disappear into the water, fresco paintings of intricate celestial depictions sprawl the entire ceiling. Three large chandeliers hang above the body of water, and hundreds of candles line the walls, bathing the room with warm light.

However, the decor is quickly forgotten when my eyes begrudgingly land on a naked lithe body amidst the steamy water. I sneer, my heartbeat rising.

Wolfgang.

Heir to Vainglory Media and its entire god-forsaken fortune.

He faces me, wet brown hair slicked back, tanned arms sprawled out beside him as he leans against the edge of the bath. Luckily, he hasn't noticed me yet, eyes closed while his head falls backward between his shoulders. Approaching him, I remove my hat and set it down on one of the small tables that I pass, the soft classical music muffling the click of my steps.

When I'm at a close enough distance, I pull out the severed finger that I've carelessly shoved into my purse and whip it at his face, hitting him square between the eyes.

That certainly catches his attention.

I find a sliver of satisfaction at seeing that blood from the finger has left a smear on his forehead. He looks ridiculous as he sputters like a dying fish, his gray-blue eyes finally landing on me. His gaze turns cold, as a sneer similar to mine pulls at his lip, revealing a gold canine and incisor to the right of his mouth.

I don't allow him the pleasure to speak first.

"One of your lackeys broke into the Grounds."

Silence coils between us like a living, breathing thing.

"Is that an accusation, Crèvecoeur?" he finally drawls, his voice rough with ire.

I cross my arms. "It's a fact."

Breaking our stare, his eyes dip to the finger now bobbing in the water in front of him. He retrieves it with only his index and thumb as if genuinely repulsed. I puff out an annoyed breath. It's not as if he hasn't touched a dead appendage countless times before. Peering at his family sigil clearly carved on the signet ring, he shrugs and throws the finger over his shoulder. It lands with a thunk against the back wall.

His expression morphs into boredom, his gaze fixed straight ahead as he resumes his relaxed pose, still naked and unbothered, arms outstretched. "I can't be held responsible for what my employees are caught doing on their own time." He yawns.

I scoff at his response.

"Oh? And it wouldn't have anything to do with what's coming up next month?" My hands land firmly on my hips. "Is this your dimwitted attempt at keeping the peace?"

My anger spikes knowing we've been warned to stay civil in the months leading up to the Lottery. That imbecilic rule. I wish I could kill him instead.

His deep laugh is so condescending that my fingers twitch, itching to pull out my dagger and stab him in the eye with it.

"Please," he says, his eyes lazily sliding to find mine. His grin turns sinister. "Why would I care about your silly little secrets," he says while his eyelids flutter closed, head tilted back as if dismissing me.

The rage that engulfs me feels like tapping into an ancient

bottomless well. I blindly let it dictate my actions like a puppet on strings. It only takes a split second for me to scan the room, noticing his robe draped over a chair nearby. I lurch for it, quickly wrenching the satin belt out of its loops and twisting it around my hands.

Right as he cracks an eye to see what I'm up to, I wrap the sash around his neck from behind, and jam one of my heels between his shoulder blades, pulling him backward. His choked gasp is almost as delicious as the sound of a dying breath. I've caught him by surprise, his legs thrashing in the water while his fingers claw at his throat, eyes widening in shock.

I smile down at him, tightening the belt. "I pray when death beckons you home, I am there to witness it," I rasp tauntingly. He's choking. It's beautiful. "I will be the first to dance on your grave."

Finally getting a finger between the sash and his neck, Wolfgang manages to push one croaked word out of his full lips.

"*Mercy.*"

2

WOLFGANG

*A*s soon as she hears her name, she releases me, acting as if her name is god-like, imbued with any real power.

Self-aggrandizing bitch.

I wheeze in a long, noisy inhale, hand to my throat. It takes me a few seconds to regain my bearings. When the oxygen finally travels back up into my brain, I spring up from the water, stark naked and *livid*.

But it's too late, Mercy is already marching out the doors, her ridiculous hat plopped back over her long black hair. I whip my wet hair out of my eyes, still breathing hard as I listen to the goading clacks of her heels on the marble floor.

She's a plague, a grotesque blight on the city I wish I could erase.

Oh, how I wish I could just kill her—collect her blood in vials, trickle it into the bath water like an expensive oil, and *soak* in it. I'd take great joy in her death. Turn it into a holiday.

Unfortunately, it's not that simple.

Lifetimes of tradition bind us together.

Our families have been feuding for as long as I can remember, but still, we rule the city together. It's how it always has been, and how it always will be.

Pravitia is ours.

But gods be damned if I enjoy sharing it with a brute like her.

My fingers linger on my throat, miffed at the thought of Mercy leaving my unblemished skin marred and bruised. I step out of the bath and shrug my robe over my shoulders, keeping it open as I retrieve the severed finger from the floor.

I didn't want to admit it openly to Mercy, but the signet ring piqued my interest. Unlike what she presumes, I wasn't purposely trying to dig up dirt on her. Besides, we've known each other our entire lives, I wouldn't need an inconsequential plebeian to do my bidding.

I would have taken great delight in breaking into her Grounds myself.

But if someone from my staff *is* sniffing around, I should be the first one to know.

Bartholomew, my thirty-something assistant, is standing on guard next to the exit. Undoubtedly, he's witnessed my spat with Mercy, but having been under my employ for a few years now, he knows better than to intervene. I press the finger into his palm. He swallows hard, his freckled face blanching as I give him a quick pat on the cheek.

"Find out who this belonged to, will you?"

It's past midnight when I stroll barefoot into the Hall of Mirrors, my hands in the pockets of my red velvet smoking jacket. The vast hall, with its vaulted ceilings, dozen bay windows, and matching arched gold mirrors on either side, is my favorite part of Vainglory Tower. It connects my living quarters to the public areas of my apartments.

I come here when I need to think. Something about staring at my reflection calms me. I'd be remiss to pinpoint my favorite feature. Everything about me is eye-catching. Delightful even. It reminds me of my own excellence. The magnificence of Wolfgang Vainglory.

I need a pick-me-up, especially after my tiresome scuffle with Mercy earlier.

I loathe to think that there was an additional motive in her barging into my bathhouse.

Today of all days.

She knew the importance. She knew it was *my* day. But Mercy is as selfish as any of us, even if she likes to pretend that some of our customs are beneath her.

There's a buzz under my skin. It's a peculiar sensation, one that is only summoned on days like these. And even if I'm accustomed to it, it still leaves me restless.

Walking up to a cushioned bench pushed close to one of the bay windows, I lift the seat, revealing a red leather violin case inside.

Playing the violin always manages to help with this *itchy* restlessness. Something about creating melodies appeases the chatter. I've never questioned it. Maybe the music connects me with something divine, a private conversation between me and the muses.

Although, I'd be hard-pressed to find anything more divine than myself.

I take the violin out and slip it between my shoulder and chin. Closing my eyes, I let the silence surrounding me take a long, slow breath as I do the same. Placing the bow against the strings, I begin to play, keeping my eyes shut during the first few strikes of the cords. When I hear the haunting notes bounce off the windows and walls, vaulting straight back into my ears, I open my eyes and gaze directly into the mirror.

It's a powerful experience to gaze at one's divinity.

I study my reflection: Jaw clenched under a short trimmed beard, brown hair slicked back aside from a few strands falling onto my forehead due to the erratic movements of my arm.

I stare and play and stare and play and stare and play ...

Until I begin to experience it.

That vague and uncanny feeling.

It's a heady but peculiar thing, and it happens when I gaze into a mirror for too long.

It starts staring back.

Reality bleeds into the imaginary, and I'm left wondering who is real. My reflection begins to feel like something wholly apart from myself.

Maybe I'm the one stuck inside a mirror.

And maybe, just maybe, I'm the mirrored rendering of this other Wolfgang.

The ego falters. It questions.

But then I close my eyes. And the heart beating wildly inside my chest, the lungs supplying sweet oxygen to my blood, they remind me who I am.

What I'm *worth*. And what my birthright as a Vainglory entails.

Then I begin to lose myself in the music all over again.

The restlessness turns into something a lot closer to *life*, the notes seeping into my skin, and charging me, enlivening me as my mind races alongside the melody.

There's no greater feeling than privately communing between me and the Self.

I let the last note stretch and whine, much longer than the song asks for.

Then it's over. I drop my arm and the silence returns.

All is quiet.

I take a deep breath and give a small bow, my reflection mirroring me.

I take another long moment to study myself.

It's intoxicating. Mesmerizing.

Then I return the violin to its case and place it back inside the bench, leaving the Hall of Mirrors with a renewed sense of tranquility.

3

MERCY

My heeled boots echo through the alley, grit crunching under my soles as I turn onto the main avenue heading toward Manor, a high-end strip club located inside an old turn-of-the-century building. Pravitia is a blur of noise and lights this evening, bursting with the never-ending humdrum of *life*. I clench my jaw, shoving a pedestrian out of my way. Even with people dying every day, this world is still dreadfully overpopulated.

As I get closer, I see the line wraps around the corner. A crowd of unlucky commoners who've been refused entry congregate on the sidewalk near the entrance just for a glimpse of something special.

Like a glimpse at one of the heirs from the six ruling families.

The paparazzis' cameras are aimed my way, my jaded glare clearly not a deterrent for these vultures as their flashing lights make me wince. My dagger beckons me from beneath my black mini skirt, throbbing against my thigh as if sentient, reminding me I could kill any of these loafers in a heartbeat.

Naturally skipping the line, eager heads turn when I walk

up to the bouncer as he quickly ushers me in. Shrugging off my leather overcoat, I fling it to an attendant, readjusting my bustier as I walk down the dark corridor, a cold stare permanently etched on my face.

Entering the main room, I let the drum of bass travel through me, the music some kind of ethereal electronica, enveloping the space within a dreamy, gothic atmosphere.

Manor doesn't irritate me like most places. If forced to leave the Grounds, it might as well be to come here. With the club's high capacity, the crowd is always a considerable one. And with the high arched ceilings and massive dance floor, it's easy to blend into anonymity.

Even as Mercy Crèvecoeur.

Sweeping my gaze across the dark-lit space, I ignore the naked masked dancers on the stages flanking the dance floor, the patrons drunk on booze and lust, and the noticeable buzz of energy that always seems to hang in the air here.

My attention snags on a man sitting on one of the sunken black velvet couches near the main bar to my left. I study him as he naively enjoys his night, eyes closed, head thrown back in ecstasy while he gets his dick sucked by a muscular blond wearing a tight patent leather outfit.

I know something he doesn't.

It's the same timeless awareness as usual, tickling at the back of my neck.

He won't last the night.

But he's a mere nick in the stream of my thoughts and I don't bother lingering on his existence.

My patience begins to wane, my jaw clenching, as I look for the one person who I specifically came here for. She's a goddess amongst mortals, it shouldn't be this hard to locate her. My eyes finally land on the redhead sitting at the bar, her white bell-sleeve dress practically glowing against the dark decor, her pale breasts nearly spilling out from the corset pushing them up.

To my dismay, I watch her grab a random clubgoer by the arm, pulling them into a kiss. They seem frozen, arms to their sides but don't appear to resist, lured into an impassioned embrace by lust herself. I audibly groan at the revolting public display but still make my way to her, irritation drumming louder than the bass under my skin. Snatching the useless rube she's kissing by the collar, I rip them off her and shove them into the crowd.

"Belladonna," I declare peevishly, trying to snap her out of her lascivious daze as I perch myself onto the stool next to her, crossing my arms.

After a few seconds, her green eyes finally snap to mine, pupils blown, cheeks pink as if she's just taken a hit of a stimulant. She lets out a small *whoop*, moaning in delight as her hand lands on my shoulder. "I needed that," she says with a sated sigh.

I brush her hand off me and snap at the bartender. He jumps when he realizes my attention is on him and hurriedly gets to work on my dirty vodka martini.

"I didn't think you'd come," Belladonna says over the music, taking a slow sip from her pink Cosmopolitan, red lipstick staining the rim.

I shoot her a glare, eyebrows pinched. "It's your birthday."

"I know *that*," she says with a chuckle, shaking her head slightly from side to side, making her copper hair shimmer in waves down her back. Her scintillating eyes land back on me. "When did that ever matter to you?"

I pinch my lips and look away, tapping my nails on the bar. The bartender has time to hand me my drink before I speak again.

When my gaze slides back to Belladonna, she's busy flirtatiously waving at someone she knows across the bar, and for a moment I catch a glimpse of why every last peasant here is enraptured with her.

"I was feeling ... restless," I say with slight disdain.

"Oh? Did you want to book a private room?" she asks with a slight raise of her brows, then her face turns mischievous. "It's been a while."

I shake my head and take a sip of my martini. "I'm just—" I can't control the scowl appearing on my face, reluctant to tell her about what happened. "One of Vainglory's idiots broke into my house last week."

Just the taste of his name on my tongue makes me want to spit in someone's face, or kill an unsuspecting fool—whichever one will assuage this lingering feeling of vulnerability smarting in my chest.

Belladonna's interest is piqued. She cocks her head. "Why?"

"I'm not sure." I let out an annoyed sigh. "I didn't realize he was part of Vainglory's inner circle before—"

She interrupts me. "You killed him," she says with a soft laugh, not missing a beat and needing no confirmation. She takes another small sip of her drink. "Are you going to try to get some answers?"

"Already tried." My lips twitch into something resembling a smile. "He claims to know nothing about it."

She studies me for half a second, then laughs. "I bet you took that well."

Shrugging, I glance around the room before answering. "Strangled him with the belt of his robe."

Belladonna snickers, her gaze filled with mischief.

"Enough with that," I say with a lazy wave of the hand, disinterested in talking about *him* for longer than I need to. "This isn't the point of my visit."

I try to focus on Belladonna but I'm distracted by someone trying to squeeze into the space behind me at the bar. Turning around, I grab them by the throat. My nails jab into their skin while the sharp tip of my dagger digs into their chin.

Their eyes widen in fear when they realize their careless mistake.

"Touch me again, and I'll sever your head and use it as a lawn ornament," I hiss.

Releasing them from my grip, I send them flying backward into the crowd. They fearfully scramble away, spilling people's drinks in the process.

I swivel back around just as Belladonna pulls out a small pocket mirror from her clutch, smoothing a finger over her plump lips and fixing her wavy hair. There's a lull in the sound of the crowd around us. It's an awed, reverent silence. Heads turn to watch Belladonna simply exist, entrapped by her divine beauty. It's like watching a masterpiece being painted in real time. Although she holds no power over me, her beauty is still a magnetizing force that cannot be denied.

Clicking the small mirror shut, she sighs. "I'm bored."

She glances around the club, her expression switching into perverse delight when she turns back to me, her eyes dancing with glee. "Let's have some fun."

She takes my hand, pulling me up on my feet, and I follow her with a huff. The kind of *fun* Belladonna is insinuating is unpredictable, especially at one of her clubs—but who am I to deny her on her birthday?

4

WOLFGANG

"Anything good today, Bartholomew?" I ask from behind closed eyelids as I enjoy my morning soak in my private bathhouse, my body submerged in warm milky waters.

Smaller than the main bathhouse, it is still just as decadent. Frescoes painted in vivid colors adorn the walls and ceilings, depicting lush sceneries of extravagant revelry.

My favorite painting has always been the one near the north-facing window. It's of a naked figure gazing into a hand-held ornate mirror. It reminds me of myself. Just like these frescoes, I provide beauty to a drab Pravitia.

My head rests on the stony edge of the bath, my face slathered with essential oils, mixed with a healthy dash of blood graciously provided by Constantine, whose family has collected it from Pravitian denizens for centuries. It's said to keep the skin young and dewy, and I am not above any beauty practice that promises eternal youth.

I hear my assistant clear his throat somewhere near my head. While I wait for Bartholomew to answer my question I take a long deep breath, inhaling the sweet floral aromas wafting up like a soothing embrace.

"Slow news day, I'm afraid," he finally says, "A few articles of you attending different soirees around town." I detect a small tremble in his voice as if worried about my reaction to his answer.

"How do they describe me?" I ask, my eyes still closed.

Bartholomew falls silent, most likely skimming over the words printed in the newspaper he's reading from. "One describes you as 'divinely flawless' and another as 'magnetically intoxicating'."

I hum, letting the words sink in. "That will do," I drawl.

I listen to scissors cutting through paper, and then footsteps on the bathhouse marble floor before I open my eyes. Bartholomew delicately places the cut-out articles into the water amidst the floating milkflowers, submerging the paper to break the fibrous substance apart with his fingers. When he's satisfied with his work, he drags his hand in the water and mixes the paper with the bathwater.

I let out a satisfied sigh, visualizing the words from the articles seeping into my skin. "*Omnia vanitas*," I say under my breath. Closing my eyes once again, I dismiss my assistant. "Leave."

"Yes, sir," he chirps before I hear his steps scuttle out of the room.

AFTER MY SOAK, FOLLOWED BY AN HOUR-LONG BODY MASSAGE, I stroll into my bedchamber naked; skin moisturized and muscles loose. With the large arched windows facing the rising sun, and the thick crimson curtains open, the early morning rays dance across the room as I make my way to the canopy bed.

Everything about Vainglory Tower has been decorated to our family's opulent standards—my private quarters especially. The gold coffered ceiling alone took a year to build. And the two hand-carved marble mantelpieces took just as long.

A pair of satin pajama bottoms has been laid out for me on the bed and I put them on before reaching for my phone on the bedside table. With a few quick taps, I put on a modern rendering of Vivaldi's *Il piacere*, the music spilling out of the surround sound speakers in the corners of the ceiling. I take a few seconds to savor the smooth, timeless violin notes before I make my way to the Hall of Mirrors. The melody follows me into the vast, empty space, the speakers connecting the music even here.

Barefoot, I relish the feeling of the morning sun's heat against the soles of my feet as I make my way to the small mat left for me in the middle of the hall. I settle onto the floor cross-legged, facing one of the mirrors. The sun warms my bare back as I begin a long series of stretches, my body backlit as I gaze upon my reflection. First my arms and torso, then my legs. I fall into a meditative state as I feel the soothing burn of my muscles being pulled and stretched.

"Sir?" Bartholomew says tentatively from the door connecting the Hall of Mirrors to the receiving room.

My gaze slices to him, my brows knitting in irritation while my body is still stretched into my final pose.

He audibly gulps before continuing, "You have a meeting in half an hour."

Letting my arms drop to a relaxed position, I sigh wistfully. *Work.*

Without bothering to answer, I stand up and stroll back into my private quarters while I mentally decide on an outfit for today's meeting.

Having decided on a burgundy three-piece suit paired with my favorite cream wing-tipped shoes, I make my way down to the second floor, ten stories below my private quarters. Most of the lower levels of the Tower are dedicated to the family business: Vainglory Media.

The only source of news and entertainment permitted in Pravitia.

Walking into the large library where the meeting is taking place, dozens of eyes shift to me—as they should—as I head for the long table, near the mosaic window. The dozen or so chairs are filled by my inner circle at Vainglory Media, all of them wearing the same signet ring. My family sigil.

Sitting at the head of the table, I give Dizzy, my right hand, a swift nod signaling her to begin the meeting. I try not to drift off as she fills me in on our most pressing affairs until finally something she says catches my attention and I spring forward in my seat, cutting her off.

"What do you mean you *don't know*?" I grit out.

Dizzy's dark eyes flash me a defensive look but she answers my question in a calm and steady voice. "I had our best men investigate Mercy's *alleged* break-in and they still came up empty-handed, we can't seem to find who this belonged to."

She delicately places the signet ring on the sandalwood table, an identical ring on her left pinky, and slowly clasps her hands together waiting for a response.

It would be an easy matter if only my most trusted wore the Vainglory sigil. Like Dizzy sitting beside me. She's been working for me since she turned eighteen a decade ago.

But the ring is worn by everyone employed at Vainglory Media, and I can barely remember the names of the ones sitting at this very table.

"Does it matter?" Marcus asks with a laugh, seemingly trying to break the tension.

My glare slides to him, sitting a few chairs down. Shocked

murmurs ripple across the room but Marcus seems unfazed. Emboldened by the longevity of his employment. Or the fact that he's a distant cousin by marriage.

In truth, I understand why he dared to ask such a question: Why would I be bothered by anything to do with Mercy? I'm not.

But it's the way he undermined me by saying those words out loud.

I continue to stare him down while I suck on my teeth, my fingers drumming both armrests. I detect the exact moment when he realizes his error. He practically *shrinks* in his poorly tailored suit. Abruptly, I stand up, fishing out my favorite fountain pen from my vest pocket, the cap flying off.

Marcus is either a complete idiot or fear has rooted him to his chair while I stalk toward him because he doesn't move an inch before I have the sharp tip of my pen lodged in his cheek.

Oh, but now? He shrieks like a banshee, eyes wide with terror, while the sound of chair legs scraping on expensive hardwood floors reverberates around the room as everyone else gives us a wide berth. While Marcus is still frozen in his seat, I use the leverage of my shoe against his chest to forcibly pull the pen out of his bleeding face.

His screams turn into a wet gurgled gasp when my second blow sinks into his carotid. This time when I remove the pen from his neck, the blood sprays onto my face and suit. Flicking my hair back out of my eyes, I lick my lips, tasting the coppery tang, and kick his slumping body along with his chair down to the floor.

Straightening back up, I take a long, centering breath. Pulling out my pocket square, I carefully unfold it and slowly wipe my face and neck. I delicately fold it back and return the pocket square to its rightful place before smoothing my hands over my tie and turning my attention to Dizzy. Her expression is hard, but she doesn't say anything.

"I don't care who broke into Crèvecoeur's property," I tell her with a trace of boredom in my tone. "You can consider the matter settled." Throwing my bloody pen on the table, it rolls toward her. She stops it with her own pen. The silence in the library is decadently thick while her eyes meet mine waiting for me to speak again. "Clean this for me, will you?"

5

WOLFGANG

*D*izzy drapes herself over my shoulder, her fingers trailing over the black vicuña wool of my sports coat as we pose for the paparazzi outside of Vore. She doesn't smile but knows exactly the right angles for the camera to heighten her natural beauty.

Like a siren resurfacing from the ocean depths, her black shoulder-length hair is smoothed back with gel, the silver of her suit reflecting the flashing lights like liquid mercury, and the plunging cleavage under her suit jacket could lure in a lot more than just wayward sailors.

She's a perfect accessory for an evening out. One I use quite regularly.

We've always made a good pair for the tabloids.

But that's as far as our relationship goes. Just another illusion for the Pravitia cannibals always hungry for more vapid gossip, something to sedate themselves with until their next hit.

As a Vainglory, I'll happily be the one to supply it.

I flash the crowd one last dazzling smile before ushering

Dizzy inside with a hand to the small of her back. As much as I adore the attention, they are not the reason I am here tonight.

It's just after midnight and the place is packed as always. Vore is one of many exclusive supper clubs and restaurants owned by the Vorovsky family around the city.

The lights are dim, candlelight dancing against countless faces while inebriated laughter and the clink of glasses rise up from busy tables. The crowd seems to pay no mind to the half-dressed burlesque acrobats perched on large swings hanging from the ceiling, lazily swaying this way and that, diamonds dripping from their necks and wrists.

I scan the dark green booths in the far corner of the room until my gaze falls on Aleksandr. He proves to be an easy mark to find tonight, his open Hawaiian shirt garish and loud compared to the stylish crowd surrounding him. I roll my eyes at the offense. The dress code never seems to apply to him—not when his last name is Vorovsky.

Turning to Dizzy still standing next to me, I hand her my credit card between two fingers.

"Indulge yourself. You deserve it after today."

I'm sure Marcus' blood wasn't easy to wash out of my suit. Nor the disposal of his body for that matter. She quirks half a smile but keeps her expression flat before taking the card out of my hand and walking away.

Ignoring the maître d', I stroll across the room, the crowd effortlessly parting to make way for me. Aleksandr spots me as I approach the table, his half-lidded gaze dancing over me. His mustache quirks up as a slow smirk appears on his face.

"The prodigal son," he drawls when I finally reach the booth. His gaze snaps to the small group sitting around the table. "Out."

They scamper like mice, emptying the booth in seconds. Sliding in, I accept the vodka on ice that Aleksandr hands me and take a slow sip. Not my usual drink of choice, but it'll do.

My gaze lingers on my childhood friend, studying him. He tilts his head, hazel eyes sparkling mischievously, waiting for me to say something, the ring on his thumb rapping on the table as he idly drums his fingers.

"Aren't you going to introduce me?" I finally say, with a raised eyebrow.

His head falls back against the booth, slowly chuckling. "Trust me, they know who you are." His snicker turns into a pleased groan, his hand disappearing under the table. "I can feel the tremble in their lips around my cock." His eyes fall back on me. "Turns me on."

I roll my eyes. "I don't need a play-by-play, Sasha," I say, using the nickname I've had for him since childhood while I take another sip of vodka.

Aleksandr's mouth curls, eyelids fluttering shut for half a second and I let him enjoy himself before speaking again.

"Have you begun the preparations?"

He keeps his head resting behind him as his relaxed gaze finds mine. "For the Feast of Fools or the Lottery?"

My eyes skate over the crowd, before answering. "Both."

His tattooed throat works around a swallow, and he slowly licks his lips as if thinking. "Preparations for the Feast of Fools are underway, nothing I can't handle," he says with a bored wave of his hand. "As for the Lottery, I'm sure my mother will inform us at the Conclave next week. Besides," His grin turns dark, "None of us are truly in charge of that, are we?"

"Indeed." My laugh is dry. "But your family has been in power for more than half of your life. You must have some apprehensions about the whole—" I pause as if searching for the next words. "*Exchange* of power."

Aleksandr smooths his tongue over his teeth. He's about to respond when he jolts slightly forward, closing his eyes and letting out a satisfied guttural hum. He falls back into the booth, his heavy gaze dreamy and slightly unfocused.

I give him a deadpan stare, waiting.

"Did you want to partake?" he asks instead of answering my question.

I stare at him some more, trying to wordlessly relay how annoying I think he's being.

Finally, I sigh. "Who is it?" Breaking eye contact, I take a peek under the table to satiate my curiosity.

I wouldn't agree to just *anyone*.

Satisfied with who's under the table, I give Aleksandr a quick nod. "They will do."

He settles into the booth looking cheerful as if excited to be sharing one of his favorite toys.

While deft hands open my trousers and pull out my cock, Aleksandr finally returns to the subject at hand. "I'm not nervous about the Lottery per se ... more morbidly curious to see which family will feud next," he says with a mocking laugh. "What if it's us?"

I flash him an agreeing look but ignore his question. "I'm sure everyone will be on edge until then." My grip tightens around the sweating tumbler, arousal shooting up my spine as a wet mouth swallows deeply around my hard shaft.

"Not to mention that the Carnalis haven't been in the same room with my family in a little under nineteen years," he adds.

I refresh my glass with more ice from the small bucket on the table, mulling over what he just said. My eyes meet his. "Similar to the six of us. We must have been children the last time we were all in one room together."

Aleks scoffs but his hazel eyes twinkle with mischief. "Let the fun begin."

I let out a moan, placing my hand on top of the head bobbing up and down under the table. Biting my lip, I regain some composure. "Speaking of — did you hear about Crèvecoeur?" I ask with a small hiss to my tone.

"Mercy? What about her?" Aleksandr responds while he signals for another vodka bottle for the table.

"Someone wearing my sigil broke into the Grounds last week."

His eyebrows dip in confusion. "Under whose orders? Yours?"

Irritation spikes. As it always does when on the subject of Mercy Crèvecoeur. "Why would I want anything to do with that brute?" I say through gritted teeth.

Chuckling, he takes a sip of his drink. "My thoughts exactly." He lets out a small sigh, looking up at the ceiling seeming to think it through. "I wouldn't dwell on it too much. Pravitians are always a little ... unruly before a Lottery." A savage darkness falls over his eyes. "Something in the air."

I let his words linger between us before my lips curl into a vicious smile, raising my glass in a toast. "*Sunt superis sua iura,*" I declare.

Aleksandr snickers, clinking his glass with mine. "*Sunt superis sua iura,*" he repeats.

6

MERCY

The weather is dreary tonight, the sky darkened by clouds pregnant with rain. If I were fanciful enough to have a favorite kind of weather—this would be it.

The leaves crunch under my booted feet as I wind through the path up to the Crèvecoeur cemetery entrance, located on the north corner of the Grounds, my three Dobermans trotting alongside me.

The cemetery is the only place where my thoughts seem to make sense—the only place where I feel remotely relaxed and at ease. I am drawn to it almost nightly. There is peace in death, and silence is a true friend to where death lies sleeping.

I enter through the arched copper gate turned green with age. It's permanently open, welcoming a never-ending queue of the dearly departed. Walking onto the consecrated grounds feels like walking through a thick veil. It's as if the spirits cloak the cemetery with an invisible barrier, and the draining noise of Pravitia is divinely left behind.

The large granite gargoyles guarding the entrance are weather-worn, the forest surrounding the cemetery slowly engulfing them. Like the earth itself grows weary of these imposing man-made structures and tries to reclaim its rightful place.

Continuing on the overgrown path, my gaze sweeps over the familiar tombstones, some with vines crawling up their facade like venomous snakes, some half-tipped over as if frozen in time and space. I don't let the groundskeeper upkeep the cemetery much. There is beauty in decay, in letting nature take its course.

Sundae circles my feet, ears perked up, tongue out, while Éclair and Truffles run around the tombstones close by, nipping at each other as they play-fight. I throw a femur far into the cemetery and Sundae bolts, sprinting to fetch it.

Naming the dogs after desserts was never my idea. I practically crawl out of my skin every time I have to utter their imbecilic names aloud. But all three never answered to anything else ever since Constantine brought them to me as puppies.

Housing the dogs was meant to be temporary—a favor for a friend. I never thought I'd keep them forever, but somewhere in the two years I've had them, I've grown … fond of them.

At the very least, they are much better companions than humans.

Sundae bounds back toward me, the clink of her diamond collar piercing the silence around us as she drops the bone at my feet. Picking it up, I pull my arm back, readying for another throw when I freeze, my arm still up in the air. Nearby, Éclair and Truffles stop in their tracks, pointed ears perked up as if trying to discern what I'm experiencing, while Sundae lets out a low growl at my feet.

I sniff the air, more as a reflex than actually picking up on anything other than the familiar earthy perfume of the Crèvecoeur cemetery. I can still sense it though—the call. The incorporeal sensation entwines itself around me like an invisible paramour.

It's time.

Back inside the belly of Pravitia, my momentary sense of peace has been replaced with bone-deep agitation. The traffic, even at this late hour, is a ceaseless drum of noise.

Needing something to do while I wait, I take a clove cigarette out of a thin silver case from my fur coat and light it. The strike of the Zippo echoes in the deserted alley, the flame illuminating the Crèvecoeur sigil—an open hand holding a flame—engraved on its side.

Even with the autumn chill, I've kept my coat open, revealing a silk slip dress with quick access to the dagger harnessed around my thigh. I also changed into a specific pair of black stilettos for the occasion. I wouldn't call myself *superstitious*, more like … ritualistic.

I have time to stub my cigarette under my pointed toe before the all-consuming feeling comes wafting around me. My eyes sweep the area until my gaze snags on a blonde walking my way. My mouth nearly waters with her approach.

Just a few more steps.

Wait.

The chatter quiets.

Breathe.

My heartbeat slows.

Strike.

I hook my elbow around the blonde's throat, slapping my other hand over her mouth as I drag her further into the alley and behind a dumpster. She tries to fight against my hold, but I'm stronger.

I don't *need* the privacy that this alleyway offers, it's not as if anyone could stop me. It's a preference. I like to keep the call of death intimate. Far from prying eyes.

I slam her into the brick wall, collaring her throat, my arm fully extended to keep her in place. Her eyes widen in alarm when she realizes who is staring back at her, a shocked, breathy *Mercy* escaping her open mouth.

I smile and cock my head.

I might not be a narcissist like a Vainglory, but I can't deny the flutter in my stomach during these short, sacred moments when my offerings recognize me.

I release my grip from her neck, but she doesn't dare move, petrified and shaking like a leaf against the wall. Delicately, I smooth my hand over her head, making her flinch as I tuck a few strands behind her ear before caressing her face with the back of my hand.

I greedily take her in like a glutton at a feast. Tears streak her reddened cheeks, plump lips trembling. Slowly, I drag my thumb through the wet tracks on her white skin and lean over, my lips grazing her jaw as her whimpering breaths reach my ears. Unsheathing my dagger with my free hand, I press a soft kiss to her mouth.

"*Mors omnia vincit*," I whisper against her lips.

Death awaits.

My blade is so sharp, that I barely need to exert any force before my dagger pierces her heart. It's a swift kill. No need to extend her fate any longer.

Unceremoniously, I pull the dagger out of her bleeding chest and step back as she crumbles to the ground, her eyes dimming.

I study her, now slumped in her last fatal repose, and take a long sated breath, the usual aggravation muted to a low dull.

Taking a silk tissue out of my coat pocket, I clean the blade before returning it to the holster on my thigh. While walking out of the mouth of the alley, I feel a raindrop fall on my cheek. I peer skyward while a few more drops land on my face.

The timing almost feels deliberate.

Like the clouds are craving a similar release to the one I just experienced.

Crossing the street, I open the back door of the idling town car. Jeremial's blue eyes study me through the rearview mirror but he says nothing as I settle in, waiting for me to speak.

"Have the body brought back to the Grounds," I order. Checking my phone, I add, "But drive me to Pandaemonium first."

7

MERCY

*P*andaemonium's rounded structure sits in the middle of Pravitia's harbor and can only be reached by boat or through an underground tunnel. The Foley family is nothing if not dedicated to showmanship, the red and white striped casino designed to look like a circus tent.

However, despite the bright exterior and colorful lights, Pandaemonium has a way of leaving whoever sets their eyes on it feeling unsettled, like staring straight into an illusion.

The message is clear: No one and nothing can be trusted—not even the naked eye.

I usually wouldn't partake in something as undignified as taking a dirty underground tunnel, but the downpour hasn't lessened since it started half an hour ago.

Wrinkling my nose at the indecipherable but somewhat concerning smells wafting in the air, I briskly make my way deeper into the tunnel, my fur coat wrapped tightly around me. The flambeaus lining the walls stretch the shadows into something uncanny, like ghosts dancing to a silent requiem.

After a sharp turn, a robust door appears, the Foley sigil—a hand with a snake coiling around its fingers—branded on the steel exterior. The large, square-headed individual guarding the entrance wordlessly lets me in with a curt nod. Ignoring him entirely, I step into a shock of bright lights and immediately don my dark sunglasses to avoid the vexing glare.

Whatever one's gambling vice, Pandaemonium can satiate the craving. A sprawling array of gaming tables takes up most of the space, while sheets of red gossamer hanging from the ceiling cloak each table, creating an illusion of privacy.

The casino's real attraction, however, is the large carousel in the middle of the room. A cyclical parade of dark-winged horses, eyes red like blood, slowly circling round and round and round while a disjointed and slightly unnerving fanfare accompanies it.

It's an eyesore.

And where Gemini Foley is known to collect his secrets.

A distinctive laugh floats up from one of the poker tables. I follow the sound, shrugging my fur coat off one shoulder as I approach.

Gemini is busy pushing a hefty stack of poker chips into the middle of the green felt table when I walk up. His hair is freshly bleached white blond, the fishnet crop top he's wearing peeking out from under a black satin tailcoat. I sit in the empty chair to his left without bothering to greet him.

His slim arms are extended, torso leaning over the table when he looks at me from the corner of his eyes with a smirk. "I was hoping you'd visit tonight, love."

I raise a shoulder in a noncommittal shrug, snapping my fingers at a passing server for a drink. "You asked me to."

Straightening back into his red velour seat, he takes a theatrical sip from his champagne coupe. His multiple rings clink against the crystal glass while his other hand is busy toying with his cards.

"When do you ever listen to anyone but yourself?" His gaze sparkles with levity as he waits for me to respond, the eyeliner smudging his bottom lashes brightening the color of his eyes. One green, one blue.

I cross one naked leg over the other and press my lips together in tempered annoyance. "I was nearby."

He hums, studying the table, then leans over to peer at my heels—the ones I specifically wear when answering the call. He grins, straightening back up. "Collecting tithe, I see?" he asks before signaling for another card.

I nod but don't say anything further.

Being his infuriating self, Gemini flashes me another amused look and gives my nose a small tap with his index finger before sprawling into his seat like a leisured king on a dais. If he were anyone else, my dagger would be lodged deep inside his pretty neck.

"Little bird told me you and Wolfie had quite the scuffle last week," he drawls.

I roll my eyes, a dirty martini finally appearing in front of me. I take a slow, savoring sip before answering. "Those little rodents of yours sure love to gossip." I wave my hand dismissively. "I'd rather not rehash it. Just the thought of him makes me ill."

"With the Conclave next week—" Gemini stops midsentence, straightens in his seat and points a black-painted nail to a player across from us, directing his attention to him. "I'd oblige you," he says slowly, "to think otherwise, love."

The man blanches. "I didn't do anything," he stutters indignantly, his eyes darting this way and that. Anywhere but my friend's piercing gaze.

Gemini's eyes flutter closed while he inhales deeply before his attention snaps back to the panicked fool. He lets out a delicious hum and says, "You lie so sweetly."

"I swear Mr. Foley, I'd never cheat!" the idiot babbles, his squirrelly eyes wide with terror.

Gemini leaps out of his seat and slowly starts to step onto

the table, mischief in his expression as the grifter shrieks, cards flying high into the air as he tries to get away when I notice a flash of pink in my peripheral.

The contact of my hand on Gemini's sleeve has him stopping in his tracks. He cants his head my way, eyes hard but a wide smile on his lips.

"Tinny will take care of it," I say flatly, nodding my head toward her.

Gemini's brows raise in delight, his head turning to watch our friend approach the table. Constantine, also known as Tinny, skips as she rounds the table in her platforms, her pink miniskirt matching the pink bows on her knee-high tights, blonde hair bouncing over her bare shoulders.

"How fun!" she says, her voice almost doll-like. "I only came here to play a round of cards, but I see the gods have offered me a little treat!" She claps her hands excitedly, her wide smile beaming. "I'd love to take care of him for you, Gem." She giggles, winking playfully before turning to a towering man behind her—donned in all black—and holds out her hand. "Albert."

The man stays rigid and stoic while handing her a morning star—a club-like weapon with a spiked ball attached to a chain. The shaft has been covered entirely in pink rhinestones, and the chain is a soft baby pink. There's no mistaking who is the rightful owner of this particular weapon.

Gemini climbs off the table and settles back into his seat, daintily raising his coupe to his lips as I take a sip of my own drink.

The insipid commoner, flanked by Pandaemonium security, has nowhere to run and visibly shakes as he awaits his fate. He barely has time to react before Constantine takes a large swing with the morning star, the spiked ball whistling through the air before it lodges into the side of his face with a gratifying crunch. Blood sprays out of his mouth, a tooth or two flying out on contact.

His body swivels abruptly, somehow getting tangled in the red gossamer hanging behind him. We watch silently as he struggles like a fly caught in sticky fly paper before finally crumbling to the ground.

Constantine hands back the weapon to Albert and straightens her pigtails with a satisfied sigh. "Back in a jiff!" Constantine sing-songs before having Albert drag the man into one of the back rooms while she skips behind him.

Gemini's gaze lands back on mine. "Anyway," he says with a hint of boredom. "What was I sayin—" He snaps his fingers. "Right!" His stare turns slightly pointed. "With the Conclave next week, I'd be remiss not to ask if you and Wolfie will manage to behave."

My scoff is mocking. "Look who's speaking."

Gemini snickers, a hand to the chest. "All part of the Foley charm, love."

"Besides," I add with a bite, "We're not the only families feuding."

His eyes narrow as if I've said something daft. "Of *our* generation, you two are the only ones who are taking it so —" His lip curls as if appalled by the word itself. "— seriously." Taking another sip of champagne, he adds, "Look at me and Tinny for example."

Their families have been feuding for as long as mine and the Vainglorys.

I cross my arms. "Whatever happened to respecting long-standing traditions," I mutter haughtily.

Gemini scoffs, his grin turning cocksure. "Since when have we ever been known to follow rules, love?"

8

WOLFGANG

Constantine's mansion, in the north end of Pravitia, would already be hard to miss just by its sheer size, but paired with the all-pink exterior, the monstrosity can surely be seen from space.

Aleksandr strolls up the white steps and opens the front door without knocking. I follow him inside at a leisurely pace, hands in my trouser pockets.

"Honey, we're home!" Aleksandr calls out from the large foyer.

He turns to me, cracking a smile and winking as if expecting me to laugh at his doltish joke. I don't, keeping my face neutral as I hear Constantine's voice from a few rooms down.

Since their families have been on friendly terms for the past century, the two have never had the hurdle of age-old feuds to overcome. Their friendship has been steadfast for as long as I can remember.

Constantine appears shortly after, looking like she tore herself out of a vintage housewife magazine. Her blonde hair falls in perfectly styled waves, a white apron wrapped tightly around her pink poodle skirt dress.

"Finally!" she exclaims, giggling loudly when her blue eyes land on Aleksandr. Running up to him with arms wide open, he catches her midway, twirling her body around before setting Constantine back on her feet. His outfit seems to mirror hers, the slacks and collared baby blue shirt echoing decades past.

"Miss me?" he drawls.

"Always," she replies with a beaming smile.

I give Aleksandr a searing side-eye but he doesn't notice, so I clear my throat. "Pleasure to see you too, Tinny," I say as I pick an invisible piece of lint off my sleeve.

Constantine's breathy giggle is unbothered. "Silly Wolfie, I'm always happy to see you," she says as she leans in to fix my silk ascot tie. I swat her away like a pesky mosquito.

Ignoring my grievance, she claps her hands together, looking at us both. "Drinks in the weapons room! Come, come."

Spinning around, she signals us to follow her down the long hall, as if we both haven't been to her house countless times.

Pink ornate sconces illuminate our path as we pass countless open doors. From the corner of my eye, I catch the room full of Victorian dolls locked away behind glass cases, it's immediately followed by the one designated for her vast human bone collection. Finally, before arriving at the aforementioned weapons room, we walk past the room stuffed with medieval torture memorabilia—my favorite.

"The gang's all here!" she chirps while traversing the threshold.

"What gang—" My words fizzle out in my throat when my gaze lands on Mercy daintily perched on a chair, a large array of throwing stars fanning behind her on the wall.

"Tinny," she hisses, green eyes narrowing to slits. The curl of disgust on her red lips and hard grip around her glass tells me she's just as cornered as I am.

"It was Gem's idea!" Constantine volleys back, pointing a manicured finger toward a grinning Gemini sprawled across a white chaise. His hair is dyed pink for the occasion, small diamonds affixed near the corners of his eyes sparkling as bright as his gaze.

Mercy's glare flares before she turns sharply around, reaches for one of the throwing stars, and launches it at Gemini's head. Belladonna lets out a high-pitched shriek, the weapon narrowly missing her as she tucks her head behind her arms. Gemini snickers beside her, gracefully ducking out of the way, the star lodging itself in the wall behind him.

"See how entertaining this already is?" Gemini says with a debonair wave of his hand.

Although Aleksandr shares a similar disdain for Mercy and hasn't been in the same room as Belladonna since his mother killed her father nineteen years ago, he seems rather unaffected by the situation. As for me, I'm stewing with irritation, chewing on my inner-lip and considering if I could just leave now before anyone notices.

Instead, I stay rooted in place, fists tight as I watch Aleksandr stroll further into the room. He plops himself beside Gemini, who takes his face in his ring-clad hands and kisses him loudly on the cheek.

Jaw clenched, my attention returns to Constantine. She stands unperturbed in the middle of the room, weapons of all shapes and sizes surrounding her, hands daintily clasped together near her waist as if performing in a pageant.

"What is the meaning of this little caucus?" I ask with a bite.

"Well," Constantine starts, turning to Gemini for what seems to be moral support. But he's too busy running his hand up one of the servants' thighs while they hand him a drink to be of any help. "We thought — with the Conclave tomorrow, and with all our parents there — or what's left of them," she says to herself, "Maybe we could present a united front for once."

"For what purpose?" Mercy asks, her tone ripe with aggravation, her clenched fingers curling into the cushion of her chair.

"Because feuds are boring," Gemini responds to Mercy with a despondent sigh. His foolish gaze then finds mine. "Besides, you're anything but boring, aren't you Wolfie?"

"Don't call me that, you pest," I growl.

Gemini holds up his hands in surrender but continues to smirk, never the one to take anything seriously.

Slowly, I turn my gaze to Mercy, who is busy ignoring me, her arms now crossed tightly over her silk blouse, her black hair pulled back into a high ponytail, leaving her neck and shoulders uncovered aside from a pearl choker. Despite the hostile body language, she seems to have accepted our current fate, given that she hasn't stormed out of the room as of yet.

I suck at my teeth while I bring my attention back to Constantine. Dragging my hand over my trimmed beard, I relent, after a long defeated sigh. "Fine. If we must."

Constantine claps with glee. "We're having croquembouche for dessert!" she says while falling into Aleksandr's lap. I find a settee as far from Mercy as possible, mentally preparing to spend an entire soiree in her dreadful presence.

AFTER A FEW ROUNDS OF DRINKS, WE MIGRATE TO THE DINING room. It's a drafty and gaudy place—including the chandelier hanging above us. Constantine spent an excruciating amount of time showcasing the hanging pink bedazzled ornaments, made from her favorite human bones specially collected for this accent piece.

I'm on my third bourbon, the servants busy clearing the plates of our last course when I feel a tingling warmth begin to bloom in my chest, the sensation slowly crawls down my spine and limbs.

I assume it's just the alcohol, finally numbing the particular *chill* I've been feeling all evening until I glance around the table and realize suddenly that something is glaringly off.

Glassy eyes. Dreamy grins. Especially when my gaze falls on Mercy, who's talking to Belladonna in hushed tones, cheeks flushed, eyes glimmering—and smiling?

"Why do I feel ..." I say to no one in particular. My words trail off, my thoughts turning ephemeral.

"Horny?" Gemini offers, his gaze reflecting a similar daze as Mercy's as he intercepts a passing servant. He drags them onto his lap, his hand up their skirt as he kisses them passionately.

"That's not what I—" I stop abruptly, letting his statement sink in, suddenly realizing that there's truth to Gemini's glibness.

Constantine laughs, taking a sip of her Mojito as she trains her blue puppy eyes my way, her tone infuriatingly innocent when she finally says, "Oh that's because I spiked our drinks."

9

WOLFGANG

"**Y**ou did *what*?!"

Mercy's scathing question hangs in the air while the table falls silent, all eyes now on Constantine, except for Gemini who is still devouring that poor servant's face. He either knew about this already or never cared if his drink was spiked in the first place.

"What?" Constantine asks, seeming to be genuinely taken aback by Mercy's reaction. "It's just some light social lubrication."

"Lubrication for *what* exactly?" I ask through clenched teeth, trying to fight through the euphoric feeling suddenly muddling my head.

"For a fun night," Aleksandr responds with a smirk. To no surprise, his gaze seems a lot clearer than the rest of us.

"You knew about this?" I hiss, sending him a cutting glare.

He shrugs, his gaze lingering on Constantine, while he circles his glass with a lazy finger.

Of course, he wouldn't care if the drinks were spiked.

"You're both acting as if you've never taken Molly before," Aleksandr says, avoiding my question.

Mercy scoffs, standing up. "Hardly the point," she spits, then turns her head to her right. "Belladonna?" she adds as if wanting support for her outrage.

Belladonna jumps slightly at her name, her eyes hooded when she looks up. Her slow, sultry smile is response enough. I'm horrified to realize that the only other person who seems to care about any of this is *Mercy*.

She lets out an enraged groan and storms out of the room.

"You'll miss the croquembouche!" Constantine yells out to her, then pouts when she ignores her.

I listen to the sound of Mercy's heels receding down the hallway before looking back at the four remaining heirs. Gemini hasn't yet resurfaced from his kiss, the servant now half-naked and full of breathy giggles.

Belladonna looks like she's searching for prey to hunt, and Aleksandr is too busy staring at Constantine like she hung the moon—and not a bone chandelier—to care.

Slowly, I push back my chair and stand up, smoothing the front of my burgundy suit jacket before clasping the two front buttons. I can feel the warm familiar buzz of MDMA getting stronger as the seconds tick by, a dull throb of lust pulsing through my veins. An urge begins to coil itself slowly around my heated thoughts.

I need to leave.

Giving the table a final glance from down my nose, I mutter, "This was certainly entertaining." I turn on my heels leaving them to whatever hijinks they have planned for the night.

I enter Manor from the back. Although I'm dressed to kill, tonight is not the night for a photo op with the vultures camped near the front door. I'm damn near delirious with drug-induced lust as I make my way through a darkly lit corridor, feverishly wondering how much Molly I ingested during dinner.

A woman in a black suit stands in front of a nondescript door, and she opens it as soon as I approach. I give her a curt nod and walk in. The entrance leads into another hallway with doors on either side. To my right, there's a reception desk, manned by a mousey-looking redhead.

"Door number six, Mr. Vainglory," she says with an assured tone, barely a glance my way.

I can hardly hear her through the blood pounding in my ears, my heart beating wildly in my chest. Stalking through the hallway, I find the proper door and barge in like a bull seeing red. The room is small with warm, soft lighting but it could be a cold, damp cell and it wouldn't make any difference to me right now.

Shrugging my suit jacket off, I throw it on the couch lining the wall. My attention zeroes in on the pair of naked legs to my left. I roll the sleeves of my dress shirt as I lick my lips, reveling in the anonymity of this type of service.

I can't see her face and upper body, hidden behind a glass divider and red curtain. The hole in the wall is only large enough for her waist to slide through, her legs strapped up with harnesses to keep her splayed open for my pleasure.

Her bare cunt is so damn inviting, I immediately fall to my knees in front of her.

I'm panting like a fucking dog, lust-ravaged and practically snarling.

The first taste of her would have brought me to my knees if I wasn't already. I give her slit a long, greedy lick and the soft muted gasps from behind the glass divider only fuel the lust throbbing through me like a supernatural force.

I tongue her swollen clit while I urgently unzip my trousers, shoving them down my thighs while I fist my painfully hard cock with desperate tugs.

Using my free hand, I circle her entrance with two fingers, her cunt wet and quivering under my touch while I continue to devour her some more, my mouth watering at the taste of her heady arousal.

Fuck.

How can she taste this fucking ... divine?

It's the drugs. It must be the drugs.

Her near imperceptible whimpers tickle my ears, urging me on. In a frantic carnal act, I spit on her cunt, dragging the spit over her clit with two fingers before pushing it into her, as if I have a feverish need to sink myself into her very pores. The wet glide of my fingers inside of her has me doubling over as I desperately fuck my own hand.

The woman behind this curtain is like no one I've ever experienced before. She's the best thing I've ever fucking felt. It's otherworldly. Hard to grasp or describe with any earth-bound word. Suddenly I don't care if it *is* the drugs in my system.

I need to feel her bare cunt around my cock—it's a matter of life or death.

Standing up, I have half a mind to start fucking her hard and fast, the urge to come just as strong as the need to sink into her perfect pink cunt.

But something stops me, like a force outside of myself whispering for me to take my time, to remember exactly how this feels.

How *she* feels.

Pleasure tickles my skin, my spine tingling when I notch my cock against her entrance. I can hear her soft, impatient breaths and I wish I could see her face, wish I could properly hear her moans dance across my neck.

But before I can sink to the hilt, something catches my attention. The heels on her feet, a row of pearls adorning her ankles.

No.

I rip myself away from the wall, almost falling backward with the speed of my action.

It can't be.

I feel sick, realizing how close I came to breaking one of our divine laws. I curse the gods under my breath while I pull up my trousers, my heart slamming against my chest, and then curse Constantine for having drugged us in the first place.

I leave seconds later, practically running out of Manor, needing as much distance from the woman behind the curtain —Mercy Crèvecoeur.

10

MERCY

My heels echo through the long empty halls of Mount Pravitia, the high arches and stained glass windows filtering the sun's rays in hues of blue, yellow, and red. The building sits at the very center of the city, a colossal gothic feat with twin spires piercing the sky as if yearning to be anywhere but here.

I know the feeling intimately.

Especially after last night and Constantine's *witless* dinner party.

I'm itching to drive my dagger deep into Constantine's gut for spiking the drinks. Acting like we were still a gaggle of unruly teenagers, instead of us being in our late twenties and thirties.

Not like that psychopathic doll would be bothered by the pain anyway.

Then came the bizarre ending to my night—or lack thereof.

Frustration prickles under my skin recalling how I was left on the cusp of an orgasm. I haven't used Manor's *lesser-known* services in over a year, but I never did think I'd experience someone leaving mid-way through.

I believe it was a man by the feel of his rough touch and thick fingers.

A man who, before leaving me high and dry made me feel ...

I can't say that sex has ever felt that exceptional before.

His tongue on my clit. His groans against my thighs. Fingers digging into my skin.

I was insatiable. Spellbound.

My stomach heats with the memories, and I quickly give my head a quick shake to snap myself out of it. Ridiculous. The drugs were certainly the cause for the heightened emotions.

When I enter the boardroom where the Conclave is taking place, I glance around the room and realize that I'm early.

Aleksandr's mother, Alina Vorovsky—the current ruler of Pravitia—stands at the head of the long quartz table, her son and husband sitting on either side of her.

Her severe expression does nothing to dull her beauty, with her piercing emerald eyes and pin-straight hair the color of sand. She stands stoic in her wine-red dress lined with fur, shoulders straight and rigid while wearing priceless heirlooms around her neck as everyday accessories.

Belladonna is already seated at the opposite end of the table, copper hair pulled up in a high ponytail, the dark circles she tried and failed to hide with makeup prove that I'm not the only one feeling ghastly this morning.

The silence in the room is as heavy as the upcoming parley.

My friend's glare and icy body language explain the pointed silence. She blames the death of both of her parents on the Vorovsky family, particularly the death of her father when she was ten years old.

Being the only other orphan amongst the six heirs, I silently take a seat beside Belladonna and wait for the others to arrive with their respective parents.

Gemini appears shortly after, accompanied by his mother. By the looks of him, I'd guess he hasn't slept a wink but still acts aggravatingly chipper, blowing me a kiss before sitting closest to Aleksandr.

Constantine is next to arrive in a burst of pink, as always, her father stalking into the boardroom first, acting like an even more impressive version of Albert.

"Morning everyone!" she sing-songs but no one responds. Ignoring the tension in the air, she sends a small wave to Aleksandr who quirks a smile before sitting to my right, opposite the Foleys.

The minutes crawl by slowly while we wait for the Vainglorys.

Alina's serious demeanor has time to crack ever so slightly. She's sighing, pressing her nude-painted lips together and looking at her watch when I pick up on footsteps approaching.

The Vainglorys arrive as a trio, Wolfgang's parents just as peacockish as their infuriating progeny. I expect Wolfgang to send me a seething glare as usual, but he avoids my gaze entirely. Taking the final available seats, the attention finally returns to Alina.

"Right," she says in an even tone, finally sitting down at the table. "As I'm sure we are all aware: Today marks the ending of the Vorovsky rule over the city of Pravitia." Her green gaze skates pointedly around the room. "As tradition dictates, during the one-week window when none of the families are officially in power, the Feast of Fools will take place on the eve of the Lottery. And *all* heirs are not only expected to attend —" She raises a finger in the air to drive in her point. "— but oversee the planning as a show of a united front for the people of Pravitia."

I scoff under my breath, and Gemini shoots me an amused

look. His mother elbows him in the ribs and he lets out a theatrical wheeze. Constantine giggles loudly, her father impatiently shushing her. I ignore all of it, my attention narrowed on Alina who's glaring at me from across the table.

"Objections, Crèvecoeur?" she says slowly, her jaw clenched.

I hold her stare, the tension between us, as well as all the families, so palpable it stabs at my lungs with every breath I take. I drum my nails on the table to antagonize her further before waving my hand toward her. "By all means, *Alina,* please continue."

I can feel Belladonna trying to conceal her laughter beside me, Alina's eyes darting to my left before landing back on me.

"You know," she states dryly, clasping her hands together as she leans forward. "Whatever little alliances you children *think* you have, just know the Lottery doesn't care about history." Her pause is so dramatic she could very well be a Vainglory. "Our gods do not care for petty loyalty amongst the different families. *This,*" she hisses with a wave of the hand around the table. "These insignificant feuds and long-standing grudges mean nothing to them." Belladonna is the one to scoff indignantly this time but Alina continues, "Worship is all that matters to them. Worship and *sacrifice.*"

A few of the parents in the room shift in their seats as if recalling some particularly uncomfortable memories while Alina stands up, and places a firm hand on Aleksandr's shoulder.

"I'll keep this brief. This meeting was always meant as a simple formality. You are all adults, I'm sure you'll figure it out. And in any case, we are available for consultation if the need arises." Her gaze falls on every single one of the heirs before finally saying, "The city is yours."

11

MERCY

As expected the Feast of Fools is a decadent, hedonistic affair. The city square, facing Mount Pravitia, has turned into a pulsing sea of bodies, spilling over into the adjoining streets like waves crashing into the rocky shore.

The commoners revel at the festivities we have so generously arranged, it's infectious and expected to be celebrated with unbound glee and devotion.

The logistics were a pestering headache to organize. Luckily we didn't have *much* to do since Aleksandr had been planning it for weeks before the Conclave took place.

However, being forced to be in the same room as Wolfgang multiple times in the past week was torture enough. Especially when he'd periodically self-indulge in his power of persuasion, like a compulsion he can't seem to control—not that he would ever want to control it. People can't help but fall to their knees and worship him.

It's revolting.

I'd rather be hated and left alone.

The six heirs, including me, are seated on throne-like chairs atop a large dais, our backs to Mount Pravitia. An intricately carved pergola especially built for the occasion looms over us, with vines and black morning glories hanging from the wooden beams.

I sigh, perching my head between my finger and thumb, while my elbow digs into the armrest, my heavy gold earrings giving me a headache.

The celebration began at dusk, and we've been loitering here for what feels like ages. As soon as the moon appeared, full and waxing, the celebration, which first consisted of a large banquet, quickly transformed into debauchery.

They always do when a Vorovsky is involved. Watching Pravitia's citizens partake in such unbridled gluttony and perversion should keep me occupied, a mild form of entertainment at the very least. Orgies in plain sight. Gorged bodies stumbling into vomitoriums. Wine served in excess. Self-control is ineffable tonight.

Instead, I'm bored witless, impatiently waiting for the second half of this idiotic feast to begin. Our private celebration will certainly be more engaging.

From the corner of my eye, I idly observe Constantine to my right, Albert standing faithfully behind her chair. Her gauzy dress is the color of cherry blossoms. She looks ethereal, her hair falling gracefully over her shoulders. My dress is similar to hers, except the color is as dark as the night around us. Constantine's eyes glimmer with delight while one of her minions is on all fours so she can use them as a footstool. If I were anyone else but me, her bright white smile would be infectious.

Aleksandr walks up to Wolfgang sitting next to Constantine. They've both donned velvet blazers for the occasion, impeccably embroidered with thin threads of gold, and while Wolfgang's is burgundy, Aleksandr's blazer is forest green.

My eyes narrow when Aleksandr whispers a few words into

Wolfgang's ear, tapping him on the shoulder before doing the same to Constantine.

She claps her hands with glee before turning to me, stars in her eyes, then yelps to Gemini and Belladonna over my chair to catch their attention. Wolfgang's pleased gaze snags on mine, but quickly turns skittish before promptly turning to the crowd.

The buzz that now seems to run through the six of us like a current tells me everything I need to know.

It's time.

HAD I KNOWN WHAT WAS TO FOLLOW, I WOULD HAVE ENJOYED MY time on the dais a lot more.

Walking through the rowdy hordes of bodies as I try to make my way through the crowded street is equal to getting my skin slowly flayed with tweezers. The city's typical wariness of us six—especially me—seems to have evaporated along with their inhibitions.

Our small group dispersed after Aleksandr gave us the okay, spilling into the crowd in different directions, giving each other an hour to find what we're looking for.

I've made my way to the west corner of the city square. The crowd doesn't part to let me through, my presence barely acknowledged. It's as if I'm simply another city-dweller partaking in the celebration.

Absurd. They should always fear me.

My fingers itch, eager to reach for my dagger hiding under my dress. I somehow manage to resist, practicing some semblance of self-control while I focus on the goals at hand.

I pass far too many plebeians mid-coitus, some on large hay bales, a few directly atop banquet tables or up against buildings. I wrinkle my nose at the egregious sight, their writhing naked bodies repulsive and uncouth. I shove as many as I can out of the way, verbally eviscerating a few as I go, when *finally*, I catch sight of something shiny.

Metaphorically at least.

He's young, early twenties if I had to guess, with strawberry blond hair that frames his face in soft waves. His eyes, the color of the ocean, crinkle at the corners while he shares a hearty laugh with those beside him.

A kind of luring attraction hums through me similar to when I feel the quiet call of death. But this feels more ... primitive somehow. Like falling prey to something much more powerful than me. As if time is dissolving and I am left standing amongst the echoes of similar memories, of countless times this *game* has been played before.

A living pawn in the gods' eternal game of chess.

My breathing slows, my mind quiets and the sound of the crowd surrounding us fades while I wait. I don't move until he does. I'm not sure how long I study him, only that the moon has time to crawl higher up in the sky before he finally walks away from the group, accompanied by another man around his age.

I follow them, eyes tracking steadily as we all dodge intoxicated merrymakers stumbling over their own feet. When they turn a corner, I speed up, not wanting to lose them in the chaos. Luckily, this side street is a little quieter, making it easier to keep an eye on them.

As I'm passing an alleyway, distracted by the potential ways I can lure the blond-haired man away from his friend, someone crashes into me, barrelling into the street like a wild, clomping centaur.

"Uncivilized *swine*," I hiss, stumbling backward, trying to gather my wits.

The arrogant chuckle that follows sends a cold shiver down

my spine as my eyes lock with Wolfgang's just as his mouth turns into a hateful smirk.

"Who are you calling such callous names, Crèvecoeur?" he drawls, jutting out his chin as he looks me up and down with unbridled disgust. "Certainly you wouldn't denigrate the Vainglory name with such slander." He looks away while straightening his blazer. "Now if you'll excuse me, you unappetizing tart, I have a pawn to catch."

He strolls down the street, and it doesn't take me long to realize he's following the same two men as I am. Quickly catching up, I keep my voice low but pointed. "He's *mine*."

"Which one?" Wolfgang asks with a small bored sigh, his gaze straight ahead.

"The blond one."

"Well then, I want the other."

My laugh is dry, my attention on the two men in front of us. "Find a different sacrifice."

Wolfgang scoffs, the tone slightly teasing, making my blood turn to a high boil. "I can't control what the gods want—and mine," he says as he points in front of us, "wants this one."

I fall silent, grinding my teeth, cursing my luck. "Fine. Let's get it over with then." I look over, finding his gaze already on mine, his gray-blue eyes narrowed as we keep walking but he says nothing. "How are we doing this?" I ask dismissively.

His smile turns roguish, revealing his two gold teeth at the corner of his mouth.

"With my intoxicating charm, of course."

12

WOLFGANG

She smells like cherry and burnt almonds. The smell wafts around me as Mercy climbs into the limousine, and it makes me practically salivate. I have half a mind to shove her back out with my wingtip shoe to the middle of the chest just so I don't have to ingest any more of her essence.

She's repulsive.

Offensive.

Downright distasteful.

Everything I am not.

I glare in her direction as she settles beside Belladonna—as far away from me as possible—her black dress fluttering around her as she crosses her legs, emerald eyes looking peeved as always.

My eyes dip down to her exposed calf. I linger on the delicate curve where her foot disappears into her stiletto, the heel designed to look like a dagger. I slowly trail my tongue over my bottom lip, remembering how her skin felt on mine.

My chest squeezes.

I look away.

Wrinkle my nose.

Vile brute.

The door opens, and a euphony of giggles and laughs replaces the stilted silence. Two bewildered Pravitians are shoved into the limousine by Constantine and Gemini.

Constantine's chosen seems to have struggled, sporting a bloody nose and a split lip. When the civilians notice who else is in the vehicle, they turn crestfallen and sit beside each other in a small huddle of shaky limbs.

I smile.

It's our birthright to be this ruthless. One I've always taken pleasure in indulging in.

Mine and Mercy's catch were easier to control. I offered the two men rose-colored glasses and they gladly took them. They're now sprawled in the corner, small sated smiles on their lips, without a care in the world. Belladonna's pick sits next to them, eyes wide and brimming with unshed tears.

I turn to Constantine. She's climbing over Gemini while he tries to grope her, both of them snickering like a bunch of drunks as she tries to fit into the empty spot beside him.

I clear my throat, trying to get her attention. "Tinny, where's Sasha?"

"Said he'd meet us there," she answers, followed by an *oof* when she finally plops down on the seat. She surveys the limousine, excitement twinkling in her blue eyes. "Can I keep mine scared?" She glances over, mischief in her smile. "I love them scared."

I roll my eyes. She's like dealing with a younger sibling. That's only a vague guess since I have no experience with siblings—none of us do—a deliberate choice made by our parents.

"No, we need them docile first," I tell her sternly.

Her shimmering pink lips turn pouty, but she follows with a wave of the hand, wordlessly giving me the go-ahead.

My eyes are drawn to Mercy, her gaze luckily on Gemini, before I course-correct and focus on the three Pravitians needing my rapt attention.

I feel the limousine pull onto the street when I snap my fingers, demanding that their eyes be on me.

As it always should be.

One by one, I gaze deeply into the chosens' eyes, my smile placating and harmless.

The warm sensation always begins at the base of my spine, tingling up to the crown of my skull. It's how I know it's working. I have them under my spell.

Their expressions fade into a blank stare, their eyes dimming.

My lip pulls up into a smirk. "Wonderful night we're having, aren't we?" I ask, my tone friendly and inviting.

I watch as their faces slowly transform into something peaceful. One of them lets out a pleased sigh, her smile growing wide. "As delightful as you are, Mr. Vainglory," she purrs.

I hear Mercy gag, and I smirk. Something about her displeasure makes a small ping of delight bloom inside my chest. It almost makes me want to laugh.

I settle back into my seat, crossing my ankle over my thigh, my smile widening.

"Let the *real* fun commence."

THE FEAST OF FOOLS HAS ALWAYS HAD A DUAL MEANING. ONE for the fools themselves, the commoners, who after countless generations have somehow still managed to keep a thread of hope that perhaps, the ruling families can be as generous as we are selfish.

We are not.

Then there is a feast just for us.

The rulers of Pravitia.

For most of the city, this misplaced hope will still ring true tomorrow. They will wake up after a night brimming with pleasure and vice. No consequences, no accountability, and they'll have only the tiniest inkling of what it's like to be us.

What it means to be this powerful.

They will go on with their lives, clinging to that ridiculous hope and somehow still believing in the fool's dream of free will.

When in reality, we hold their fate in our hands.

Our private soiree is taking place in the Vorovskys' sprawling gardens. The large hedge maze looms behind us, a backdrop to our entertainment. I yawn, stretching my arms over my head, and lean into the cushioned chair as I survey the banquet table. It's a veritable feast of roasted chickens, glazed hams, and root vegetables dripping in butter, all served on gold and bejeweled platters.

I'd be a glutton if I took even one more bite.

Besides, I need to keep my wits sharp for tonight's final act.

I glance over to the six Pravitians we plucked from the crowd earlier tonight. They're seated at a smaller, but just as lavish, banquet table next to us.

Unbeknownst to them, they are partaking in a much truer reenactment of the Feast of Fools. I've made them believe they are one of us. Special. Deserving of respect. I've made them *feel* the power we hold every single day; while their entire existence has been to act as jesters dancing for our entertainment. Even now, while gorging on their last meal, they feel no humiliation, no sense of degradation.

Instead, they feast.

Just like us.

Never like us.

The sound of gold cups spilling over and porcelain

breaking has me glancing back to our small group. Gemini has climbed atop our table, kicking centerpieces out of his way as he struts like a peacock, the loose collar of his white linen shirt revealing the tattoos across his chest. His smile is wide and playful while his gaze is dark and mocking.

"The city is ours," he says with exaggerated grandiosity, repeating what Aleksandr's mother told us a week ago. Placing a hand on his hip, he leans his body forward as he wags a scolding finger at the five of us. "Our gods do not *care* for petty loyalty." He pouts. "Do not *care* for family feuds. All that *matters* is worship and sacrifice." Constantine bursts out in a fit of laughter at the spectacle. Picking up a cup yet to be spilled, he holds it up in the air in a toast. "If it's sacrifice they want, then it's sacrifice they will receive." His glittering eyes flick to my seat, his voice turning conspiratorial. "Vainglory, care to do the honors?"

13

WOLFGANG

The waxing moon is high above our heads, soft light caressing our faces as if the moon itself yearns to be a part of this divine moment with us. We have gathered at the center of the maze, the large statue of an archer with his arrow pointing to the sky, covered in moss and vines, lording over us.

The six helpless fools are facing us. Faces smooth of worries.

Still unsuspecting.

Still so trusting.

The silence is filled with febrile anticipation. One look to my right tells me Aleksandr is feeling it too. His grin is feral as he stares at his sacrifice with promises of slaughter in his piercing gaze while Constantine paces beside him like a wild animal, the spiked ball of her morning star swishing in the air to and fro.

There is an electric energy humming through the six of us, tying us together with an invisible thread. I've never felt so attuned to them. Never felt so *connected*.

Time has finally come to lift the veil. To break the spell and remind our fools that we were never friends but foes all along —hungry wolves starving for blood.

It only takes a small breathless instant to release them from my hold. An effortless snip of the leashes I had collared around their minds.

They blink. Startled. Confusion sweeps over their faces as they look around before their gaze finally lands on us. They must notice the predatory glint in our eyes because the realization of where they are, and *who* they are with, ripples across their faces like a deadly crashing wave.

"Boo," Gemini says with a sneer.

Constantine giggles as she continues to pace in place. A few whimpers float up in the air like weightless mist, and the thrill coiling in my stomach turns into something much larger— much more lethal.

I clear my throat.

Terrified eyes turn to me.

"I suggest," I say with a slow drawl, "you run."

Gemini's sacrifice bolts as soon as the words are out of my mouth as if she was somehow waiting for the order. The soft sound of her bare feet on grass marries with her harried breath, as she quickly disappears into one of the tall hedged paths surrounding the maze's center.

Gemini barks out a wicked laugh but doesn't run after her. "I think I'll give the little rabbit a head start," he says to no one in particular.

We all plan to do the same.

The hunt doesn't start until they've all successfully scurried away.

It takes a few seconds for the others to follow suit. But finally, they all make a mad dash for different paths, some stumbling over their own feet, slamming to their knees before hurriedly pushing themselves up and continuing their escape.

While we wait, Belladonna, Constantine, and Mercy step out of their heels and remove their earrings while the men step out of our dress shoes, readying for the eventual sprint around the maze.

My gaze flits to Mercy, still in her black dress, her dagger visible around her exposed left thigh. My eyes dip down to her bare feet, toes painted red.

"It's time for us to take what's ours," Aleksandr says ceremoniously as he slowly rubs his palms together.

Before any of us move, we share a final, loaded glance.

Like taking a long deep inhale before a guttural scream.

Then finally ...

We commence.

THE SERRATED KNIFE I SPECIFICALLY CHOSE FOR MY SACRIFICE hangs loosely in my grip as I stroll through the maze. The same knife my father used when he first partook in the Feast of Fools, bestowed to him by his father before him.

It's been a little more than half an hour since the fools skittered like mice. I caught my little rodent within ten minutes of the chase. But it was much too fast. I wanted to prolong the kill. Prolong the sick thrill thrumming through my veins. So I let him go. But not before biting half his ear off and slicing my knife through his right eye as punishment for being such an easy catch. I can still taste his blood on my tongue, the echo of his screams like a delicious, haunting melody.

With my free hand, I trail my fingers over the bush beside me, the hedges over twelve feet tall. I've worked up a sweat, the sleeves of my black shirt rolled up, the collar unbuttoned. I'm growing eager, knowing that next time I catch him, it will be for the kill.

I cock my head and listen. I know he's close. No matter how

hard he tries to hide, there's a subtle, but powerful, force guiding me to him.

An agonizing wail suddenly rises up from the depths of the maze, then another. My breathing turns shallow, my heart beating faster as if the harrowing screams are pumping me full of unadulterated adrenaline.

When the silence returns, I hear a rustle of leaves.

Turning my head, I follow the sound.

Another rustle.

A low chuckle rumbles through my chest while I begin to run, knowing he'll soon be in my grasp. I spot a figure dart across the opening of the path and I speed up, knife in hand. Turning the corner, I find him stumbling haphazardly through the maze attempting a futile escape.

The dreadful mite doesn't stand a chance.

I tackle him from behind and he goes down hard. Flipping him over, I climb over him with effortless grace, dodging his vain attempts at a struggle. Taking his left arm, I lift it above his head and jam my knife straight through his wrist, the blade burrowing into the earth underneath.

He howls in pain, tears streaking through the blood from the wound across his eye. Pinning his other arm under my leg, I grab his face with one hand, squeezing his cheeks together. His skin is slippery under my touch, wet from blood and tears.

I let out a small tut, followed by a few tsks. "Have a bit of decorum," I say casually while I dig my finger into the wound on his face. His howls turn to wailing pleas. "No one likes a bellyacher."

Leaning over, I pull the knife out of his wrist, his screams only intensifying. Tugging his shirt up, I slowly dig the blade into his soft stomach, carving a W with the sharp tip. My eyes skate up to his face, and I flash him a grin. "I hope you're honored," I say as I spread the fresh blood over his stomach with my open palm. "To be marked by a Vainglory before you die."

I hear another terrified scream from a few paths away, and my fingers begin to tingle with anticipation. My smile widens. I bury my blade in his gut. His eyes grow wide, his shocked gasp dying on his lip as I pull the serrated blade up to his ribs.

Pulling it out, I slam it back down, this time through his heart, breaking through the sternum. The knife squelches through blood, bones, and organs as I stab him repeatedly. I am enraptured by the sight of my sacrifice slowly waning beneath me. I don't stop when his eyes turn glassy and lifeless, only when my arm grows heavy and tired.

Pushing myself off the corpse, I try to catch my breath as I wipe the blood dripping over my eye with the back of my hand, knife still in hand. I take a few haggard steps forward and fall to my knees.

I peer up at the moon and grin foolishly.

I feel light-headed—intoxicated even—as I try to repress the uncontrollable laughter bubbling in my chest.

A small tingle at the back of my neck has my gaze jumping to movement ahead.

A few yards away, Mercy appears at the mouth of the path, cloaked in moonlight and gore. She takes a few steps and then stops, her dagger loosely clutched in her hand. Her dress is ripped, uncovering the swell of one of her breasts, strands of her black hair, wet with blood, sticking to her face.

My breathing slows as I silently take her in, reluctant to alert her of my presence.

I've never seen her so ... at peace before.

Her eyebrows are smooth of any divots, green eyes devoid of their usual hardness. She wipes the blade of her dagger on her tattered dress while smiling up at the moon before she walks down the opposite path.

I stare at where she disappeared for much longer than I care to admit.

After a few minutes, I find the strength to stand up and exit the maze before the adrenaline plummets and the bone-deep exhaustion takes over.

I need my beauty sleep.

Because tomorrow, the Lottery begins.

14

WOLFGANG

The wild power pulsating inside of me since the Feast of Fools last night has only ramped up in intensity and urgency now that I've stepped inside the cavernous hall where the Lottery takes place.

I've never seen the space with my own eyes—none of the heirs have—needing to be a minimum of eighteen to participate. Being the eldest of the six, I was just shy of seeing the hall nineteen years ago.

The stone is cold under my bare feet as I step further into the hall, furtively looking up and around, slowly taking it in. The vast cavern is on the lowest subterranean floor of Mount Pravitia, lit up entirely by torches and candles, the flames dancing alongside the shadows on the walls.

It's made mostly out of marble with a soaring arched ceiling, and at its center is a large circular platform crafted entirely of black obsidian, the inky hue seeming to swallow any light that comes near it. The space around the circular platform is split into six sections, one for each family.

A crowd has already gathered, and countless pairs of eyes

turn to watch our approach to the large platform as we file in, one after the other.

Although this is a sacred and private ritual, all immediate and extended family members over the age of eighteen are required to attend. Typically, I relish being the center of attention, but today, the weight of their stare feels tender against my skin.

I split from our small group to join the Vainglorys. Walking past cousins I haven't seen since prep school and uncles I was convinced were dead, I make my way to the front of the group, only a few steps away from the platform.

Other than a few throats being cleared and muffled coughs, the silence is ominous. It's as if it has wrapped itself around the very molecules in the air and is whispering our fate in our ears.

When all heirs have joined their respective families, a woman steps onto the platform, her long tunic dress as black as the obsidian under her bare feet. Her white hair is plaited into a crown around her head, the wrinkled skin around her pale blue eyes painted gold. The six sigils of the ruling families are tattooed on her aging skin, three on the inside of each forearm.

Although I've never seen her before I immediately recognize her as the Oracle.

The adjudicator of the Lottery.

The silence was already potent before she stepped onto the platform, but now that she is standing at its very center, it feels like it could suffocate me if I would only let it.

"Heirs," she says with a stern voice, looking straight ahead. "Please come forth."

My heart pounds in my chest when I follow her order and step onto the platform, the obsidian stone surprisingly warm.

We are all equidistant from each other, standing at the edge of the platform, dressed in similar ceremonial garb. The men are shirtless, donning a simple pair of white pants, while the women wear a white dress with a plunging neckline and exposed back. Our accoutrements reveal our family sigil tattooed on the entirety of our backs.

A small emblem to honor our gods.

A glance around the platform tells me we are all equally feeling the gravity of the moment—I have never seen Gemini and Constantine this serious.

My gaze lingers on Mercy to my left. Her face is smooth and impassive.

I look away.

The Oracle stays silent long after we've settled into our respective places. I wipe my clammy palms inconspicuously onto my pants as I wait for her to speak and swallow a hard lump when I finally hear her voice echo magnanimously through the hall.

"It has been six thousand nine hundred and forty days since our last communion with the gods." She pauses and spins in a slow circle as she takes the time to look every single one of us in the eyes.

When my turn comes and her blue gaze connects with my own, a cold jolt travels down my spine. Her eyes shimmer with ancient knowledge so powerful that even a Vainglory like myself would not feel worthy of its secrets.

"Gathered before us today are the fresh faces of a new epoch." Her smile is sudden; wide, and unsettling. "Faithful servants to our all-powerful gods. From this handful of souls the next ruler will be chosen—allowing a new god to reign over Pravitia for the next six thousand nine hundred and forty days." With a slow curl of her hand, she addresses Aleksandr first. "Aleksandr Vorovsky, heir to the last ruling family, servant of the god of excess, and slave to no vice." Stepping up to him, she presses what looks like a small coin into his palm. Turning to the next family, she continues, "Constantine Agonis, servant of the god of torture, and invulnerable to pain."

Just like with Aleksandr, she hands her a coin. Constantine's cheeks pinken, her expression turning coy as if being addressed in this manner is making her bashful.

"Gemini Foley," the Oracle says, "Servant of the god of trickery, and impervious to all lies. Belladonna Carnalis, servant of the god of lust, and wielder of all carnality." She hands them both a coin. Her gaze falls on Mercy, whose face is still a blank mask. "Mercy Crèvecoeur, servant of the god of death, and conduit to the afterlife." She accepts her coin with the same leaden expression.

Finally, the Oracle's attention swings to me. My breathing turns shallow as I try not to make a sound, sweat beading on my forehead. "Wolfgang Vainglory, servant of the god of idolatry, and wielder of persuasion and worship." When the coin makes contact with my palm, I glance down and realize it's engraved with my family's sigil.

She returns to the center with soft steps and falls silent once more.

The anticipation is a deliberate kind of torture to which I doubt even Constantine isn't impervious. I've been waiting my whole life for this moment. The Vainglorys have not been in power for over a hundred years.

It's our time.

My time.

Our gazes are all trained on the Oracle as she closes her eyes, bringing her chin up while her palms are open, arms close to her body on either side of her.

Time seems to slow to a halt as we wait. The limbo feels especially great since we heirs don't know the exact process of the Lottery, only the sacrifice we must complete. I sneak a glance at Aleksandr but he's studying the Oracle intently, eyebrows dipped into a severe arch.

I'm concealing a small sigh when my back begins to sting. I don't have time to question the sensation before the smarting turns into an intense burn. I choke on a loud wheeze, eyes watering as I fall to my knees. If I didn't know any better, I'd think my back had caught on fire.

As soon as I make contact with the floor, the coin flies out of my hand at the same time as the flames from the many torches and candles extinguish, plunging the room into total darkness. I barely hear the small gasps emanating from the crowd as I try to contain my pained whimpers, writhing in agony. The light returns in a burst of flames and then falls back to its normal state.

With it, my pain evaporates.

I'm sucking in breaths, panting in exertion as I try to force my mind to focus back on what is in front of me.

The Lottery.

Suddenly, it dawns on me.

Looking up, I find the Oracle's glare trained on me, my coin in the center of her palm. I scramble to my feet, my heart beating wildly.

"The gods have chosen," she says in an even tone. "Idolatry shall rule next."

I can't contain the bewildered laugh that falls out of my mouth, turning to my parents who are beaming with pride, my mother smiling wide while my father nods beside her.

"Vainglory," the Oracle says, calling my attention back to her. "By your hand, a Vorovsky must die. Please declare your sacrifice."

My smile falls, gaze swiveling to Aleksandr. All I find is quiet resolve. He knew this moment was coming just as I did. The chosen must always select their sacrifice from the past ruling family. I can't deny that I've deliberated who I would choose, especially considering our close relationship. It leaves me questioning if friendships can ever thrive in the city of Pravitia.

Whose death would cause the least ripples between us?

I look past my friend, to his family behind him. His parents are out of the question, my gaze skating over them to finally fall on one of his estranged cousins.

I lock eyes with the eldest. He must be in his forties with a bowl cut that should be worthy of a mercy killing in the first place.

"Boris Vorovsky," I declare loudly.

The last vowel has barely passed my lips when Boris' head whips backward, Mercy's dagger lodged deep into his left eye. Shocked gasps rise from the crowd as his family disperses around him, his body crumbling to the ground.

Dead.

15

MERCY

*E*ven from across the room, my aim is perfect. My trusted dagger, which I refused to take off even here, sinks into Boris Vorovsky's eye like warm butter. I can feel death's cold embrace wrap itself around his body even before he has time to collapse to the floor.

I might have not known which family was next in line, but one thing I *did* know was who would be sacrificed. I felt the call as soon as I walked into the grand hall. Death swam around my head, whispering the fate of the Vorovsky cousin, like it had done my entire life.

His death didn't need to be by my hand—I answer the call as I please—but Boris' fate was as inevitable as the Lottery.

However, the sacrifice *needed* to be mine. I was ready to betray whichever family was chosen next, the only thing that mattered was gaining control of Pravitia for myself. It just so happened that the gods chose the most execrable of us all.

Wolfgang whips around to find me smirking. His blue-gray eyes narrow into slits. His naked chest rising quickly, breathing hard like a bull at an inane rodeo.

For a long loaded beat, everyone is frozen in place.

Until Wolfgang breaks the spell.

"You *bitch!*" he growls, charging toward me with surprising speed until he lunges forward and tackles me to the ground.

Even with the wind knocked out of me, I manage to fight back while Wolfgang hisses like an aggrieved street cat as he tries to wrap his hand around my neck. Curses fly out from his lips but they barely register as I struggle to wrestle him off me, my nails leaving scratch marks on his cheek and neck.

The scuffle doesn't last long until Wolfgang is finally dragged off me, but not before he grabs a handful of my hair pulling me up with him. "Bonafide ape, let go of me!" I shout while I try to get out of his grasp.

The Oracle's voice rises high up above the commotion. "Cease your childish squabbles *immediately*." Her tone is measured but the warning is unmistakable.

Once again, everyone freezes. Wolfgang releases my hair from his grasp as we both look over to where the Oracle is standing.

Her lips are pinched, hands clasped tightly together in front of her while her disapproving glare surveys the crowd. "Everyone out except the six servants." There's a small ripple of protest coming mostly from the Vainglory family. The Oracle's stern gaze slices to their faction. "I said *out*."

While we wait for everyone to file out, I distance myself from Wolfgang. My scratch marks, red and swollen on his left cheek, send a victorious thrill through my veins.

Pretending that his seething glare isn't sizzling through me, I rake my fingers through my hair and straighten my white dress. I ignore any Crèvecoeur looking my way—uninterested in the judgment of distant family members who never visit.

When the heavy double doors have closed, and we're left standing in a semi-circle around the Oracle, it's Aleksandr who speaks first. "What in all six gods was *that*?"

"Count your fucking days, Crèvecoeur," Wolfgang adds with a hiss, hands in tight fists, his knuckles turning white.

I scoff, unperturbed. "You can't touch me, Vainglory. I would have killed you long ago if that was the case."

The ruling families don't follow many laws but even this one has us all staying in line. Called *damnatio memoriae* or damnation of memory, the six heirs are forbidden to kill each other. The disgraced servant, along with the entire family, is wiped out and eliminated from all records if this law is broken.

Even I'm not daring enough to tempt the wrath of our gods to that extent.

"Quiet," the Oracle says somberly.

I snap my mouth shut and wait for her to speak again.

Gemini, Belladonna, and Constantine haven't said a word, but by the look on their faces I can tell they're as taken aback by my actions as Wolfgang and Aleksandr.

"These are unprecedented events." Her blue gaze slides slowly to mine. "No one has ever been asinine enough to sully the ritual in this manner," the Oracle says, her jaw clenching again and again.

"The sacrifice is the only thing the gods *truly* care about," I say, cutting through the accusatory silence. "The power is rightfully mine."

"They chose *me*," Wolfgang spits, taking a step toward the Oracle.

"Please," I throw back, "because of a silly flying coin?"

Wolfgang's mouth opens on a fresh new insult, but we're both silenced by the Oracle before I have the honor of hearing it.

"*Enough*," she says with aggravation, looking at Wolfgang and me. "You both must be entirely moronic to believe that you'd have the last word." She closes her eyes. "The gods will decide."

I cross my arms, pretending this is a mere annoyance, but

my heart is slamming against my chest. Six pairs of eyes lock on the Oracle while we wait for her verdict. The flames lighting the hall begin to flicker, and the air around us shifts into something more ... dense.

My coin, now on the ground, begins to vibrate before flying into the Oracle's open palm.

Finally, her eyes fly open.

"You shall rule together," she declares, her voice slightly disembodied.

Startled, I take a step back. Wolfgang lets out a livid shriek and flies into another fit of rage, attempting to lunge for me again, but Aleksandr grabs him by the shoulder, pulling him back hard. He whispers in Wolfgang's ear, both of them glaring at me, and whatever he says seems to calm his friend down.

It's over in a second, and I turn to the Oracle, eyes pleading. "But—"

There have *never* been co-rulers in the history of Pravitia ... I never even considered the possibility. I curse at my prideful short-mindedness.

"The matter is settled." Her gaze is threatening. "You dare tempt fate? Then accept the consequences," she says, expression hardening. "It could have been far worse, Crèvecoeur." Pointing to the far corner of the room, she adds, "The new rulers will dispose of the sacrifice. The rest of you, follow me out."

My eyes flick to Wolfgang who is still seething, and I stomp across the cavern to the corpse before we're completely left alone, pulling my dagger out of Boris' face. Keeping an eye on Wolfgang, I wipe the blade with the hem of my dress, the blood seeping into the white threads.

I refasten the dagger to my thigh but not before ripping a slit in the dress in case Wolfgang plans on doing anything rash and I need quick access to my weapon.

"Let's get this over with," I say, referring to the body at my feet.

Wolfgang is still standing in the middle of the platform, arms crossed, chin high. He doesn't deign to look at me when he replies, "You wanted this so badly." His lips curl in disgust. "You deal with it."

I puff out an irritated breath but don't bother arguing. The less I interact with him, the better. I crane my neck to where the Oracle pointed. It appears to be a large stony well of some kind.

Lifting the cadaver's feet, I wedge them under my armpits, coiling my hands around his calves and start to pull. The only sounds heard in the hall for the next minute are the body getting dragged across stone floors, mixed with my impatient pants and heated curses while Wolfgang stands petulantly on the platform.

Finally, after a few stops to catch my breath, I make it to the corner of the room. Wiping sweat from my brow with the back of my hand, I peer down the well, breathing hard.

It's more like a gaping hole in the ground, with barely any ledge surrounding the cavernous pit. I'm assuming it's filled with the sacrificial skeletons of past Lotteries.

Getting on my knees, I give the body a few hard shoves and it topples over the edge. The seconds between the fall and the sound of the body landing at the bottom confirm that the pit is deep. Letting out a tired sigh, I stand up and startle when I realize Wolfgang is standing right next to me.

"Needs to be said," he drawls, his words sharp and pointed. "You look like a whore in that dress."

I don't have time to react before he shoves me hard in the chest. I lose my footing, my body pitching backward as I fall straight into the pit.

16

MERCY

It takes me less than three seconds to hit the bottom. I barely have time to think, my mind shutting off as my survival instincts kick in. The hole is too wide for me to even try using the stone walls to stop myself, and ultimately my back slams into a hard mass of bones, painfully stealing my breath away.

Although I'm fighting a *far* too human and irrational hysteria of being at the bottom of a pit of skeletons; the scream I let out while falling still echoes against the walls, and I'm embarrassed by my blatant show of weakness.

Especially in front of a Vainglory.

Egregious self-serving scrote.

I don't bother to call out his name. I know he's already left.

Because I would have done the same.

I bare my teeth, wincing as I suck in sharp, harried breaths while making a mental tally of my body's current state. It's pitch black down here, the only light source is the mouth of the pit high above, but I'm far too deep for it to travel to me.

A sharp pain coming from my left arm has me hissing loudly, and I blindly grope at my arm to find that a piece of bone has lodged itself into the muscle of my forearm. Forcefully pulling the bone out, the pain travels up into my neck, and I let out a desperate scream knowing that, this time, no one will hear my revolting frailty.

Flipping over to my stomach, I try to push myself up, my left arm giving out under my weight.

I continue to fight through the abhorrent hysteria, sucking down air through my nose and then out through my mouth but end up gagging on the putrid smell surrounding me.

Get yourself together, Mercy.

It's just a pile of bones. I've seen much worse. I've *done* much worse.

I manage to get myself up on both feet, the bones shifting under my weight making it difficult to keep my footing. My eyesight has grown accustomed to the dark yet, I only see shadows, my hands in front of me barely visible as I try to reach the stone wall.

I bump into something a little more ... fleshy and immediately know I've found Boris. Thinking his corpse might help me reach up a little higher, I plant my feet on his stomach and step onto his wide chest.

My hands fumble against the wall and by the feel of the uneven raised brick, I think that I might stand a chance of climbing out of here. But not before I get rid of my long manicured nails. I start with my thumb, clamping my teeth down on the nail. Chewing and then ripping it off, I spit the piece out and then move on to another finger until finally, I've done both hands.

Digging my fingers into the grooves between the stone bricks, I struggle to pull myself up, my left arm throbbing with excruciating pain, the warm drip of blood coating my skin. It takes a few tries but my bare feet manage to find a foothold beneath me, and I let out a shocked laugh, surprised that my plan is working.

Oh so slowly I begin to climb up, sweat prickling my skin as my harsh breathing fills the air.

I've only made it up a few feet before my grip slips and I fall backward into the pit of bones.

The rage that flares at my defeat nearly suffocates me.

I curse Wolfgang's entire lineage while I scramble back to my feet, even more determined than before. This time, I make it a little further up before crashing back down.

I lose count of the times I try and subsequently fail.

I lose count of time itself as my attention is solely focused on climbing out of this rotten well.

I'm catching my breath before my umpteenth attempt when I hear Constantine's voice float down to me.

"Mercy, darling, are you down there?"

"Tinny?" I say a little too desperately. Looking skyward, I can barely make out a shadow of what looks like a wave of a hand.

"Mercy!" she replies with her usual glee when she hears my voice.

"How did you find me?" I can't help but ask.

"Wolfie sent me — said you'd probably die down there if I didn't." Another shadow appears beside hers. "I brought Gemini as reinforcement!"

"Are you okay, love?" Gemini asks.

I suppress the overwhelming sense of relief I feel hearing both of their voices while my fury at Wolfgang still scorches my insides. I know the only reason he even sent Constantine in the first place is out of pure selfishness—most likely fearing *damnatio memoriae* more than he fears me.

"Just get me out of here," I bark loudly.

They both mutter something that I can't make out, and I stew in my indignation while I wait. Seconds later, Constantine's voice travels back down to me.

"We're sending down a rope, tie it to your waist and we'll help you climb out!"

I grope at the dark, eventually finding the rope. Tugging it further down, I loop it around my waist, yelling out that I'm ready after making sure the knot is secure.

It takes great effort, but they manage to heave me up the well as I hold onto the rope while shuffling my feet against the stones. When I arrive at the top, they hook me under my arms and drag me out and onto the cool marble floor. Trying to hold on to the waning amount of dignity I have left, I quickly clamber to my feet.

Gemini gives me a slow once-over, my breathing loud in the silence. "You look positively ghastly," he finally states, "and what did you do to your *nails*."

Smoothing the matted hair out of my face with irritation, I narrow my eyes. "Whose fault is that?" I ask with a snarl. "I'm going to stake Wolfgang's head on a *pike*."

"You both are quite homicidal for two people who can't kill each other," Constantine states, pursing her lips in amusement.

I glare at both of them, their mirth making me ill. "There are worse things than death," I answer before storming out the door.

A FEW HOURS LATER, I'M BACK AT THE GROUNDS, BANDAGED AND showered. The wound on my left arm needed a few stitches, but it was nothing Jeremial hadn't done before.

Padding into my lofty bedroom, I cinch my black chiffon robe around my waist, the billowy sleeves lined with ostrich feathers. I let out a small whistle and hear the clacks of my dogs' claws before seeing all three strut in.

I gingerly crawl onto my satin sheets, the dogs jumping up

after me. Sundae curls up beside me while Truffles and Éclair settle down at my feet with small sighs.

Now that the adrenaline of the Lottery—paired with a forced trip down a sacrificial pit—has started to seep out of me, my body is heavy with exhaustion.

The fury that fueled my many attempts up the wall has simmered down to a quiet rage. I'm sure that Wolfgang expects me to retaliate quickly. If that's what he believes, then it only proves how little he knows me.

Because revenge never expires.

Revenge never forgets.

Scratching Sundae behind the ear while she nuzzles into my thigh, I sigh deeply. Dread is slowly slithering its way up my throat at the thought of what comes next.

In the upcoming days, as the new ... co-ruler of the city, I will have to move into Mount Pravitia, alongside Wolfgang.

Most of the lingering rage roiling inside of me is directed at myself.

How could I have been so *idiotic*?

So bold to think I could outplay our gods at their own timeless game.

I could refuse to move and rule from the Grounds—let Wolfgang have Mount Pravitia.

But not only would I never want to *let* Wolfgang have anything, I would undoubtedly miss out on valuable information. I would rather slit my own throat than give a Vainglory the upper hand. Not to mention that moving into Mount Pravitia is a long-standing tradition—and I think I've tested the gods enough for an entire lifetime.

Although this particular defeat hurts worse than having every bone in my body pulverized, I must accept my fate: For the next nineteen years, Wolfgang and I are linked together, whether I want to accept it or not.

17

MERCY

Three days later, Jeremial pulls up to the back entrance of Mount Pravitia. It's late in the evening, and although this is a private street, I don't trust that it will keep the parasites from trying to capture exclusive pictures of the new ruler of Pravitia.

I keep my wide-rimmed fringed hat on my head to cover my face as Jeremial opens the car door for me to step out.

The news of there being two rulers broke yesterday.

The entire city was shocked.

I'm sure Vainglory Media painstakingly controlled how the story was covered. Outside of the six families, no one knows how the power is handed down. Only that it happens every nineteen years, and that—until three days ago—there has always only ever been one sole ruler.

According to Gemini, the break in tradition has sent ripples of intrigue through the entire city, creating a buzz of gossip and speculation.

I have no patience for any of it.

The commoners can yak all they want—at the end of the day, it doesn't change that I am still *one* of their rulers now.

The thought of having to share this new Crèvecoeur epoch, and with a Vainglory no less, certainly dampened the victory. Still, a small thrill zips down my spine when I step into Mount Pravitia. My recklessness paid off—I now hold the city in the palm of my hand.

I make my way to the sixth and top floor of the building where the ruler's private chambers are located. It's a sprawling collection of beautifully designed bedchambers, living quarters, and receiving rooms, meant to accommodate a large family. Children of the ruling family are expected to live here until they turn eighteen—or until power passes to another god.

Our parents' generation was the first to decide to solely have one child, so as to prevent the potential anguish of one of their offspring being sacrificed at the Lottery. They offered the gods heirs to continue the bloodline—the six of us—and nothing more.

I hear quickening footsteps behind me and I turn to find one of my servants, who I put in charge of moving my belongings into the ruler's chambers, looking flustered and wide-eyed.

"Miss Crèvecoeur, there's uh—" She swallows hard, her red lipstick desperately needing a retouch. "There's an issue with the living situation."

Slowly removing my hat, I hand it to Jeremial beside me and I quirk an eyebrow.

"*What* issue?" I say slowly, my shoulders tensing, as I slowly readjust my elbow-length leather gloves.

She seems to shrink in size, and I must admit, I'm pleased by the fear she seems to harbor for me. She stutters but eventually says, "Mr. Vainglory has already claimed the ruler's chambers as his."

I bare my teeth at the sound of his name, pinning her with my stare. "Where are the rooms?"

She points a shaky finger in the direction she just came from. "Through there, Miss Crèvecoeur."

The doors open to an enfilade, a series of connected rooms aligned with each other, which permits me to see all the way into the ruler's bedchambers at the very end.

My gaze snaps to Jeremial. "Wait here."

I pass through three opulently carved doorways before entering the fourth and final one, only to find Wolfgang lounging on an imposing four-poster bed like a king without a throne, wearing nothing but a pair of black silk pants.

"Crèvecoeur," he drawls, not bothering to look up from the tabloid magazine he's flicking through. "Still alive, I see."

I ignore his provoking dig. "The ruler's chambers are *mine*," I growl, my gloved hands tightening into fists.

Wolfgang's gray-blue gaze moves up slowly to meet mine, and every muscle in my body tightens. His glare is hard but seemingly unbothered by my anger. Chuckling dryly, he rolls off the bed. "And what makes you think that?" He slips into a crushed velvet smoking jacket but leaves it open as if purposefully wanting to showcase his toned chest with a dusting of hair and the defined muscles disappearing into his silk pants.

"I deserve it."

His lip curls into a sneer revealing his two gold teeth. "Bold statement from someone who *cheated* her way into power," he says while stalking toward me.

I straighten my shoulders and lift my chin as he approaches, standing my ground.

"A sacrifice is a sacrifice," I spit out coldly. "I was just quicker."

He snarls, his hand snatching my left arm as he tries to drag me closer to him. His hold tightens around my still-smarting wound, and I can't help but hiss in pain. I purposely chose to wear long gloves tonight to hide the bandage around my forearm. I didn't want Wolfgang to learn that his little stunt had left me injured.

The room falls silent, Wolfgang's gaze flicks down to where his hand is still tight around my arm, and then back up, studying me. I clench my jaw, trying with all my might to appear unbothered but I'm beginning to sweat from the pain.

Smoothing his tongue over his teeth, he lets me go and steps back. The relief is immediate, but my arm continues to throb.

The air between us crackles with tension as we both glare at each other.

"I have three dogs," I finally say, sticking my chin out.

Wolfgang's mouth forms into a mocking grin. "To your point?"

"I need the space," I retort.

He slowly crosses his arms over his bare chest as we continue to stare at one another.

I'm bracing myself for a never-ending showdown when, to my surprise, Wolfgang sighs dramatically and concedes. "Fine, you tiresome brute," he says through gritted teeth, "but the bathhouse is mine."

He clips my shoulder as he passes me, heading for the door. I turn, tracking his exit. "Why would Mount Pravitia have a bathhouse?" I say in mock derision.

Swiveling around, he leans his hands on either side of the doorway, his abs rippling with the strain. His eyes narrow, a burning stare pinning me to the spot.

"Do you forget that the Vainglorys once ruled Pravitia from these very rooms?" he asks. His gaze trails down my body, then back up. "How could you? It's how our feud started in the first place." Pushing himself off the doorway, he gives me one last peeved look before walking away. "Only now, I have a legitimate reason to hate you."

18

MERCY

I rouse to angry rain pattering against the windows, thunder rumbling somewhere in the distant Pravitia cityscape. Sundae lets out a low whine and tries to bury her wet nose under my arm. With my eyes still closed, I gently shush her, blindly finding her warm body and patting her reassuringly on the stomach.

"It's just thunder, silly beast," I mumble.

It's been raining all week. It began the night I moved into Mount Pravitia and hasn't let up since. It's as if the gods are as disappointed in us as I am with myself. I'm usually not bothered by anything as insignificant as the weather, but it has left me ... on edge. The dogs have been restless ever since we relocated. Being forced into new surroundings, paired with the unrelenting thunderous rain, means they've kept me up most nights. Especially when I haven't had the time to take them back to the Grounds for our nightly walks in the family cemetery.

They don't like change.

And neither do I.

But here I am, the purveyor of my own life-altering circumstances.

Sundae continues to nudge me, and I audibly groan into my silk pillows. Pushing myself up, I sit and throw my legs over the side, squinting toward the windows to find the sun barely risen and blanketed by heavy clouds. The sound of claws against wood makes me turn my head to find Éclair and Truffles near the door, pawing to be let out.

With a sleepy sigh, I put on my open-toe feathered slippers and don my chiffon robe over my nightgown before letting them out. The door is hardly opened before they bound through the enfilade and disappear, Sundae not bothering to move from her spot in bed.

Taking the time to freshen up in the ensuite, I inspect the wound on my arm. It's still sore but healing, and no longer needs a bandage. Surely, it will leave a scar and I press my lips together at the thought that Wolfgang has managed to leave a permanent mark on my skin.

I don't bother to change before I give my thigh a quick pat, followed by a short whistle commanding Sundae to follow me out of the ruler's chambers. Her head pops up from where it's been resting on her large front paws, ears perked up before she jumps down and trots up to my side.

Walking through and out of the enfilade, I head into the East Wing. It's still quiet this early in the morning, the drum of the rain dulling the bustling sounds of the servants only now beginning to set up for their morning duties.

Entering the atrium where breakfast is served, I stutter to a stop when I notice a lone figure sitting at the head of the large oak table, the dark clouds outside the floor-to-ceiling windows casting a long shadow over his body.

"What are you doing with my dogs?"

Wolfgang lets the corner of his newspaper fall, his blue-gray eyes slowly lifting to where I'm standing. Even at this hour, his brown hair is perfectly coiffed, beard trimmed and manicured. The scratch marks I left on his cheek are fading, but it pleases me to see his face still scarred just the same. He's wearing another one of his smoking jackets, his chest bare underneath.

His assessment of me is quick, but I do notice the dip of his gaze to my open robe. I cross my arms, but his eyes still linger a second too long on my short nightgown before he tilts his head to the side of his chair where both Éclair and Truffles are sitting, tails wagging.

Traitors.

Straightening back up, his attention returns to whatever article he's reading—most likely about himself—before he rasps, "I have nothing to do with those things." He takes a slow sip of tea. "Fiendish creatures, just like their mother."

My irritation spikes but I let his comment fade into the sound of the rain, now echoing louder against the countless windows of the atrium. I had the fortune of avoiding him at breakfast all week, but I see my luck has finally run out. Crossing paths outside of mandatory meetings was bound to happen. Still, the familiar aggravation when around him buzzes under my skin.

I walk to the opposite end of the table and sit, black tea poured and served before I even have time to call the dogs to my side, except for Sundae who is already settling at my feet under the table.

"The usual," I say to whoever is serving me while reaching for a copy of the Pravitian Digest. I typically don't bother with the news, especially when I know that the Vainglorys are behind every single word circulating in the city's news cycle.

Their family's power isn't as straightforward as people care to think. It's not *simply* the power of persuasion and glamor—like how he hypnotized those six Pravitians during the Feast of Fools.

No.

It runs much deeper. Their power seeps through any kind of media they create. Especially useful to keep the masses compliant and submissive. Their persuasion through media is an advantage that all six ruling families indulge in daily.

Each family wields a power connected to the god they worship. Passed down from firstborn to firstborn, they are the only viable heirs to continue the family lineage.

Like me and Wolfgang.

Luckily, our powers do not work on each other. And considering that we are the first generation not to have any siblings, the powers—and subsequent immunity—have been passed down to us.

This means the Vainglorys' power over the media does not affect me.

I avoid consuming any of their media simply because it's an unappealing pigswill full of praise for the man sitting across from me. Nonetheless, I would rather pretend to read his precious Pravitian Digest than stare at Wolfgang for another damnable second.

The silence between us is as loud as the storm brewing outside, punctuated by the intermittent crinkle of a page being turned or a cup being placed back on its saucer.

Eventually, the servant returns with my breakfast; two pieces of brown toast, fried eggs, and caviar. Taking a bite of toast, my gaze inadvertently falls on Wolfgang who seems to have stopped reading and is now studying me eat.

"Problem?" I say tersely after swallowing.

His head turns back to the newspaper and he simply shrugs as if dismissing me. I furrow my brows but continue to eat until my attention pauses on his half-eaten plate discarded beside him.

Caviar, eggs, and toast.

My bite turns to wet cement as I swallow it down my throat realizing we share the same taste in breakfast.

"We have a meeting with Claire from the Pravitian Digest at ten a.m.," Wolfgang declares.

I startle out of my thoughts, my gaze lifting to his closed-off face, eyes still on his newspaper.

"What for now?" I mutter, a heavy dose of impatience spiking my tone as I sip my now tepid tea.

The week has been full of dull people and mandatory meetings, and I long for some time alone back at the Grounds. Or even a night out with Gemini or Belladonna.

From the corner of his eye, he sends me a subtle but exasperated look, and my gaze flicks to his mouth, his tongue dragging over his bottom lip.

"Puff piece to officially announce our—" he pauses, mouth curling upward, his attention back on the silly article he's reading. "Co-rulership."

Carefully, he folds the newspaper and lets it fall on the table with a slap. Smoothing his hand over his short beard, he takes a long sip of tea, and my eyes can't help but dip—*again*—to his Adam's apple bobbing as he swallows. Standing up, his silk pajamas hang low on his hips as he presses his curled fists onto the table. He leans his weight forward and pins me with his stare.

"You might be plotting my demise behind closed doors." His mouth transforms into a snarl. "I certainly am plotting yours. But you'd be *advised* to act like we are nothing but a harmonious team when in public. Understood?"

I slam my cup on the table, tea spilling over. "Don't you dare give me orders, Vainglory. You are not, and never will be, above me."

His stare is glacial as he lets the thrumming silence settle around us until his snarl turns into a hostile smile. "I cannot wait for your downfall, Crèvecoeur. The day your god finally comes to retrieve you, to *humble* you through the one thing you love more than yourself—death, *oh*," Wolfgang says with a cold laugh, gold canine appearing at the corner of his mouth. "I will spend my days dancing on your despicable grave."

With a turn of his heels, he storms out, and it's on the tip of my tongue to yell back a similar threat, but I swallow it back down, trying to tamper my erratic heartbeat, already so sick of our childish squabbles.

I would rather watch him slowly bleed out from a knife to the gut.

Yes. That would be much more satisfying.

I let the image calm me down and finish my breakfast in peace, as I dread the upcoming morning interview.

19

WOLFGANG

*A*dding the final touches to my outfit, I fix the gold collar chain on my bespoke three-piece suit and study my reflection in the imposing floor-to-ceiling mirror. I had the thing specially brought from Vainglory Tower. If I were to concede the ruler's chambers to Mercy, I'd at least have some comforts from home. The mirror was one of them.

A pinch of irritation flares behind my ribcage. I shouldn't have let her have the rooms so easily. Not after what she did to me. I somehow got caught in a moment of atrocious human weakness. When I held her arm and she flinched, I could tell she was injured. The fall into the sacrificial pit must have been the root cause of her wound. Although every part of me, down to the very last atom, wanted to see her suffer, I let go. As if pulled by an invisible force.

What was it about her pain that made me sway?

Whatever it was, it made me relinquish the quarters, and the nauseating perfume of regret has been trailing me ever since.

Those rooms should have been *mine*. Instead, I'm living in

the family quarters like someone's powerless spouse and not like the proud gods-ordained ruler of Pravitia.

My mouth contorts with disgust as I take a small step back, continuing to study myself in the mirror. My gaze finds the fading scratch marks on my cheek just above where my beard begins.

I'd have someone killed for much less, let alone *disfiguring* my image like Mercy did.

Ineffable barbaric creature.

There are only two things that have kept me from spiraling into constant fits of rage this week while having to share the same space with Crèvecoeur. One is the subtle knowledge that Mercy isn't as comfortable in the public eye as she lets on, just by the way she carried herself in meetings all week indicates this. She might have craved the power attached to such an eminent title but the woman is a misanthrope at heart.

I might not know her intimately but we still grew up in the same circles. And I'm willing to bet my entire family fortune that she'd rather spend her time with her precious corpses than have anything to do with the public aspect of being our gods' ascended ruler.

As for me? I was quite literally born for this.

Speaking of ... *intimacy*—although my apathetic feelings for Mercy have been lit with the fires of genuine detestation since the Lottery—I have yet to forget what happened the night before the Conclave.

Admittedly, the feel of her warm, tight cunt around my fingers might have blurred the edges of my feelings toward her —if only for a few days. An infatuation that was hard to stomach and lined with a healthy dose of self-loathing.

Luckily, her coup at the Lottery wiped away any lingering attraction.

And now, withholding my knowledge that it was me behind

the curtain that night is the only other thing keeping me sane. I'm not certain I would have ever considered disclosing it to her before the dire shift of our entwined fates happened. But now I can use it as a valuable chess piece, one that I can't wait to play, if only to mess with her head and wrestle some power away from her cold, usurping hands.

It's late morning but it might very well be the dead of night with how dark the skies above us are. The rain pours down in sheets but Claire—who is conducting the interview—*insisted* on a photo-op outside of Mount Pravitia. Unfortunately, despite the miserable weather, I had to agree. The building is the physical manifestation of our newly acquired power.

The four large umbrellas interlocking above our heads held up by Vainglory Media staff manage to protect us from the cold wet rain. Still, I'm much too close to Mercy for my liking. And my loafers are getting wet.

Cherry and burnt almonds.

I can almost taste it. It's as if the rain has created a barrier between us and everything else and Mercy's scent has nowhere to go but up my nose.

I can't stand it.

I want out from under these umbrellas, and let the rain cleanse me of the stench.

Claire, with her perfect blonde updo and pearl necklace, smiles up at me as she stands to the side but still out of the rain, while the photographer readies himself for a picture.

Being the professional, she tries to fill the silence with endless dribble but I'm barely listening, Mercy's silence is louder than any noise outside of Mount Pravitia.

She might not enjoy the attention, but at least she dressed

the part. Never in anything but black, she looks impeccable in a sleek dress that falls just below her knee. The only color on her pale white skin is a hint of blush on her cheekbones and pouty red lips. I nearly choked on my breath when I noticed she was wearing the same pearled stilettos as the night of Constantine's little psycho soiree. I've been avoiding looking at her feet since.

"Ready?" the photographer mumbles from behind his camera.

Simply having the lens pointed at me has me falling into a pose like second nature, my hand effortlessly landing on the small of Mercy's back like I've done countless times before with other women.

I feel her stiffen and I flinch, realizing my mistake. But with a quick look at the small crowd gathered around us despite the weather, I know I can't remove my hand now without it looking suspicious. By Mercy's lack of reaction, I realize she's heeding my warning—we must look like a team, not enemies. A part of me wants to take advantage of this moment, to taunt her like a cat to a dying mouse.

How far could I take it before she snaps?

It's a fleeting thought.

Because my palm *burns* as if my skin itself knows I shouldn't be touching her. My charismatic smile never slips while the consecutive flash of the camera momentarily blinds me, my fingers curling into a fist behind Mercy's back.

"Marvelous," Claire says, her nude lips spreading into a beatific smile as her brown eyes bounce between Mercy and me. "You two look like *quite* the pair. Let's finish this interview inside shall we?"

Mercy seems to choke on Claire's remark but pulls away without saying a word. Snapping at one of my employees to follow her with one of the umbrellas, she turns and storms up the large entrance steps.

My eyes can't help but watch her disappear inside as I gingerly bring my palm up to the rain. It practically sizzles with relief when the drops hit my skin. Taking a few lungfuls of air free of Mercy's perfume, I collect myself, securing the Vainglory mask even tighter over my face before following her inside.

Sitting on the far edge of a velvet settee, Mercy on the other side, we face Claire in the drawing room of the ruler's quarters. We've been answering her vapid questions for the last three-quarters of an hour. I was the one to vet the questions personally, but they're boring and superficial nonetheless.

I'm uncertain if it's the change of scenery or the implicit safety of knowing the answers to the questions before they are even asked, but Mercy has been considerably warmer in attitude since the interview began. An untrained eye could hardly tell she lacks any media training by how she's answering Claire's questions.

I just might have underestimated her yet again.

Claire asks a final question; something to do with our upcoming inauguration, and I respond with barely a thought, my answer already perfectly crafted.

"Alright then," Claire says, "I think we have everything."

Relieved, I move to stand up, but I notice her pause as if considering something. Her head tilts to the side before she inches closer to the edge of her cushioned seat, her eyes sparkling with renewed interest. "One last question before we wrap up, if I may?"

I press my lips together before answering. Her curious demeanor tells me this question is improvised. My eyes slide to Mercy, and she gives me a small nod. I give Claire the go-ahead with a wave of my hand before I stretch out my left arm across the back of the settee. I realize too late that my hand is now only inches away from Mercy's shoulder, and I curl my fingers into a fist to widen the space between us.

"I would love a statement from our two rulers on the pamphlets that have been found circulating the city." Claire watches us carefully, and then adds, "The ones calling for an uprising against the founding families."

20

WOLFGANG

The room falls silent. The air turns into frosted ice, and I can practically see my breath when I let out a small puff of air. Claire's gaze lingers on mine, then moves to Mercy whose facial expression doesn't betray any of her inner thoughts.

The only small tell in her cool exterior is the twisting of one of her rings around her finger. I have a knee-jerk reaction to place my hand over hers, and I'm thankful I'm just far enough away not to follow through.

My attention returns to Claire. Something about her body language and the careful way she delivered the question informs me that it was not meant to be incriminating.

She's just merely doing what I employ her for—reporting. My eyes slide to Bartholomew standing near the door. His eyes are wide, thin lips pressed together, gaze ping-ponging from me to Claire. His alarmed expression, however, makes me question if *he* knew.

I'll deal with the weasel later.

I break the tension by letting a warm chuckle roll off my lips while I smooth a hand over my trimmed beard and stand up.

"Claire, darling. An insurrection?" I ask, my voice as sweet as honey. Straightening my suit jacket, I button it closed while my hard stare pins her to her seat.

My power tingles up my nape. The tether between us tightens. My grasp on her psyche strengthens. Her expression turns soft. Malleable.

"That would be a waste of everyone's time, don't you think?"

Her eyes appear slightly dreamy when she answers. "Of course."

I clasp my hands together. "Now that's all settled," I say slowly, having trouble keeping the ire out of my tone, "The interview is over."

With a flick of the hand, I dismiss my staff, except for Bartholomew. I turn my back to the exiting crew and stare out the window at the dark rainy Pravitian skyline. I ignore Claire's parting pleasantries, my jaw clenching harder with every passing second until finally the clatter of her heels and the shuffle of assistants following her out fade into nothing.

Swiveling on my heels, I stalk across the room, slamming Bartholomew into the wall. I feel his yelp vibrate against my palm as I hold him steady by the neck.

Mere inches from his face, I growl, "You knew." I slam him harder into the wall, his head bouncing against the portrait above us, nearly knocking it off the wall. "Give me one good reason why I shouldn't gouge your eyes out and feed them to the dogs."

His gaze widens, sweat trickling down his temple. "I — I had planned to tell you, Mr. Vainglory, I s — swear, I really was." He swallows hard before continuing to babble, "But with the Lottery and — and the exchange in power, I was just waiting for the right moment. You already had so much on your plate. Forgive me, sir. I — I was going to tell you, I promise I was."

"Wolfgang." Mercy's tone is sharp, and my impatience spikes with her interrupting me.

I twist my head to the side, teeth bared, catching Mercy's gaze from the corner of my eye. She's stood up from the settee, her expression now a lot more transparent, revealing a worried crease between her eyebrows. I say nothing, waiting for her to speak again while tightening my grip on Bartholomew's throat. Something about hearing his pained gargles calms me somewhat.

"We should speak in private."

Logically, I know she's right, but every muscle in my body is singing for bloodshed. When Mercy sees I'm not moving, her gaze turns slightly miffed as she lets out a small puff of air and cocks a hip.

"I don't need Gemini's ability to sniff out a lie to know Bartholomew is telling the truth." She gives a small wave of the hand toward him as if proving her point. "He's as loyal, and pathetic, as ever."

I feel Bartholomew's head vehemently nod in approval, and I suddenly want nothing more to do with the boy. I give his body one last hard shove before releasing him. "Tell Dizzy to meet me in the boardroom in an hour." I try not to get enraged even further, knowing that my second-in-command has most likely kept this from me as well. I'll deal with her later.

He scampers to the door like a fearful little mouse.

"Oh, and Bartholomew?"

"Yes sir?" he chirps, shoulders straightening.

"If you ever withhold this kind of information from me again," I grit through clenched teeth, "I'll let Constantine debone you like a roast duck for her personal collection. Understood?"

"Yes, sir. Understood, sir."

As soon as he disappears, I turn my attention back to Mercy.

"And *you*," I say heatedly as I step toward her.

Her black brows lift in surprise, but she quickly schools her expression and doesn't move an inch, carefully standing her ground.

"Did you know about this?" I snarl, now crowding her. "Thought you could make me look bad in front of Claire? Or maybe ..." My face is much too close to hers. "You're behind all of it. Planning another coup, are we? Now that you realize this kind of power shouldn't be shared?"

Her dry laugh scratches my heated skin. In her heels, she's nearly the same height as me but her eyes still slowly lift to mine. She juts her chin out and regards me with a sneer.

"Do you hear yourself, Vainglory? You're being paranoid. *Pamphlets?* Please. Don't make me laugh." She tries to give me a hard shove, but I snatch her wrist before she can even hit the mark. "Let me go," she hisses.

"Or what?" I taunt. With her free hand, she tries to go for the dagger on her left thigh but I slap her hand away. "You'll try to threaten me with your *little* dagger?"

Mercy might be clever but she's still weaker than me, and I take advantage of that fact by slamming us onto the table behind her. With my upper body, I force her backward, her dress bunching up and over her knees. Before she can react, I slide my free hand over the top of her left thigh trying to reach for her dagger.

"You insipid waste of air," she barks, "Get off me!" She struggles against me, trying to pry my arm away.

I snicker as I savor feeling her struggle under me, my anger morphing into something much wilder. A carnal metamorphosis pulsing full of lust. "I recall you declaring that I wasn't and would *never* be above you, Crèvecoeur."

Her reaction is almost comical. She lets out an infuriated shriek before her hand flies to my throat. I laugh when she squeezes hard, lacking the strength with just one hand to do anything but give me a pleasurable shiver down my spine. Hiking her dress even higher, my palm finally catches on her dagger, and my laugh deepens.

"I wonder," I muse, my finger tracing the leather harness over to her inner thigh, "if your dagger has ever marred that perfect skin of yours." Mercy continues to struggle against me, baring her teeth. It only makes me grip her wrist even harder, my body pinning her to the table as I shove a knee against her thigh, widening her legs. "I wonder," I continue slowly, trying to keep my voice controlled, but now much more serious than before, "if that blade has ever tasted the life force of a cold-blooded Crèvecoeur."

My hand slides higher, and I allow one finger to trail upward and slowly drag across her lace-covered cunt. Her breath hitches and my gaze flies to meet hers, her eyes wild with flames. She grows still under me, and my finger lingers over the dampening spot near her entrance.

Mercy's breathing is just as fast as mine, and when her mouth falls slightly open as if wanting to say something but deciding against it, my eyes dip to her red-painted lips. It's a split second but it's enough for my cock to twitch in my slacks, and suddenly her skin on mine burns worse than it did before.

In an instant, I let her go and take a large step back while Mercy breathes heavily, barely moving from the table, eyes wide and full of what is most likely scorching internal turmoil.

Similar to mine, I'm sure.

"Right," I mutter, dragging my hand over my beard and forcing a bored look over my face. "I'll have Dizzy look into it."

I turn to leave, but Mercy's icy voice freezes me mid-step. "One day soon you'll wake from your precious beauty sleep in agony and realize that I've cut off both your hands for *ever* daring to touch me."

I conceal the small amused twitch on my lips, and from

over my shoulder, I say, "You better go recite your violent little poems to a more impressionable audience."

21

MERCY

"So no matter who the gods chose between us six, you would try to steal their rule?" Gemini asks casually as he strolls into the large kitchen which is located near the atrium in the East Wing.

After the day I had with Wolfgang, I needed a ... friend. Gemini jumped at the opportunity to visit the ruler's quarters, and after a few hours of gossip and martinis, he dragged us out of my rooms for a midnight snack.

"Yes," I answer with no remorse as I follow him into the kitchen. Gemini heads straight for the wall of state-of-the-art fridges, his black boots squeaking on the polished floor. "Even you."

"I always knew you were a cold-hearted bitch," he says with amusement while opening a fridge at random and poking his head inside.

"Don't pretend you ever wanted to rule in the first place," I volley back as I approach him from behind.

He swivels around to look at me, now holding a bowl of cherries. "I am a slave to chaos, love," he says with a grin, shooting me a wink with his green eye, a subtle smear of eyeliner tinting his lower lashes. He pops a cherry in his mouth. "Besides, power doesn't suit me."

Placing the bowl on the marble island, he turns back to the fridge, continuing his search for the perfect midnight snack.

"I don't know if it suits me either." The words stumble out of my mouth before I can even process them while Gemini yells out, "Jello cake!" I freeze and hope to the gods he didn't hear me.

Closing the fridge with his hip, he places the green cake beside the bowl of cherries.

"That looks revolting," I say, pretending I didn't just admit something vulnerable.

"It's a delicacy." His gaze lifts to my face, his eyes narrowing. "Something's wrong."

My chest tightens and I suddenly feel like crawling out of my skin.

I try to unclench my jaw before I speak. "Nothing's wrong."

Gemini pushes himself up and sits on the marble top. His legs, clad in black and white striped pants, swing idly as his head tilts to the side, studying me. "You're lying."

His comment is nonchalant, but it makes me want to smash every breakable thing in this place. I turn to the drawers to have something to do, away from his prying gaze, and begin to search for a fork so he can eat his ridiculous jello cake.

"Your power doesn't work on me, Gem," I mutter, getting more and more flustered with every wrong drawer I open.

"Good thing I can read body language then," he says with a laugh.

"Nothing is *wrong*," I repeat through gritted teeth, fruitlessly opening another drawer. "It's just that—"*Nothing feels right.* "Why can't I find one single *thing* in this godsdamn place!" I jerk the handle far too hard and the drawer flies off its tracks, dozens of kitchen tools clanging to the floor.

The silence settles between us, my breathing much too loud for what I've been letting on.

Slowly, my gaze slides back to Gemini, and he flashes me a sly lazy smile. His tone is innocent when he asks, "Looking for this?" He holds up a fork having already started to eat the cake. "If I had to guess, Wolfie is getting under your skin," he mumbles around his bite.

The mention of Wolfgang's name has me stomping my heels like a child, kicking at the fallen whisks and large metal spoons just to tame some of the fire burning behind my chest.

I soon realize how ridiculous I must look and stop. I avoid Gemini's gaze, smoothing my hair back into place while the silence returns in the kitchen.

"I know you'd rather never share your secrets, love. But at least give me *one*," he says smoothly.

My eyes fall closed as I take a long deep breath and slowly exhale. Finally, I look over to Gemini. Leaning on the counter facing him, I cross my arms.

"Nothing is … easy," I relent with a slow sigh.

He offers me a fork and holds out the cake between us. I press my lips in irritation but grab the fork, stabbing it into the gelatinous monstrosity and take a half-hearted bite.

It's not as bad as I expected.

"What, exactly?" Gemini responds with a small puff of laughter. "Working with a Vainglory?"

My throat tightens recalling our last encounter, earlier today. I could have fought harder, kneed him in the groin at least. But something about his touch made me pause. His exploratory fingers between my legs felt almost … familiar. His hands on me should make me want to kill him. Instead, I was mortified that his touch had aroused me and that he could feel how wet I was.

I shove the thought away before glancing up.

"The gods are punishing me, Gem. That's the only explanation as to why I would be stuck ruling with the man I hate most."

Gemini snickers. "Maybe start with owning up to your mistake." He twirls his fork at my face. "Cunning Cee-Cee, thinking she could outplay the gods."

"Careful," I say, "or that fork could end up in your thigh."

He grins while eating another bite, studying me, then finally says, "What's troubling you most?"

"Wolfgang," I grit out, crossing my arms again. "This all looks effortless to him. The endless meetings, interviews, photo ops," I add with exasperation. "I'm not good with people."

I brace myself for another of Gemini's flippant remarks but instead, he says, "I don't know, love. Sounds to me like maybe the solution is as simple as *actually* becoming a team, instead of simply pretending to be one."

My laugh is bitter. "Don't be so foolish. There won't ever be a time when Wolfgang and I will be friends, let alone partners."

WHEN GEMINI LEAVES AN HOUR LATER, I'M HEADING BACK TO MY rooms when I hear a noise floating up the stairs leading to the lower floors.

It's more than just a noise …

It's—

Violin?

Intrigued, I walk down the flight of stairs, my chiffon robe drifting behind me as I descend. I end up on the fourth floor and while I head down the drafty corridor, a prickle starts to tingle at the base of my neck. I realize I'm walking straight for Mount Pravitia's bathhouse.

The violin notes become clearer with every step I take. The slow realization that it must be Wolfgang playing makes my heart speed up in itchy anticipation.

Still, I'm unwilling to believe that a Vainglory is capable of such raw beauty—such enrapturing melodies.

On soft feet, I approach the arched doorway and peer inside.

The room is lit with countless candles, the flames flickering alongside the shadows as if swaying to the melody. Wolfgang, wearing his customary silk pants low on his hips, has the violin tucked under his chin, eyes closed shut and eyebrows squeezed in concentration. A few strands of brown hair fall over his forehead as he plays with abandon, his torso swaying with the music, abs contracting with the movements as if the violin dictates what his body should do or go next.

He looks ... so unlike himself.

Like a devotee kneeling at the steps of musical worship.

As if the music itself has cracked through his perfect image to reveal something much, much deeper. As if his mask is missing. And all that is left is ... Wolfgang.

And he is breathtaking.

My stomach flutters. It makes me want to turn around and run. Pretend I've never witnessed him like this. Pretend that all that exists is the Vainglory persona.

But I can't move.

I'm transfixed by Wolfgang and his violin.

Standing under the moonlit window, barefoot. He plays with abandon.

And still, I can't move.

The melody stirs something deep inside of me. It makes me want to rub my chest and try to soothe the ache.

Wolfgang's eyes suddenly fly open.

My heart slams against my lungs as he pins me to the spot somewhere between the shadows and the darkened doorway. If I didn't know any better, I'd think he was using his power of persuasion on me.

Wolfgang continues to play, hooded gray-blue eyes burning

a hole through me as I dig my fingers into the cold stone of the archway next to me.

    The music halts.

    My breathing stops with it.

    Slowly, his hand holding the bow falls to his side. Phantom notes still waltz between us, our eyes interlocked. The echoes of his music whisper to me a story I long to hear more of.

    The silence turns deafening. Wolfgang continues to stare, his expression a stone facade. Betrayed only by his darkened gaze and quickened breaths as his chest quickly rises up and down with exertion.

    I force myself to blink.

    To break whatever *spell* this is.

    Without saying a word, I turn around and leave.

22

MERCY

My skin is on fire. Feverish hands burn a path even hotter down my body.

One squeezes my breast over my silk slip. The other smooths over my stomach.

Down the crook of my thighs. Between my legs.

My orgasm builds and builds and builds.

Until—

I tumble out of sleep, a needy moan slipping out of my lips. My eyes snap open and I freeze, my body turning to stone while silence softly settles like silt at the bottom of the ocean.

I rip my hand away from between my thighs.

I was ... dreaming.

Nausea roils in my stomach when I realize I was dreaming of *him*.

I can hardly bear the thought. Thankfully the dream is elusive. It fades the more I try to pick at the details. But oh— does my body ache with the invisible memories of his hungry touch. I let out a large sigh, trying to focus on anything but the tormenting throbbing in my clit.

The rain still pattering against the windows. The hard

thrum of my heart. The dogs' soft breathing in their beds. Éclair's snoring. The silk sheets smooth over my skin.

My core squeezes with need.

Gods be damned.

This isn't working.

I let out a dramatic huff and stare at the vaulted ceilings. Try as I might, my mind drifts quickly to the one thing I'm trying to avoid as if caught in the eye of a storm.

The one memory that has been anything but elusive.

Wolfgang playing the violin.

It's nearly been a week, yet I can trace the curves of his flexing muscles playing that blasted instrument with my eyes closed. I ache with the desire to feel his hard body under my fingertips. They tingle at the forbidden thought. The image haunts me like a ghost wishing to come back to life. If only I keep paying attention to it.

We've barely said a word to each other since Wolfgang pinned me against that table.

That should please me.

Instead, something about his pointed silence has left me on edge.

Luckily, I'm saved from having to further dwell on such vexing feelings when suddenly every wayward sensation in my body shifts. A cold pleasurable chill ripples through my limbs, ending at the crown of my head. A sated smile slips over my lips as I push myself up in bed.

The call.

From the only god I will ever serve with abandon.

My beloved god of death.

It beckons me now to do its bidding. Inviting me to walk the line between this life and the next, my dagger collecting souls with every bleed of the blade.

It's been far too long. I haven't purposely killed since the Lottery—that was over two weeks ago. Warmth settles over me, the promise of death like a calming balm over my frazzled nerves.

A FEW HOURS LATER, I'M BACK IN MY ROOMS, CONSIDERABLY MORE relaxed and freshly showered. The kill was a little messier than expected. A probable outcome when they struggle. I might have been a tad more aggressive this time too.

I needed the release.

I needed the quiet of a kill.

I came back to Mount Pravitia to change into something a little less gory but plan on visiting the Grounds so I can cremate the corpse.

Still only wearing my velvet bathrobe, I pad out of the ensuite and into my bedchamber. My gaze lands on a vase of black orchids on the small writing desk near the door. I stutter to a stop and study them from afar. They must have been delivered when I was in the shower, most likely because it's my birthday today.

Not that I celebrate such a thing.

When I step closer, I notice the card attached to it and pick it up to read. My eyes trail over the handwritten note.

It's signed from Wolfgang. Offering his birthday wishes.

When the words sink in, I fling the card across the room as if it had spontaneously combusted. A swarm of butterflies explodes in my stomach, my heart drumming loudly against my ribcage as blood rushes through my ears. The calm I felt after answering death's call is now replaced by something closer to an embolism.

Why on earth would he—

My gaze lands back on the card, now on the floor near the bed.

It's made out of thick papyrus, dyed red.

I press the heel of my palms into my eyes and groan out loud.

How could I have been so foolish?

Picking the card back up, I inspect it closer.

Constantine. Known to dip her stationary in the blood of her victims.

I ignore the minute pang of disappointment at the realization.

Even the handwriting is hers. I take a quick sniff. It's perfumed. How did I *ever*, even for one single moment, think this was from Wolfgang?

I must be losing my fragile grip on the threads of sanity.

Constantine and her pointless pranks. Silly doll, I'll wring her neck next time I see her.

Not that she'd remotely care. She'd probably enjoy it.

It proves quite hard to intimidate a servant of the god of torture successfully. Especially when she can feel no pain, physically or emotionally.

Letting out a large sigh, I fish my Zippo out of my purse and light the card on fire, dropping it in the empty waste basket near the table.

I need respite from this place. I can't think straight.

My mind aches for the peace only the Grounds and a walk in the Crèvecoeur cemetery can offer.

CHANGED INTO A LONG-SLEEVED CORSETED DRESS AND BLACK lace gloves, I pass through the drawing room, the dogs following me toward the stairs.

"Heading somewhere, Crèvecoeur?"

Wolfgang's baritone voice slithers out from somewhere behind me, and I'm grateful I manage to hide the shiver that hearing his voice creates.

Slowly, I turn to face him.

My eyes travel up his aubergine pinstripe suit, pausing on his fingers fidgeting with his signet ring on his left hand. Finally, I meet his serious gaze, and my stomach dips. I'm mortified, unable to control the flash of heat burning up my body at the sight of him.

"Yes."

"We have a meeting in half an hour," he says with far too much authority for a mere *co*-ruler. "Logistics about the inauguration," he adds with a dismissive wave of his hand.

I cross my arms. "Then postpone it."

He chuckles softly. Humorless and with a hint of a threat as he takes a few steps toward me. "What could *possibly* be more important than the very thing you double-crossed me for?"

My jaw clenches as I flash him a bored look. "Your hurt feelings are getting old," I snap, "Move on, already."

He lunges for me. He's fast, but this time I'm faster.

My adrenaline spikes when my dagger digs under his chin, the skin taut under my blade. This time his laugh is a little heartier and it skitters down my spine like a cold shiver. Éclair lets out a low growl beside me.

Wolfgang's breathing turns heavy, matching mine. It's the only thing I can hear, as if even the silence cloaking the room tries to give us a wide berth. We're at arm's length, but even from this distance, I can smell the vanilla in his cologne. It muddles my head with desire and I swallow hard.

I twist my wrist, my eyes glued to his as the blade softly pierces the skin. Wolfgang hisses, revealing his gold canine and incisor, but his grimace slowly turns into a leering grin as he keeps still, his blue-gray eyes swirling with unspoken threats.

"I'm starting to think," I muse, tracking the small drop of his blood down the blade. "That *damnatio memoriae* is a lesser punishment than suffering nineteen execrable years with you."

Releasing him, I bring the blade to my mouth. I'm mystified

as to why I even do it. Wolfgang's darkened gaze widens, seeming just as surprised as I am. It doesn't prevent me from slowly licking the blade, my tongue collecting his blood into my mouth.

His taste, inexplicably sweet and with a tang of iron, explodes on my taste buds. I suppress a moan, my body engulfed by a roaring ripple of flames. Wolfgang studies me intensely, his chest still rising quickly as he swallows hard, his mouth falling open as he tracks my tongue glossing over my bottom lip.

I take a step back, my mind ablaze just like my body.

"I need to visit the Grounds," I finally say, my voice much too soft. "There's a body, I need to — it's private."

Wolfgang's voice comes out hoarse, the rise and fall of the words laced with a staggering amount of need. "Let me come with you."

23

WOLFGANG

I am not sure how I got here. And I don't believe Mercy knows either.

One moment we're at each other's throats and the next I'm sitting on a bench in a dark barren room watching Mercy fiddle around with a corpse, who she's donned in all white.

There's a small twinge of pain on the underside of my chin that pulls me out of my thoughts and without taking my eyes off her, I bring my hand up to rub where she nicked me. Forbidden heat travels up my spine at the memory of her licking my blood off her blade.

The throaty groan she thinks I didn't hear. I don't know how I resisted the urge to slam her against the wall and taste myself on her tongue. Bite her lips and taste her blood in turn.

My responses to her actions are becoming steadily more confounding. And asking to witness the private worship of her god might be the most bewildering to date. But the fact that she accepted perplexes me the most.

I wonder if she could still taste my blood when she breathed out a small defeated *Yes*. I don't think she would have ever allowed it if we weren't both so rattled by what had just transpired.

I'm still waiting for the trap.

Maybe she'll burn my body next.

But for now, I sit and watch.

She's propped the corpse on a chair and is now carefully brushing their long blonde hair.

"What exactly are you doing?" I finally ask.

"I said not to speak," she answers dryly, not bothering to look at me, too busy forcing the corpse to sit upright atop the metal chair.

I fall silent.

She combs the hair back. Ties it into a bun. Adds a bit of rouge on the cheeks. Places the hands gently on their lap. Blue eyes open and glassy.

I disturb the silence again.

"You can't expect me to keep my mouth shut when you're doing ..." I wave my hand toward her. "Whatever *this* is."

Her emerald gaze slices through me, her eyebrows dipped into a severe frown, but she says nothing while continuing to fuss over her kill.

"Looks more like something Tinny would do," I add while crossing my arms.

Mercy lets out a long, loud sigh. "Better than pruning in a bath while plebeians pay you compliments like a vain little wolf," she snaps as she steps back to survey the results. My lips twitch into a side grin, amused with how easy it is to annoy her.

"Tinny isn't the only one who likes to keep mementos," she finally explains, walking to a small armoire. Other than the bench I'm sitting on and the chair where the corpse is placed, it's the only furniture in here. She opens one of the doors and pulls out a camera that looks like it was made before I was even born.

I study her while she focuses on putting in a fresh roll of film. Her long black hair is swept back over her bare shoulders, a diamond necklace resting delicately across her neck. The tattoo of her family sigil—an open palm holding a flame—takes up most of her back and disappears underneath her corset. We were all made to get our family sigils tattooed on our backs when we turned eighteen, the same year that we were officially eligible for the Lottery.

When the camera is wound and ready, she adjusts the lighting so it's mostly aimed at the corpse. I hold my breath, trying to add respect to the moment while she takes a picture.

Then a few more.

"Do you do this every time you kill?" I ask softly once she's done.

She turns to face me, and I'm struck by the absence of her usual stern expression. As if something about this ritual has softened her edges.

"Only the ones I've been specifically called to," she says.

I give her a questioning look, unsure of what she means.

She fiddles with the camera, avoiding eye contact while she answers, "There are layers to my relationship with death. I can sense when someone is about to die." I nod, aware of that side of her powers. She puts the camera back into the armoire and shuts the door. "But some souls, my god asks me to deliver personally, like this one." She finds my gaze, her face still soft and open. "Those are the ones I burn myself. The ones I keep pictures of. It's also why I collect tithe all year round."

I realize then what she means. Aside from Mercy, the rest of us collect tithe for our gods on specific occasions called Tithe Season. It occurs four times a year. The last one was during the autumn equinox, the next will be during the winter solstice. Mercy, on the other hand, is free to collect anytime, anywhere. Makes me wonder if this is partly why she carries herself with such superiority. Nonetheless, I can't deny the warmth blooming in my chest hearing her share this private part of her with me.

I study her for a beat before asking, "What do you do with the pictures?"

"I keep them in a box."

"That's it?" I say, a little surprised.

She shrugs but says nothing. Walking to the exit, she opens the door. "Come," she declares, "Time to watch the flames dance."

WE STARE AT THE FIRE IN DEAD SILENCE AS THE CORPSE BURNS. Mercy's nearness crackles against my skin while I keep my hands in tight fists inside my trouser pockets. The smoke burns my eyes, and I suppress a cough. I wonder if the smell will stick to my clothes but keep my mouth shut, knowing the importance of ritual.

When Mercy deems her worship completed, she changes from stilettos to lace-up heeled boots and leads us out into the Crèvecoeur cemetery, her three Dobermans bounding up the path with us.

The sun is setting behind the heavy gray clouds. The rain has finally let up, but the soil beneath our feet is muddy and wet.

"I didn't wear the right shoes for this," I say with a haughty sniff.

Mercy pulls her fur coat closer to her face, her expression looking pensive. "Do you even own shoes for this?"

I purse my lips at her small dig but stew in silence because she's right. I am not one for nature—or panting, slobbering dogs for that matter.

I watch as two of them chase each other, while the third doesn't leave Mercy's side. My gaze sweeps around the cemetery, taking in the decaying tombstones and crooked trees bending halfway into the uncovered path.

"This is it?" I ask, scrunching my nose. "We simply walk aimlessly?"

A small puff of air leaves her lips. "Yes."

"Interesting," I mutter, the crunch of our shoes over dead leaves accompanying the heavy silence.

One of the two dogs chasing each other suddenly runs up to me and drops a bone at my feet. Upon closer inspection, it appears to be a humerus. I stop in my tracks and give the dog a side-eye. It sits at my feet, peering up at me expectantly while its tongue lolls out of its mouth.

"What does it want?"

Mercy's giggle is so soft that I almost miss it. My eyes snap to her, convinced I must have heard wrong. There's an ephemeral smile on her lips as she stares down at the dog, gone as soon as she looks up and finds me staring.

"She wants to play fetch. Throw the bone," she says, her tone still carrying an amused lilt to it.

I eye Mercy warily. Taking out my ostrich-skin gloves from my pockets, I carefully slide them on. Picking up the bone with two fingers, I ask, "Is this from a grave?"

She shrugs, giving one of the dogs a scratch behind the ears. "Perhaps."

"How tasteful," I mumble before reluctantly wrapping my hand around the humerus and letting it whistle through the air. The dogs bark excitedly, racing after the bone as if it still has some meat on it.

"I'm sure you've done far lewder things than touch an old bone in a cemetery, Vainglory. Quit the act."

My first urge when I hear her provoking words is to shove her into whatever half-dug pit I can find and fill it with dirt. I stop in my tracks when I find her piercing gaze fixed on me. Studying me amidst old graves, half of her face cloaked in shadows. The fire burning behind her irises propels me back to when I found her spying on me in the bathhouse. And I suddenly realize the intent behind her three last words.

Quit the act.

Because I know what she saw that night when I played the violin.

She's seeking the man behind the mask.

24

WOLFGANG

While the sun set over Crèvecoeur cemetery, Mercy informed me that Gemini wanted her to come visit him at Pandaemonium. In addition to a century-long feud between our two families, I've never been particularly fond of Gemini. But that didn't prevent me from telling Mercy I would accompany her.

"Great opportunity for a candid photo-op of us," I said.

She studied me, a small wave of curiosity rippled over her face in the way she lifted her eyebrows and pressed her red lips.

I wasn't interested in dwelling on the small lull of peace this day had brought forth between us. Thankfully, she didn't either and simply nodded.

Now here we are, in Mercy's town car, each of us staring out of the window on our respective sides of the back seat.

Except.

I'm carefully watching her from the corner of my eye, my thumb cradled under my chin and index finger resting near my temple. It's like being confined in a tight space with a deadly predator. Even if I'm just as much a predator as she is, it doesn't remove the vague but uneasy feeling pulsing inside my chest when I look at her.

My eyes flit down to her feet. She's changed back into pumps, and there's a pinch somewhere deep in my gut when my eyes skate over the dainty row of pearls wrapping around her ankles. It's those same damn stilettos again. Must be her favorite pair.

My fingers twitch on my lap, and I flex my hand around my thigh while my mind replays feverish flashes of Mercy splayed wide open, her skin supple under my touch.

Heat curls up my spine, my gaze smoothing up her fishnet stockings to the slit in her dress where her dagger is proudly displayed. Then upwards to the swell of her breasts pushed up high by the tight corset around her waist, until I end up staring directly at her jeweled eyes already trained on me.

I don't look away. Don't pretend I wasn't just caught surveying her physique.

Instead, I just continue to stare. The carnal ache building and building.

My breathing turns slightly harried. The molecules in the air charged with whatever untapped need I *know* we're both experiencing.

She stares back, her expression just as serious as mine as her face falls in and out of shadows whenever we pass a city light outside.

"Jeremial," Mercy says, cutting through the silence, her gaze still fixed on mine. "Stop the car. We can walk from here."

Breaking eye contact, I look out the window. We're just a few blocks from the harbor. I'm unsure why she's having him stop here, but I don't protest, needing the fresh air of the cold Pravitia night.

Burnt almonds and cherries.

Jeremial quickly parks and steps out to open the door. Being closest to the sidewalk, I exit the town car first, smoothing my palms over my suit jacket before holding out my hand for Mercy to take.

After sliding to my side, she pauses, one leg halfway out of the car, before reluctantly putting her hand in mine. The weight of her palm sends a shiver up my neck, tingling up to the crown of my head, and I drop her hand as soon as she's successfully out of the car and onto the inner side of the sidewalk.

This is ridiculous. I need to get a grip on these runaway reactions I keep having. Clearing my throat, I rub a hand over my beard and avoid eye contact.

I should be feeling nothing but the white-hot heat of Mercy's treachery.

Not whatever nonsensical attraction this is.

I stuff my hands into my trenchcoat and follow Mercy down the street, noticing her body language slowly change into something a lot more stiff now that we're away from her home and back in the heart of the city. Like watching her step into a dress made of invisible chainmail, she shields herself, the calm presence I saw her embody at the Grounds completely erased away.

It reminds me of my own mask. Or the *act* as Mercy puts it.

Maybe we're not as different as I initially thought after all ...

I listen to the click of her heels on cobblestones as we turn a corner when something drags my attention away from Mercy. My hand snaps out to grab her wrist, making her stop in her tracks.

Her head turns to the side, and she glances down to where I'm touching her, her icy glare skating up to mine. "What?" she grits, forcibly removing her arm from my grasp.

I cock my head, trying to find the errant noise again. "I thought I heard my name."

Muffled laughter spills into the alleyway just a few steps from us, and I perk up, irrevocably pulled to follow the sound. I put my finger up to my lips signaling her to stay quiet and indicate for Mercy to follow me with a wave of my hand. She mumbles a few words under her breath but doesn't balk.

At the far end, there's a backdoor cracked open. The laughter intensifies, cheers and yelps intermingling together. It sounds like a small crowd has gathered inside. From my vantage point, it appears to be the back room of some inconsequential business, but there's a small stage in the corner, big enough to fit half a dozen people.

It takes me a few seconds to realize that it's a play of some kind. And a few more seconds for the embarrassment to entrap me like quicksand made entirely out of shame. I gape in horror while one of the actors, dressed up in a vain and pitiful attempt to look like me, approaches a crass version of Mercy.

I chew on the inside of my cheek, my jaw clenched so hard that pain shoots up my temple.

"You *bitch!*" Wolfgang shrieks on stage, pulling Mercy's hair as they tumble to the floor.

A chill traverses down my spine. It's a crude reenactment of the Lottery. I watch in rapt mortification, forced to relive how Mercy usurped my gods-given right to rule alone.

They wrestle onstage and the crowd laughs, entertained by my biggest failure.

The murderous rage exploding inside of me nearly topples me over.

I need to raze this abomination to the ground, need to kill every single person in this room. I take a large step inside but I'm immediately stopped by a hand on my shoulder. Hissing like a snake, I turn around to shove Mercy off me, but she manages to have both her hands land on my collar, pulling me back from the threshold and pushing me into the brick wall of the building.

She surprised me but I quickly regain control, swiveling us

around, her fur coat fisted into one of my palms as I slam her into the wall, her hands flying off my trench coat.

"Another one of your sick little jokes, Crèvecoeur?" I growl through clenched teeth.

Mercy's mask is uncracked, her expression as smooth as a statue's. "Don't be dense," she says with irritation. "You're the one who walked into this alley. Not me."

I slam her into the bricks again. "First the pamphlets, now this? How on *earth* would a troupe of classless thespians know what happened at the Lottery? How could they possibly know?"

Her eyes narrow, lips pressing into a hard line. "I wasn't the only one there that day. Why would I leak this kind of information?"

I bare my teeth, my face mere inches from hers. "Why?" I say incredulously. "Nothing is sacred to you but your private rituals and miserable little death-dolls." My chest pushes against her breasts as her scent wraps itself around my throat. "And because sullying my image would work wonders for your own, wouldn't it Crèvecoeur?"

"You're out of your mind." She tries to shove me off but I'm too close for her to get good leverage. "Get off me," she spits.

I don't let her go. Strained seconds pass in silence while we glare at each other. Laughter drifts out from the open door and I flinch.

I can't stand looking at her for a second longer. Stepping back, I leave her in the dark alley.

I have more pressing issues at hand.

As soon as I turn the corner, I call Dizzy and order to have my men come round up the troupe. I need every single one of these traitors to suffer.

25

MERCY

*I*t only took Wolfgang two days to arrest the troupe of actors and plan their public demise. We haven't had a public execution in over a decade, but Wolfgang was adamant about his choice, especially this early into our rule. I agreed without much resistance. Although, if it were me, I would have approached this headache much more privately. I don't need irrelevant witnesses to exact my revenge.

Death is my audience.

The air crackles with jubilant energy. I can practically smell the anticipation of the crowd gathered in the town square in front of Mount Pravitia. They're just as bloodthirsty as the rest of us. Even the children. Packed like sardines, half of the city wriggles shoulder to shoulder in the hope of sneaking a chance to witness the spectacle.

And what a spectacle it is.

Having public executions less than a month after the Feast of Fools has sent the masses into a frenzy. The macabre event was announced and broadcasted on a twenty-four-hour cycle all over Vainglory media leading up to today. Wolfgang, of course, kept the real reason secret. It's not hard to make up probable cause in the city of Pravitia.

Wolfgang has barely acknowledged my presence since we came across the clandestine play. It's grating, especially when attending meetings with the rest of our staff. His employee Dizzy has acted as a middleman between us and I'm just about ready to slit her throat just to steal a reaction out of Wolfgang.

In other matters, we've yet to find out how the information was leaked. It's becoming clear that we have a rat amongst us. We might not have said it out loud, but I'm sure both Wolfgang and I are hoping that these executions will frighten whoever is behind this back into submission.

And if they don't?

I'll just have to seek them out and kill them myself.

It's insufferably sunny this afternoon. It hasn't rained in two days, as if the gods are finally warming up to us mortals again. A similar stage to the one erected for the Feast of Fools stands a few yards away from the stairs of Mount Pravitia, the troupe of actors lined up at the forefront on their knees, hands tied behind their backs.

All six of them are sobbing, beseeching for forgiveness, which only seems to make the crowd more frantic while the families of the condemned scream hysterically for them to be saved from the front row.

It's a beautiful sight.

Of the ruling six, everyone came to show support except for Belladonna. She's not one for group activities, especially when Aleksandr is attending.

I would have done the same if I didn't have to preside over the executions with Wolfgang in a show of unity. I hide behind large black sunglasses as I stand with Gemini on the left side of the stage. Always the one for theatrics, he showed up wearing a black top hat, a small mourning veil covering half his face, and a silk scarf hanging loosely around his neck.

He's as giddy as the crowd before us.

Constantine, who's standing with Aleksandr to the right of the platform has managed to upstage Gemini, appearing to have come back from time-traveling to the late 1700s. Blonde hair curled high above her head, pink feathers and bows adorning her *pouf* while her dress is a cloud of taffeta, embroidered with pearls and lace.

Wolfgang, dressed in a red velvet suit jacket with black satin lapels, stands proudly in the middle of the stage. He prowls behind the six kneeling with a smug smile painted over the curves of his lips. Typically, as a servant of the god of torture, public executions are Constantine's domain, not mine. My god is more subtle than hers. Death does not seek retribution, only dissolution.

But Wolfgang asked to be responsible for the death of at least one.

Death is all around us, I can practically see the chains tugging on their souls. But in such a large crowd, the six on stage are not the only deaths I can sense, there's another soul my god will claim today, lodged somewhere in the thick of bodies.

There's no fixed method for these executions. Wolfgang can kill however which way he wants, and curiosity pricks at the base of my nape as he strolls up to the table with an array of weapons, waiting to see which one he will choose.

There's an underlying current of anticipation rumbling inside of me; I've never watched Wolfgang kill before. The air shifts, as if the whole city is taking a collective breath while we wait for his decision.

We all crane our necks while his fingers slowly curl around a wooden handle, finally brandishing an axe into the air. The crowd bursts into cheers at the promise of bloodshed, the true life force of Pravitia.

Snapping his fingers at the guards flanking the stage, Wolfgang orders them to bring the man who dared to impersonate him during the play to kneel over a small chopping block, stretching his neck against it. The sobbing continues, but no one important pays it any mind.

Especially Wolfgang, who has now taken off his jacket and rolled the sleeves of his black shirt. He's leisurely swinging the axe in the air as he positions himself perpendicular to the soon-to-be corpse. He holds up his free hand, his gaze on the crowd, and the masses fall to a murmured hush.

The anticipation now prickles up my arms, my heartbeat quickening as I watch Wolfgang gently place the sharp blade against the man's neck. He straightens his shoulder, placing both hands on the axe handle. He takes a slow breath. Then another. Finally, he raises the axe and brings it down with force, his broad shoulders straining against his shirt, the muscles of his forearms protruding with the effort. The squelching crunch of the blade slicing through muscle and bone merges with the crowd erupting in crazed cheer.

But the kill is not over, only half of the man's neck has been severed. The force of the blow has sprayed blood upwards into Wolfgang's face, and the image of him has a smoldering heat twinging low in my stomach. I lick my lips in anticipation, slowly taking off my sunglasses, needing to see him as clearly as I can, hypnotized by the sight of him like this.

Swiftly, he raises the axe again. The second blow detaches the final tendons keeping this man's head on his body, successfully beheading the actor who impersonated Wolfgang.

Because there is only space for one Wolfgang on this wretched earth.

The head falls, rolling haphazardly toward our end of the stage, and the crowd roars even louder. Handing the axe to one of the guards, Wolfgang strolls up to the head and picks it up by the hair. Raising it to his shoulder, he grins widely, blood splatter dripping from his face as the crowd caterwauls for their ruler. I ignore the pinch of jealousy in my heart at the sight of him so comfortable basking in the crowd's approval.

Keeping the head raised, he turns toward it. His darkened gaze snaps to mine before his lips touch its cheek for a chaste kiss.

A small gasp tumbles out of my mouth, my heart stuttering inside my chest as I watch in rapture as he softly presses his lips to the severed head, his eyes glued to mine.

It only lasts a few feverish seconds. Before I can gather my wits, Wolfgang has flung the head back on the ground and sauntered offstage toward Aleksandr and Constantine.

Ripping my gaze away from Wolfgang, I turn to Gemini who is staring at me, mischief dancing in his eyes.

"What was—" he starts to say but I cut him off.

"Give me your scarf," I bark, practically ripping it off his neck.

Giggling, he swats me away but still hands it to me.

"Don't follow me," I order before storming off stage.

Putting my sunglasses back on, I wrap the scarf around my head, managing to conceal my identity somewhat, and slip into the crowd hoping the frenetic energy and the collective focus being on stage will allow me to fly under the radar.

My senses are muddled but heightened, and my breathing isn't slowing down. I refuse to acknowledge the steady throb of my clit while I replay the burn of Wolfgang's gaze on me. I usually avoid crowds but something about the anonymity of thousands comforts me right now. Slipping through bodies, I find a spot to stand and look back to the stage.

Wolfgang has disappeared and Constantine, with her ridiculous outfit, has taken his place. She prances on stage in front of the remaining five, taunting them with a finger as she deliberates who she will choose next.

Suddenly, two firm hands coil around my waist from behind me, a hard chest pushing into my back. Between the split seconds it takes for me to reach for my dagger, I notice two things: The Vainglory signet ring on his left pinky finger and the smell of Wolfgang's cologne, smoky with a hint of vanilla.

My actions continue to dumbfound me as I abruptly stop in my tracks, my breath catching in my throat. A quick survey of the people around us confirms my suspicion—even though I'm sure Wolfgang has done nothing to try to conceal his identity, the crowd is ignoring us. He must have persuaded them to look away.

I swallow hard but don't look over my shoulder. Instead, I continue to watch Constantine, who has finally chosen her next victim, her trusty bedazzled morning star in hand, the spiked ball swinging idly in the air.

With one hand, Wolfgang tugs the scarf down from my head, his breath hot against my earlobe, a slew of pleasure-filled shivers prickling my neck. He presses his hips against me, his hard erection against my ass, both palms slowly burning a path up and down the front of my tight skirt.

"You know," he says while his fingers dance over my hips to the back, finding the zipper. "I wish it was you kneeling on that stage." His voice is coarse but full of heat as he slowly unzips my skirt. I can hardly bear the thought that I'm letting him touch me like this.

But the thought of stopping him is even harder to bear.

My heart slams in my chest. I can feel myself getting wet, my clit now an aching and demanding pulse. I don't move, arms firmly crossed over my chest while I barely acknowledge his presence except for a subtle grind against his cock. His left hand splays wide just above my core, pinning me even harder against him while the other hand slithers under the now loosened waist of my skirt and over my thong.

His short beard tickles my sensitive skin, his mouth still so close to my ear. "I've imagined killing you countless times," he groans, his cock digging into my ass. He wastes no time, his fingers slipping under the lace, letting out a throaty groan when he finds me drenched. I bite my lip, concealing the whimper lodged somewhere in my throat.

My eyes are still trained on Constantine. She's already swung her weapon across the woman's face and is now grabbing her by the hair, pulling the sobbing actress back up on her feet while her jaw hangs loose and bloody.

Wolfgang tuts, circling my clit with two fingers. "Don't you have any shame, Crèvecoeur?" His hand travels further down, dragging his fingers through my soaking slit. "What's making you so needy?" He thrusts two fingers into my pussy, the palm of his hand grinding against my clit and I bite down on another moan. "Couldn't possibly be me, could it?"

Frustration bubbles up in my chest but it's quickly chased away by unbridled lust. Unable to think clearly as his fingers deftly pump in and out as he continues to whisper his heated threats into my ear, his cock grinding against my ass as if chasing his own relief.

"You know," he says, his tone laced with carnal need, "I thought nothing could ever come close to the idea of watching you die."

Wrapping his hot mouth around my pearl earring, he tugs forcefully, and the pain mixed with the perverse need to come by Wolfgang's touch sends shivers dancing down my spine.

My eyes are still fixed to the stage. The woman is now a mangled mess of shredded skin and muscle, she's skittering on the ground attempting to get away from Constantine but she has nowhere to hide.

Wolfgang's fingers slip back to my clit, wet with my arousal. His lips return to the shell of my ear. "But then I witnessed you watching me take a life." His slow circles over my clit become harder and tighter, and I start to feel myself tip over the edge. My hips begin to follow his movements as my head falls backward onto his shoulder, palms flying to his thighs, my sharp nails digging into his trousers and the hard muscles underneath.

I can barely breathe, can barely swallow.

I'm chasing the smooth cadence of his words almost as much as his touch.

Constantine delivers the final blow to the woman's head with a wide beatific smile and unceremoniously moves on to the next person with a small skip in her step.

"And then I experienced the intoxicating thrill of your rapt attention," he growls into my ear. It's my turn to grind myself against Wolfgang's hard cock, and this time I'm unable to suppress the low moan that follows. My hand wraps around his wrist as my orgasm furiously builds and builds. "And now I wonder if anything will ever come close to that feeling ever again." I can feel his battering pulse under my palm. "The thought makes me sick," he spits.

My mouth falls open as the pleasure explodes in a burst of blinding bliss, and my knees almost buckle under the weight of my climax. Wolfgang fucks me with three fingers through it all, the palm on my stomach digging into me.

"My ruin." His delighted hum feels almost perverse while his fingers are still deep inside of me. The tip of his nose trails up my neck. "Aren't you glad I made you come this time?" he muses. He pitches his hips forward, reminding me how hard he still is. "Remember, Crèvecoeur?" His body tenses while his mouth remains next to my ear. "When you served your cunt up on a silver platter for me at Manor?"

I freeze, my mind still on fire, a small *What?* tumbling over my lips.

His chuckle is filled with darkness. "Pretty little crescent moon you have tattooed on your hip," he taunts hoarsely before ripping his hand out of my skirt and shoving me away, leaving me breathless and keening.

By the time I've turned around, he's disappeared into the crowd

26

MERCY

"I once gouged someone's eye out just two doors down from here," Constantine sing-songs as she walks through the entrance of our personal seamstress' studio, the door held open by Constantine's pet, Albert. It's a small space, with heavy black curtains framing the windows and a busy floral wallpaper covering most of the space.

"Am I meant to be surprised by that?" Belladonna responds with a hint of disdain as we both walk in after her. "I bet it would be easier to list off places around Pravitia where you *haven't* maimed anyone."

Belladonna's coldness towards Constantine could easily be explained by old family feuds but in truth, she just doesn't understand Constantine's appeal and only tolerates her in small doses. I'm usually the one who forces her into it—like today. Constantine, however, has never cared about what other people think of her or bothers to keep track of the feuds between the six ruling families.

She giggles and turns to face us, pleated pink skirt twirling. "That's a good point, Bee."

Temperance—seamstress to the ruling class—appears from

the back wearing a gold mumu, her curly brown hair pulled into a chignon. She's been ancient for as long as I can remember; I'm always half-surprised when I don't feel death lurking in the shadows anytime I visit her. "Girls!" she says theatrically. "Always so lovely to see you."

She walks up to me first and places her hands on my shoulders, giving me two air kisses before sweeping her gaze up and down, seemingly taking me in.

"Power is becoming on you, my dear," she says.

Her tone is far too warm for my comfort. I ignore how her compliment makes my chest tingle while I give her a tight-lipped smile, quickly removing myself from her grasp. Not bothered by my lack of response, she moves to the two others before clasping her hands together, multiple rings clinking, and surveys all three of us.

"Just shy of two weeks until the inauguration," she muses. "You didn't give me much time."

"Oh Tempie, I'm sure the dresses will be as breathtaking as always," Belladonna chirps.

"I've been busy," I say under my breath at the same time.

Typically, I would have Temperance come to me, but I desperately needed out of Mount Pravitia this morning.

The executions were just yesterday, but time seems to have stopped, subjecting me to a cursed limbo state where I'm incessantly haunted by Wolfgang's final words and the unnerving pleasure of the ghost of his touch.

Wolfgang was the man who left me high and dry at Manor.

How did that even happen? Was it on purpose? Or just a baffling and horrifying coincidence? And *why* did he not say anything sooner?

All questions I should confront Wolfgang with. Instead, I'm avoiding him. I can't stand the thought that he kept this hidden from me for almost a month.

His move was calculated. He knew he had the upper hand.

My hand twitches near my thigh, visions of gutting him from cock to throat dancing behind my eyes. Still, and unnervingly so, the same confusing flame glows brightly deep in my gut. The thought of his mouth on my skin resurfaces in my mind for the umpteenth time since he so viciously whispered the words into my ear.

A small shiver courses down my body at the memory of the night in question.

The anonymity of his tongue on me.

Hot and needy. His warm lips sucking my clit. Fingers digging into my thighs. I've never remembered a tryst at Manor so vividly before. And it had to be ... *him*.

"Mercy?" My eyes snap to Belladonna. "Are you even listening?"

I keep my face neutral, but inside my heart rate triples, incensed that I just got caught daydreaming about Wolfgang. My gaze sweeps the room and I realize Temperance has disappeared into the back, leaving us alone while both Belladonna and Constance have settled on the purple couch near the wall of mirrors.

I grumble a *What now?* and sit on the opposite couch, facing them.

Belladonna lets out a small sigh, copper hair tumbling down in soft waves over her chest, her long-sleeved crochet dress the color of daffodils. "I *said* that we haven't done anything for your birthday this year, we should celebrate," she says with a smile.

I cross my arms and look away. "I'm in no mood to celebrate," I answer.

"Oh please," she replies with a soft laugh. "Stop being so—"

"Incredibly boring," Constantine says for her.

Belladonna tongues her cheek. "What Tinny said."

My eyes narrow, turning to Constantine. "That reminds me, thank you for the flowers," I bite out sarcastically.

She giggles into her hands, her two high ponytails falling into her face. "How did you know they were from me?"

"You weren't subtle, you dunce."

"What flowers?" Belladonna chimes in.

My gaze slips to hers. "Tinny sent me flowers," I say flatly. "Signed them as if they were from Wolfgang."

Constantine bursts out into an even deeper laugh and when Belladonna joins in, I'm mere moments away from clawing both their eyes out.

Temperance returns and interrupts my violent impulse. Ignoring their fits of laughter, she directs me with a wave of her hand to the small podium facing the mirrors.

"How has it been?" Belladonna asks, a bit more seriously this time.

I peer at her through the mirrors while Temperance busies herself with double-checking my measurements. I chew on my lip before asking, "Being in power? Or having to share with ..." I pause, the words sour on my tongue. "Wolfgang?"

"Both?" she replies with a small inquisitive shrug.

My mind can't help but tumble back into the memories of yesterday—and even earlier yet, and I'm appalled all over again. I mull over my response, keeping my expression flat.

"Bearable," I finally say.

It's a little after midnight when I arrive back home.

I shouldn't call it *home*, but my aversion to the word won't change that Mount Pravitia will be my official residence for the next two decades.

The dress fitting only lasted a few hours, but I was reluctant to return so early in the evening, instead stopping by Gemini's just to waste some time. I refused to answer any of his probing questions about the loaded gaze Wolfgang and I exchanged when he held up the severed head to kiss.

I will keep those secrets to my death—and even longer still if possible. Gemini grumbled about the irony of having me as a best friend but eventually dropped the subject, distracted by some vapid gossip only he could manage to care about.

The living quarters are quiet as I make my way through the enfilade, the staff having retired for the night. I walk into my bedchambers to find them empty.

I do a quick sweep of the room just to make sure but can't find my dogs anywhere.

I stand idly for a beat in the doorway before the back of my neck begins to prickle with an errant thought.

They wouldn't.

I turn on my heels, backtracking through the row of rooms, in a temperamental huff, and head for the West Wing. I know exactly where Wolfgang's living quarters are located, but I've never had a reason to step foot in his wing before now. It's just as lush and decadent as everything in this place, just a little smaller than mine are—and with a lot more mirrors.

I approach his bedchamber with hurried steps and a clenched jaw, but when I hear a muffled groan, I skid to a stop. I hold my breath, my heart slamming in my chest. Through the cracked door, I peer into the room. Only the warm light from his bedside lamp illuminates the space, and my eyes immediately land on Wolfgang sprawled in bed. He appears to be naked, gold satin sheets covering most of his lower body, except for …

Except for.

My mouth falls open. Slowly, my hand reaches my lips as I begin to covertly watch him from the small opening. Gripping his cock in his palm, his head rests on the headboard behind him as he pumps up and down his hard shaft with a tight fist, the muscles in his arm and naked chest tight with exertion.

A moan falls from his mouth, and my clit throbs as if in answer. In the way his jaw is clenched, and eyebrows furrowed, he seems angry, fucking his fist with a barely discernible rage.

I step closer.

His free hand grips the sheets, and a low curse traverses his lips before his movements turn more frantic as he fucks his cock even faster. He comes with a long hiss, his head falling downward, abs growing taut while the cum pulses again and again all over his stomach.

My body is aflame, my mind a ruined mess.

When his dark gaze snaps to mine, I fall deeper into the blazing inferno. A shocked gasp dies somewhere in my throat, but I don't try to escape his scrutiny.

I hold his icy stare as I count the quick rise and fall of his chest.

"Perverted little creep," Wolfgang growls, his hand still loose around his cock. Slowly, he drags his finger through his release, a sinful and crooked smile appearing on his lips. "Next time you want to slither into places you don't belong, I'll force-feed you my cum with your caviar on toast, really make it a delicacy."

His sharp, degrading words only manage to stoke the raging flames even higher, my clit aching to be touched. Instead, I reach for the handle and slam the door in his face.

27

WOLFGANG

I find Aleksandr sitting in the dark, facing a large aquarium, the bluish lights from the tank flickering over his face. He is staring sightlessly at his pet axolotls. Curious-looking salamanders with gills circling their wide heads like a crown—they always appear to be smiling.

Mercy would hate them.

The thought jumps from the shadows like a fanged nightmare. It makes me stumble a step as if the thought itself has morphed into a bunched carpet under my feet. Luckily Aleksandr seems lost in thought, he usually stares at his axolotls when he needs to think. He's sprawled on his couch in the sunken living room, his burgundy tracksuit a stark contrast against the white leather.

The fact that I'd think of Mercy's likes and dislikes over something so anodyne as Aleksandr's aquatic pets makes me grind my teeth as I step down into the conversation pit.

"Something on your mind?" I ask.

I subtly try to sound like I'm not the one who's plagued with unwanted thoughts.

Of that pest no less.

And of how *unbelievable* it felt to have her eyes fixed on me while I fucked my fist. I can't deny she was the reason I was so hard and desperate in the first place. I've been stroking my cock raw since the executions two days ago. And every time I come, her name permanently tattooed on my lips, I promise it will be the last.

It never is.

My reality has slowly begun to sink in ...

I'm doomed to be forever riddled with this *cancerous* lust for Mercy.

Aleksandr's hazel eyes slide to mine as I unbutton my suit jacket before sitting on the couch facing him.

"Not particularly," he says, answering my question with a quirk of his mustache. His head rests against his thumb and finger, the low beat of music filling the space between us. Falling silent, he studies me and a cold shiver trickles down my spine. I've never been able to hide much from my best friend. And his gaze seems to convey that very fact. "I could ask the same of you," he finally states.

Within one single breath, I consider sweeping everything under the same metaphorical rug I tripped over earlier and reply with a generic response about the woes of being a new ruler.

Instead, I reply with a question that has been weighing on me for a lot longer than I care to admit. "Have you ever wondered about the consequences resulting from breaking a divine law? The one which forbids two heirs to marry? Or—" I clear my throat, feeling like I'm crawling out of my skin. "Consummate?"

Aleksandr's gaze turns wistful, his eyes flitting back to the aquarium. "Yes."

We don't have many divine laws, and even a lawless bunch

like us would never dare to break them. The consequences would be too dire.

The most infrangible is the vow to never kill a servant of the gods, which would result in *damnatio memoriae*. Then there's the vow to never mix our bloodlines and to only marry outside of the ruling families.

We've always assumed that the latter included any kind of sexual relationship between us. But the punishment for breaking this law has always been unclear, and I've never had any desire to look into it until now.

But ever since the night at Manor with Mercy, I've been brazenly toying with the boundaries of this gods-given law, half expecting to be struck dead at any moment.

And yet ...

"What do you think would happen?" I gently probe.

Aleksandr's gaze returns to mine, eyebrows narrowing. A small smile appears on his lips. "Why the sudden interest, Wolfie?"

I don't bother answering at first, holding his teasing stare instead, my expression flat while my heartbeat doubles in rate behind my bespoke suit. Then I relent and give him a small crumb.

"Crèvecoeur and I have been ... playing with fire," I say slowly, chewing on my words.

He sits a little straighter, a large palm smoothing over his mustache before he speaks again. "I thought you two were feuding behind closed doors?" he says drolly.

I huff out a breath. "I never said otherwise."

I expect him to press me further—or continue to mock me at the very least—instead, his eyes burn with unanswered questions of his own.

His chuckle slowly dies before turning thoughtful. "We've never had co-rulers before."

My gaze drifts to the three axolotls lazily swimming in the

water, then back to Aleksandr. "What are you implying?"

"Have you not wondered how Mercy walked away unscathed from her little coup at the Lottery?" Irritation flashes across his expression as if angered on my behalf and something inside me quiets somewhat. "Maybe the gods have a larger plan for you two ..." Then he adds almost hopefully, "For us."

I tap my index on my thigh while I ponder on what he just said. "Or maybe they've grown bored of us, and they're merely toying with their servants for entertainment," I reply flippantly followed by a long sigh.

Aleksandr's phone dings beside him. Picking it up, his eyes begin to glimmer. "It's Tinny," he mutters while he reads her text. "Says she's at Vore with Mercy and Belladonna to celebrate Crèvecoeur's belated birthday." His grin turns mischievous when he raises his gaze upwards to meet mine. "In the mood for a little fire?" he asks far too casually.

I pretend the dip I just experienced in my stomach has nothing to do with Mercy's name. My mind sticks to the mention of her birthday, and I try to wrangle the thought before it sears my brain like a hot iron, but I'm too slow. *Why didn't she tell me it was her birthday?*

"Surprised Belladonna would ever step foot in one of your clubs," I say, avoiding the obvious.

He shrugs before standing up. "It seems like not just our gods are acting out of character lately." He gives me a small flick of the head while pocketing his phone. "Let's go."

VORE IS JUST AS BUSY AS ALWAYS, THE SCANTILY CLAD ACROBATS faithful to their posts high up on their cushioned swings. I follow Aleksandr through the parting crowd, slightly miffed that he didn't bother changing out of his tracksuit.

I spot Constantine first, a beacon of pink and sparkles even in this dark lighting, dancing by herself amidst the circle of booths and tables in one of the VIP sections. I don't bother fighting the burning urge to locate Mercy in the sea of people. I find her sitting a few seats over, chatting with Belladonna.

As Aleksandr and I walk up to the bouncer guarding the area, my throat grows dry at the sight of the skin-tight leather pants she has on, her dagger on display over the leather. Unusual for her but just as striking as her typical dress or skirt, her tits spilling out of her black lace bustier, red painted toes in five-inch stilettos.

Gods help me.

I ignore the crowd in the VIP section, most of them witless and power-hungry upper-class drones hoping to one day marry into the ruling families anyway. My eyes stay on Mercy, her gaze now tracking my movements, flawless face stoic as I sit at an empty table near her. I meticulously endeavor to keep some distance, our seats connecting into one long booth with a vacant table between us.

When a bourbon on ice appears on the table moments later, I break eye contact with Mercy and wrap my hand around the sweating glass just for something to hold, my body thrumming with heightened tension. And if the truth wasn't so maddening to swallow, I'd admit that the tension was sexual in nature.

I survey the area while I take a slow sip of my drink, the smoky alcohol warming my chest as I swallow it down. Aleksandr has joined Constantine as she continues to dance, now practically using him as a stripper pole. I notice Dizzy, her body half in the shadows on the opposite side of the crowd, kissing a blonde on the neck, her hand up her dress.

The patrons seem particularly uninhibited tonight. Although, I wouldn't expect anything less at a club like Vore. The establishment is an extension of the god of excess. Aleksandr finds pleasure in witnessing the perverse and gluttonous needs of others. He instigates it, seeks it, and revels in it. His power is an ironic one. He himself can never be satisfied, whether it be from food or drink, and try as he might, he will never experience the freeing release of inebriation. He is but a humble spectator to the hedonism of his adored god.

When my attention returns to Mercy, a man now sits in Belladonna's seat. I can't see his face, only that he must be whispering something into her ear by the way he's leaning into her. A stunning rage fizzles under my skin as I watch his hand trail up her arm, his fingers caressing over the scar from when I pushed her into the pit.

When I hurt her.

Me.

My body locks in a tight fury when my eyes snap to the Vainglory sigil on his signet ring.

I react from somewhere beyond my rational mind. Standing up, I fling the table out of my way, glass shattering to the floor.

From the corner of my eye, I see Mercy looking up in surprise as I stalk over to where she sits. I don't glance her way, too busy reaching for an empty wine glass and smashing it against the table, breaking the stem off. I feel the sting of broken glass in my palm but don't linger on it.

The next series of events happen in a flurry of movements but I cherish every second. I've never been one to shy away from murder, but this one feels a lot more personal than most, and heat scorches up my spine knowing Mercy will be witnessing it all.

His eyes widen when I grab his collar with a snarl, dragging him off of Mercy and out of his seat. Gripping the broken wine stem in my fist, blood from my cut now dribbling down my fingers, I shoot my arm backward to gain some momentum. His arms fly up to protect his face.

And inside the small liminal moment before I bring my arm back down, my crazed gaze flicks to Mercy. Her mouth is open in slight shock, but I don't miss her pinkening cheeks and rising chest. I shoot her a dark grin and then plunge the broken stem deep into the man's unprotected neck. Pulling it forcibly out again, I make sure the spray of blood doesn't reach Mercy. And I ram the stem back into his neck.

Again.

And again.

And again.

Finally, I let the body drop to the floor.

I shrug my shoulders as if shaking off a crick in my neck and pull out my pocket square, wiping the excess of blood from my cut palm. I fix my suit jacket and sit down.

Mercy tries to stand, but I grab her by the back of the neck and pull her backward onto my lap, letting out a few small tsks near her ear. The fragrance of burnt almonds and cherries is just as heady as always.

"He was one of yours," Mercy says through gritted teeth, staring straight ahead and refusing to look at me.

Her legs straddle my left thigh and I hook my arm around her waist, pulling her back tighter against my chest. "All the more reason to kill him," I answer heatedly.

"This isn't what a *united front* entails," she growls, her nails digging into my thigh through my trousers.

I reach for her pack of clove cigarettes on the table, lighting one up with her Zippo next to it. "Look around, Crèvecoeur," I say with a bored wave of the hand, the corpse at our feet now being carried out without any brouhaha. "No one cares."

I take a long drag, my left arm still firmly hooked around Mercy's waist. I slowly blow out the smoke while Mercy twists her torso toward me and turns her head to the side, my gaze locking with hers. Her green eyes smolder and with it my cock strains against my trousers.

I bring the cigarette up to her lips, my fingers still stained red, and to my shock she lets her plump lips fall open for me, her shoulders relaxing ever so slightly. My fingers burn with the heat of her skin and my gaze is fixed on her mouth as she slowly wraps her lips around the filter and takes a deep drag. As her lungs fill with smoke, her back melts against my chest and I wonder if having to suffer the wrath of our gods would be less painful than seeing her like this and not being able to do anything about it.

"Now tell me," I whisper into her ear as she tilts her chin upward, blowing out the white smoke. "You knew that the useless heap of muscles and bones was about to die, didn't you?"

Upon hearing my question, she tries to rip herself away from me. But it's futile. I laugh darkly as she struggles against my lap. My breath feathers over her neck, and I don't miss her skin pebbling as my thumb idly rubs circles on her waist.

She straightens her back, head now facing forward, but answers my question. "Yes, I could sense death around him."

I'm suddenly made aware of a subtle rock of her hips against my thigh.

I hum deep and low as I place the cigarette in the ashtray. When I lean back toward Mercy, I graze my fingers over her inner thigh before I settle us back into the seat. I savor the hitch in her breath and the subtle grind of her hips. I can practically feel the heat of her cunt through her leather pants. The feeling is a blissful kind of torture.

I trail my hand up the valley of her breasts and then her neck, cradling my palm and fingers just below her chin. "Why act so surprised then?" I rasp before sucking her earlobe into my mouth.

A hushed gasp tumbles out of her lips while she pushes her ass into my cock, her hands gripping the booth on either side of my leg. I let out a low groan, her cunt beginning to grind harder into my thigh.

"I didn't know it would be by your hand," she answers dismissively, but she can't hide the tremor of lust in her voice.

Her hips begin to rhythmically rock back and forth, and my balls are so tight they ache. I let go of her chin and grab her waist, helping her pitch her hips, my fingers digging into her flesh.

"I don't need you to explain to me in words how watching me kill him made you feel," I hiss into her skin while my own skin burns and burns and burns. "Considering how you're currently fucking my lap, you sick little fuck."

Mercy laughs.

She laughs ...

It's small, barely noticeable, but the noise leaves me momentarily stunned.

"And what about you?" she says a little breathlessly. She slides her hips forward and reaches back to palm my hard cock. It throbs painfully in response. I bite down on a growl as my lips blaze up her bare throat. "Desperate wolf, wanting the one thing he can't have."

Again, she tries to wriggle out of my grasp, but I'm stronger and fueled by the irritating sound of her last words. "Let me go," she bites out, her burning gaze clashing with mine.

Her chest heaves, and my fingers dance over the curves of the top of her breasts before saying, "What makes you think I want anything to do with a feral creature like you?" My hand moves down her stomach, over my linked arm, and grazes over the seam of her leather pants. She doesn't say a word, but her lips part when I put pressure over her clit. It's a slow taunting circling motion, her eyes burning as I do so. I then splay my entire palm over her cunt, pulling her hard against me. "The very thought of you is a plague I'd rather not *catch*," I spit, finally unhooking my arm from around her waist and pushing her off my lap.

She falls onto the booth, but I avoid the glare she's most likely directing my way and stand up. I ignore my erection, straightening my cuffs before exiting the area, suddenly needing fresh air before I do something I'll regret until my last rightful breath.

28

MERCY

The rain has returned. It batters steadily against the windows, the wind howling as if mourning a dying lover. It's late evening, and I'm lounging on one of the couches in the library in my quarters, my bare feet curled up under me.

To my left, the large fireplace crackles softly with flames and embers while my dogs slumber atop the wool rug in front of the mantelpiece.

Two of the four walls of the library are floor-to-ceiling bookcases, some books as old as our family feuds. There's a large section dedicated to the Lottery records and the resulting nineteen-year rule. Reading about classified information and family secrets I haven't been privy to before would usually thrill me, but the book balancing on my lap is as entertaining as a dull knife to the eye. The words blur, my thoughts much too volatile for any of it to make sense.

Wolfgang is ignoring me again. It's been nearly a week since he last had his hands on me. The night at Vore when he killed one of his men for touching me.

Heat curls low in my stomach at just the thought. It incenses me. I should carry out my own execution for even daring to keep track of time in this manner. Every day I'm repulsed by how easy it is to let my mind wander to the few times I've felt Wolfgang's touch on me.

And yet ...

I find myself emerging from memories without any concept of time, trapped in the echo of inconsequential moments like when his hand found the small of my back in the pouring rain.

I slam the book closed with a huff and throw it beside me on the couch. Propping my chin into my palm, I sigh, my gaze idly lingering on the rows and rows of our family history.

I wonder if ...

I can barely finish the thought. Irritated that I would even entertain any of Wolfgang's recent erratic behavior and how it's only left me wanting more. But try as I might, curiosity prickles my skin.

This library must have a book detailing the divine law that forbids us from mixing our bloodlines. And if fornication never leads to procreation, would we be punished? I can't believe that Wolfgang and I would have been the first to have—I swallow hard, barely wanting to admit to myself, but alas—an attraction to one another.

Quietly, not wanting to wake the dogs, I uncurl myself from the couch and stand up. But I only make it a few steps toward one of the shelves when I feel the air shift.

I stop in my tracks, my head slightly cocking to the side, eyes narrowing.

The sensation is similar to when I feel the call, but it's not quite the same. It takes me a few seconds to remember where I've felt it before. Then it hits me.

The Oracle.

SHE SITS STOICALLY ON A SETTEE IN THE DRAWING ROOM, BACK straight and palms flat on her thighs over her gray tunic. It seems she knew I'd be called to her, and she has been patiently waiting. I sense my god of death drifting around her, but I know it's not her time. If I could sense all six gods, I'm sure I would make out their presence here too. She is their mortal vessel after all.

Her eyes are streaked with the same black and gold as when I first saw her. They slowly slide to watch me enter the room. The weight of her observation makes me tighten my chiffon robe around my waist and cross my arms.

I'm not sure if I should speak first.

The room is tense with silence as I deliberate.

She wordlessly signals me to sit across from her, and I do as I'm told. I wring my hands together as we sit, not one word yet exchanged. Until I finally crack.

"Are we waiting for—"

She holds out her hand for me to stop. I snap my mouth shut.

Time crawls forward. I count my heartbeats as we sit.

Footsteps approach the drawing room and I start counting those instead, until Wolfgang finally appears, wearing an embroidered smoking jacket.

I'm disgusted by the small leap my heart takes when I see him.

According to the small flinch and low hiss he lets out when he notices the Oracle, I don't think he knew who was waiting for him here. His eyes snap to where I'm sitting for half a second, his jaw feathering, before jumping back to the Oracle.

She gives him the same wordless signal, motioning him to sit beside me. He stands, fists tight against his sides for a second too long, until reluctantly lowering himself onto the settee.

A snail could run laps around how slow the seconds seem to tick by.

Finally, she speaks.

"The gods are agitated," she says, her voice much louder than expected.

I wince while Wolfgang shifts beside me. My stomach sinks, suddenly anxious that the gods know exactly what we have been up to. Cold sweat prickles my forehead.

"Agitated?" I repeat slowly, keeping my expression unperturbed. "How so?"

Her blue gaze flicks to mine. And again, I feel myself shrink under her scrutiny.

She presses her lips into a thin line. "There's been chatter of a rebellion."

Wolfgang laughs dryly. "A rebellion?" Crossing his arms, he sits back into the settee. "Nonsense."

The air shifts and I can feel my god's presence like a pulse inside my chest. Still, I can't help but feel sheepish relief that the agitation is not about our most recent indecency.

The Oracle's eyes narrow, her attention now fully on Wolfgang.

"Foolish mortal," she grits, "Power is not everlasting. It can always be taken away. You are nothing but playthings to the gods." She stands, clasping her hands together. "Handle this," she orders. "I do not wish to visit you again."

With those parting words, she shuffles out of the drawing room, leaving us in tense silence.

I cross my arms in petty defiance, stewing over her words, my heart drumming in my ears. How dare she speak to us like that. Treating us as if we're unfit to rule.

But then again.

First the pamphlets, then the play, and now this?

Maybe the Oracle *is* right, and we're not taking this as seriously as we should.

"What do you—" I begin to say, but at the sound of my

voice, Wolfgang briskly stands up and marches out of the room.

I watch him disappear through the doorway, and let the frustration wash over me, sighing loudly as I look up to the ceiling in exasperation.

Killing him would be much easier.

29

WOLFGANG

I focus on the vibration of the music strumming through and then out of me, the violin wailing out a tale fraught with angst and yearning. My fingers move swiftly over the strings, my eyes pressed closed in concentration.

I don't typically prefer this type of melody, but the twinge in my chest is only growing stronger the more I ignore it, and I don't know what else to do but play. I'm being driven to insanity, and I'm not quite sure if there's anyone else to blame but me.

Except—

A prickle at my neck makes me snap my eyes open.

Mercy stands on the opposite side of the water from me, the bathhouse cloaked in darkness, with only a few candles and the silver gleam of the waxing moon outside illuminating the room.

My treacherous heart skips a beat, and I almost start playing off-key. I catch myself just in time and instead start playing even more fervently as I take her in from afar.

Her face is bare, wearing the same short black nightgown and chiffon robe as when the Oracle visited us earlier. It was childish of me to storm out, but I could hardly stand being in the same room as Mercy.

I'm plagued with the thought of her cunt sheathed around my dick. Plagued with the thought of her telling me all the ways she could kill me while still letting me fuck her.

I despise her.

I crave her.

I will have her.

Her eyes reflect the flickering flames of the lit candles, her stare just as ardent as mine. The violin music fills in the silence between us, the air shifting into a living, breathing thing. It growls and moans and begs for attention, but all I can do is watch Mercy.

She undoes her sash. Her movements are deliberately slow. I swallow hard. First falls the robe, fluttering delicately around her bare feet. Then her fingers slide under the thin strap of her nightgown, letting it slip over her shoulder. Then goes the other strap. My throat goes dry. Her eyes burn. A small shimmy of her body. The dress falls. And my violin nearly falters once again.

The sight of her ...

If I didn't know any better I'd think she was the servant of the god of lust for how affected I am right now. Or even my own god of idolatry, for my sudden and blinding need to worship her.

My chest begins to rise and fall faster and faster as I hunger over her naked body. I trace the shape of her with my gaze, the curve of her plump breasts, the smooth lines of her stomach, the swell of her hips, the small crescent moon tattoo near her pubic bone.

She starts for the stairs leading down into the water, never breaking eye contact.

I continue to play, the notes building and building and building.

Step by slow step, the water rises higher up her legs, until she's covered up to her waist. She glides up to the opposite side from where I'm standing and faces me, leaning her back against the edge. Her gaze darkens when her hand disappears under the water, and by the subtle fall of her mouth and the gentle flutter of her eyelashes, I know exactly what she's doing.

I experience a sudden and maddening hysteria watching her touch herself in front of me, unable to actually *see* her fingers, let alone her cunt.

The music stops.

I practically throw the violin across the room in my haste.

Already bare-chested, I tug my pants down, briskly taking them off before storming down the stairs and into the water, now just as naked as Mercy.

Her eyes narrow in challenge as I approach her and although I'm bedeviled by desire I notice the small grin of victory she's trying to conceal.

She thinks she's gained power over me.

"You vile little whore," I can't help but hiss.

Her laugh is mocking and before I can reach her, she dives and disappears under the water. I slam my fist in the water, splashing myself in the process, but I'm too strung out to care.

She reemerges a few seconds later, at the opposite end of the large bath. My cock hardens as I watch her smooth her hands over her wet slicked hair, breasts bouncing with the movement as water lazily drips over her face, her jaw, her lips.

My muscles coil tight, jaw clenched and teeth grinding.

Her gaze snaps to mine. "What's wrong, Wolfie?" she says tauntingly as she idly glides through the water. "Displeased to see me in your *precious* bathhouse?"

The pet name sends an unwanted shiver down my spine, and I begin to slowly approach, my eyes on her like a predator with their prey. "When in these waters, you should be tithing to *me*, Crèvecoeur," I say slowly.

She scoffs. "Tithe to you?" she replies, giving the water a small flick of her fingers. "You mean compliment you? Is that really what pleases your god?" Her eyes track my movements while we begin circling each other. She pouts mockingly. "Your bloodline is a farce."

I bare my teeth, letting out a low growl. "You're one to speak, you morbid freak."

She lifts an eyebrow at my attempted jab but acts unbothered, her gaze idly watching her index finger glide back and forth on the surface of the water. Her sparkling eyes lift back up, and I notice the subtle cocksure grin at the very tip of her lips. "Maybe you should tithe to me, instead."

I grow still, a mere foot away from her, my hand curling around my cock as I begin to slowly stroke the ache away. Her gaze dips down, then flutters back to my face. "Come here, and I will," I say, my voice deepening with pleasure.

She falls silent for a few slow breaths, her face falling into her usual serious repose. "I don't trust you," she finally says.

I chuckle dryly, my head falling back slightly while I continue to stroke my cock under the water. Straightening back up, I pin her with my stare. "What is there to trust, Mercy? That's not why you came to me tonight, is it?"

Her attention falls back to where the water and my stomach meet, seemingly deliberating her next move. The hard swallow indicates she's made her decision. Moments later, she glides like a nymph through the water and *finally* stands in front of me.

"You want me to tithe to you?" I whisper harshly, my balls aching with her proximity.

She studies my face, and her eyes shutter with something I can't quite place before she finally nods.

I grow still, the silence between us urging for someone to speak, until I finally heed its command. "I'd rather never see my own reflection again, than ever compliment you," I grit out.

She startles just long enough for me to successfully snap my hand out, grab her by the throat, and dunk her into the water. Her limbs flail as I keep her under, the glee in having her this compromised is incomparable.

When I gauge she's had enough, I pull her out of the water but keep her firmly in my grasp, my fingers now digging into the flesh of her arms. She gasps, mouth wide open and eyes closed as she tries to swallow down lungfuls of air. It doesn't take me long to push her down again, but not before she lets out a shriek that makes my cock ache with vicious satisfaction.

Seconds tick by and waves form around us as she thrashes in my arms. I could easily drown her. Have her greet her god with lungs full of water. But as I deliberate, I realize that maybe *damnatio memoriae* is not what I fear the most, but the fleeting thought that Mercy and I are destined for more.

It makes me want to drown alongside her.

Instead, I pull her back up by the hair and slam her into the edge of the bath. She's choking, water and spit dribbling down her chin as she gags out the water she must have accidentally swallowed. I use her disorientation to my advantage and press my body against her, my hand firmly around her throat.

"Do you think I'd yet to forget how much of a conniving bitch you are, Crèvecoeur?"

"I'll gut you alive for this," she seethes, her eyes burning with hostility, trying but failing to push me off her.

I bring my free hand down to her left thigh. "Oh but where's your dagger now?" I ask, slotting my thigh between her legs.

She manages to slap me across the face before I wrestle both wrists into my grip, extending her arms above her head, making her arch her back over the edge of the wall. With her new position, her hips press against my throbbing cock while her breasts jut upwards. My gaze dips to her peaked nipples, and we both fall silent, breaths ragged with impassioned exertion.

Before I can talk myself out of it, I lean down and suck her wet nipple into my mouth. A small gasp tumbles out of her lips and my thoughts evaporate into pure animalistic need. She's not struggling in my grasp anymore, and I take the opportunity to transfer both wrists into one hand. With her nipple now between my teeth, I slip my cock between her legs, sliding my hard shaft up and down her warm cunt.

Her gasp transforms into a moan, and I press her even harder into the wall at the sound.

"Why didn't you fuck me when you had the chance?" she asks breathlessly.

Her words surprise me, obviously referring to that night at Manor, but I'm having a hard time concentrating on anything but her wet skin against mine. I let her wrists go, lifting her by the ass and making her wrap her legs around my waist, slamming us back into the wall.

My hands slide over her wet skin and I'm fucking starving. Her fingers coil into my hair at the base of my neck, tugging hard, but I ignore the sting as I slot my cock against her slit and then begin to circle the tip around her clit. With my free hand, I grip the back of her nape and make her look at me.

"You know why." My voice is pained with need. "*You know why,*" I repeat again, groaning through my teeth while the tip of my cock slides much too close to her entrance.

Her mouth falls open, and I mimic her while her hand slides down to my arm, fingernails digging into my scorching skin. The threads of reason are unraveling and I'm moments away from slamming my cock into her. I can hardly recall the reasons why I shouldn't.

I thrust her upwards and out of the water, her ass landing on the edge while I push myself out, now desperate to see all of her if I can't *have* all of her.

I manhandle her body, somehow knowing she'll let me, and lay her flat on her back against the wet tiles, water sluicing over her skin. I thrust her legs open and give her cunt a long slow lick, growling like a madman as I do so. She lets out a low whine, and I'm blind with greed.

"My ruin," I breathe against her clit, sucking it into my mouth before straightening back up quickly, bending her knees, and pulling her even closer to me. I catch her gaze in mine while I slowly circle her entrance, soaking the tip of my cock with her arousal. "My terrible demise."

Her bent legs fall open even wider, her eyes a burning inferno as her hand finds her swollen clit, her face transforming into shocked rapture. "Your downfall," she moans, voice thick with need.

My eyes slide to her *bewitching* cunt and watch as I slide the head of my cock inside, letting out a small whimper at the sensation. Her back arches upwards and my thighs begin to shake with the effort it takes not to thrust into her. I wrap a hand around my shaft, the other digging into her hip, and fuck myself while I'm barely sheathed inside.

"Despicable little thing," I spit while my arousal rises and rises. Anger spilling into aching desire, spilling into the uncontrollable seduction that is Mercy Crèvecoeur. "Look at what you've made me do."

I slap her clit hard, and her breath hitches with need, her eyes trained on me, eyebrows creased in pleasure as I feel her flutter around the head of my cock. I can barely breathe, terrified to move except for the furious pump of my hand. Until I feel the orgasm crest like a deadly wave and slip out, ropes of cum spilling over her fingers and clit while her hand continues to move in hurried circles, merging my arousal with hers.

I'm a mere shell of myself, my psyche shattered into a million little shards. Breathless. Captivated. Enraptured by Mercy's glistening cunt and the way her back arches even higher when she comes on a long moan.

It only takes a single moment before the glacial silence returns as if she conjured it herself.

She opens her eyes, her hard glare clashing with the rose in her cheeks.

She slaps my hand away from where it is still resting on her thigh and stands up. I remain kneeled at her feet, too stunned to move.

I slowly look up to meet her gaze. Her expression is thoughtful but stern.

"We are both damned," she says softly, her tone resolute.

She gathers her things, slipping her robe over her naked body, and walks out without another glance my way.

30

MERCY

A month has passed since I was forced into co-rulership with Wolfgang, and I've yet to fully acclimatize to all the attention.

The crowds of people. The countless pairs of eyes. The roar of mish-mashed energies grating on my senses. At least in a crowd as formidable as this one, death is never far. I can always count on the steadfast presence of mortality to quiet my nerves. It lingers, ever-present.

My attention shifts from the tens of thousands of Pravitians in front of us to Wolfgang standing beside me on stage. Always so at ease under such adoration. His smile is wide and beaming, the sun glinting against his gold canine and incisor.

We haven't been alone in the same room together since the bathhouse … incident, nearly a week ago. It's as if we're both hoping that if we don't acknowledge the breach in rationality we fell victim to that night, maybe the gods won't notice either.

Even if I'd love nothing more than to put all the blame on Wolfgang, I can't. Not when I was the one who taunted him into acting on his baser instincts.

I regret it. But it's not exactly for the most obvious of reasons.

The regret is perfumed by how it felt to experience him in the most erotic of intimacies, leaving me yearning in ways that I cannot explain. The stretch of my pussy around the head of his cock. The heat of his cum on my clit. I've never felt this type of desire before. I am no stranger to pleasure, to the carnal and sensual, but no one from my past compares to Wolfgang.

Almost as if a part of me had always known him like this, and I was simply revisiting the feeling. The selfish greed has turned into an ache that speaks only in words laced with Wolfgang's primal essence. An invisible string has somehow attached itself between us, and I can feel the tug no matter where he is. Even if we've done nothing but ignore each other.

I wonder if he feels it too.

Or is this what madness feels like?

It can never happen again. I have tested the gods enough.

I've been on edge all week. Unable to sleep, pacing the library at all hours of the night, waiting for something to happen. Waiting for my punishment. For *our* punishment. I dredge up the worst-case scenarios: the stripping of our power, banishment—death? But it's been nothing but the constant drone of meetings and dress fittings.

And now here we are.

At our joint inauguration.

The first of its kind.

Behind us sit Gemini, Aleksandr, and Belladonna in hand-carved thrones, their parents sitting alongside them, including Wolfgang's. Mine would be in attendance if they hadn't died in a house fire eleven years ago.

Constantine's chair is empty as she prepares for the bloodletting ritual at a table just a few feet from where we are standing, her father standing by her side.

Everyone on stage donned the color gold for the occasion.

I've been in my gold dress for less than an hour, but I already miss the comfort of my all-black wardrobe. My outfit is constricting, the gold chainmail sewn over my corset weighing heavily over my ribcage. I can barely take a full breath without feeling like an elephant is sitting on my chest.

Maybe it's why I feel so awkward standing here like this.

Or maybe it's the fact that Wolfgang hasn't touched me once since we've stepped into the public eye. Not even the skin of his fingertips has grazed my dress, and I'm deeply embarrassed to admit that maybe the feeling of his touch could help ease some of my discomfort.

Constantine's father turns to face her, presenting her with a red jeweled ceremonial dagger, and kisses her softly on the head before she takes it from his hands with reverence. It's a small but important moment between them—of power being transferred to the next generation.

Dressed in all gold, her appearance is just as startling as mine without her signature color. Her dress is less intricate than mine but just as beautiful, the afternoon rays glimmering against the satin. Finally, she begins to walk toward us in small assured steps, the dagger now resting on a small velvet cushion atop the flat of her palms, two small empty vials on either side of it.

"Hi," Constantine whispers excitedly when she's taken her last step, now standing between the two of us, Wolfgang facing me.

I don't bother to answer, my stomach in knots.

Constantine's expression turns into something slightly more serious, her eyes bouncing from me to Wolfgang, whose gaze I'm still avoiding. She tilts her head, her blonde hair falling off her shoulder, as if in thought. Finally, she holds the dagger in my direction, still resting on the ceremonial cushion.

"Here," she says innocently.

My eyebrows lift in surprise before knotting in confusion.

"Here what, Tinny? You're the one overseeing this ritual," I answer just low enough for only the three of us to hear.

Her smile returns, this time with a lot more mischief. "My ritual, my rules. You'll collect Wolfgang's blood and he'll do the same to you."

This time I don't avoid Wolfgang's gaze, his steely eyes clashing with mine. I swallow a hard lump in my throat, my stomach in knots now that his full attention is on me. He seems just as taken aback as I am.

"This isn't how the ritual goes," he says, his gaze slicing back to hers.

Constantine shrugs, still holding the cushion. "We've never had co-rulers before. We are already breaking tradition by having two families celebrated today." She holds up the cushion toward me again. "Why not create our own?"

She looks up to the sky.

And I'm sure everyone in attendance follows Constantine's line of vision.

It's why we've all congregated outside of Mount Pravitia in the first place.

A small sliver of darkness stains the sun—a shadow slowly growing in size until eventually, it will engulf the sun like a dragon swallowing a ball of fire.

"Enough of your dilly-dallying, the eclipse is starting. We don't have much time," she urges.

My gaze falls back to Wolfgang, his expression unyielding, but he gives me a small nod while he pushes the sleeve of his double-breasted gold suit up to reveal his left wrist. My heart flutters at the implication, and I swallow hard.

I reach for the cool ivory handle of the dagger. The shadows of the eclipsing sun dance over the blade as if urging me on.

I turn to face Wolfgang as day slowly turns into night. The crowd grows quiet, but for once I'm barely aware of it, my attention solely focused on my fingers curling around his wrist. My skin is electric from finally touching him after this long, my heart fluttering in my chest like an animated bird.

I press the blade against his skin but before drawing blood, I lift my eyes to his. They burn. My fingers squeeze harder around his arm. The blade breaks the skin. I continue to burn under his glare. His lip twitches as if in pain, and I finally look down at the blood slowly pooling around the tip of the blade.

His life force.

I emulsify into a flaming ball of lust at the sight.

Trying to keep my expression calm and steady, I hand Constantine the dagger and she gives me a vial in exchange. Wolfgang lifts his arm over it, opening and closing his fist to make the blood flow faster. Drop by drop, it falls into the glass vial and with every drip I am reminded how it felt to taste it on my own dagger's blade.

Unusually decadent and laced with animalistic desire.

Wolfgang's blown pupils tell me he might be recalling the same memory. I never told him how good his blood tasted, but seeing me react to it seemed to have had a similar effect on him.

When the vial is full, he staunches the bleeding with his pocket square before taking the offered dagger and wiping the blade clean.

By the time Wolfgang's hand touches the thin skin of my wrist, the sun is but a black orb. Darkness has cloaked the city in hushed silence.

It only lasts a few seconds. Just long enough for Wolfgang to whisper *My terrible demise* under his breath and for me to feel the welcomed pain of my blood set free, the blade warm against my skin. I can't help but let out a satisfied sigh as I track Wolfgang's tongue sliding slowly over his bottom lip. Night turns back to day while I hold my wrist over the vial, my blood pooling slowly into it.

The sun returns and it's over.

I let Wolfgang press his pocket square tenderly over the small wound, so close to the fresh scar I now have from him pushing me into the sacrificial pit. My eyes are incapable of looking away from his smoldering, yet icy, gaze. I barely register Constantine walking back to the small table near the side of the stage, vials and dagger in hand.

Once again we are alone, standing before the people of Pravitia.

But this time I can feel Wolfgang's thumb smoothing over the scar, his Adam's apple bobbing around a tight swallow.

The air shifts.

I break our gaze, looking at the crowd, then at the families sitting behind us, while the feeling only intensifies. It takes me a moment too long to realize what's happening.

My dear god of death whispers the answer into my ear.

I look back at Wolfgang in alarm.

"We need to—"

I don't have time to finish my sentence before an explosion sends me flying backward.

31

WOLFGANG

The smoke burns my eyes, choking me from the inside and out. I can barely think, the ringing in my ears distorting my senses. It dulls the screaming and wailing surrounding me like a deadly ripple of sound.

I've been flung into rubble, the stage now blown to bits. I try to move but my thigh throbs in pain, and I grit my teeth. Looking down, my eyesight still blurry, I find some kind of shrapnel lodged into the muscle. Without much rational thought, I pull it out. Removing the ragged piece of metal out of my thigh has all my senses rushing back simultaneously, and I cry out at the pain, snapped back to reality.

The screaming intensifies, the smell of burning flesh making me gag. I look around, trying to gather my wits. By the look of it, I must have been out for a few minutes. The crowd in the city square has dispersed but what has been left in its wake is mayhem.

Blood, death and …

"Mercy!" I bellow. The sudden terror of finding her dead has me pushing through the pain and standing. I take a few wary steps, my injured leg slowing me down.

Through the thinning smoke, she appears standing amidst the chaos, blood dripping from a gash near her temple and onto her ripped gold dress. I shout her name once more, stumbling over the wreckage, trying to get to her. But she doesn't seem to hear me, her eyebrows knitted in worry as she looks all around her, a faraway look dulling her eyes.

"Mercy," I press when I finally reach her, gripping her upper arms so she focuses on me.

"I can't find Gemini," she says, her voice sounding far away while she continues to avoid my gaze. "I can't find Gemini," she repeats under her breath.

"Mercy," I urge, giving her a small shake. "Look at me, you're bleeding," I say as I frantically survey her face and body, pushing her hair back to examine the cut.

Her eyes finally snap to mine. "I'm fine, it's just a ..." she trails off, her attention now behind me. "Gods be damned," she breathes.

My stomach sinks before I turn around and find Constantine pinned to the ground, her lower half crushed under a large beam. Given she doesn't feel pain, I'm not surprised to find her conscious. But the absence of pain doesn't negate the severity of her injuries. Belladonna is kneeling beside her, holding her hand while Aleksandr and Constantine's father are struggling to move the beam off her. But by the look of their failed efforts, it's much too heavy for them to do alone.

Guilt digs its claws into my chest when I realize that my best friend's well-being hadn't even crossed my mind until now. Nor that of my parents. Who, with a hurried glance around the bombed stage, are nowhere to be found.

I grab Mercy by the wrist. "Come. We need to stay together."

Her vacant expression tells me she must be in some kind of shock. She nods, and I slide my hand down from her wrist, intertwining our fingers together. I try to ignore the piercing throb in my thigh, as she follows me without any resistance, weaving us through the rubble.

"Sasha!" I yell out when we're close.

His head swivels around until he locates me. "Wolfie," he says in relief. "I couldn't ... Tinny ..." he mutters when I reach him.

Mercy kneels beside Belladonna, reaching over to smooth a few bloody strands away from Constantine's forehead. They exchange a few words, but I can't make out what they're saying, only that Constantine looks a lot less bothered than she should be, acting like this beam is but a mere nuisance.

I pull Aleksandr into a quick embrace. "Are you okay? Are you injured?" I ask while giving his body a quick survey after we pull away.

He ignores my question, his gaze hard. "You need to leave, Wolfgang. And take Mercy with you," he says urgently.

"But Tinny," I mutter, slightly stunned which then morphs into irrational panic. "And my parents," I add, "I can't find—"

Aleksandr cuts me off. "They're fine, they're with ..." Grief quickly flashes through his eyes and he clears his throat. "My mother is dead."

I curse through clenched teeth while I drag my palm over my face. "Who is responsible for this?" I seethe.

"We don't know," he answers quickly. "Even more reason for you to seek shelter."

"But—" I begin to say.

"Now," he orders, his expression unusually stern.

I stare at him for a moment, but eventually relent and move to kneel close to Constantine. I mutter a few comforting words into her hair, pressing a kiss on her cheek before telling Mercy we need to go while dragging her up to her feet.

"I'm not leaving Tinny like this," she says, pulling herself away from me.

"We're still in danger," I grit out, "This isn't the time for recalcitrant behavior."

"Wolfgang is right," Belladonna says softly, touching Mercy on the shoulder. "You need to find safety. This was clearly a deliberate attack."

"What about …" Mercy starts, vulnerability rippling over her face.

She never finishes her sentence. Instead, she falls silent, sharing a wordless exchange with Belladonna before her shoulders drop as if accepting her impending fate.

She turns to face me directly, her gaze deep with a slew of warring emotions—concern, anger, sadness, grief. I'm struck by her beauty even here amidst the madness, blood staining one side of her face, soot and dirt smeared on her skin and dress.

"We did this," she says, her voice cracking around the rise and fall of the accusation. My heart squeezes, barely managing a hard swallow. Her words sting but ring true and I struggle to fight through the weight of the guilt. "We did this," she repeats in defeat.

I huff out a haggard breath and try to tune out the pained cries still polluting the air around us. Family members crouched over bodies trying to staunch the flow of blood. Citizens carrying the injured away from the blast site. Dead bodies being lined up near the Mount Pravitia steps.

I keep my gaze locked on Mercy as I take her hand in mine and lift it to my lips. "This wasn't our gods," I utter low before pressing a gentle kiss to her skin. But even I don't quite believe my statement.

Mercy chews on her bottom lip, panic marring her face but says nothing.

"And besides," I add with a resolute sigh while navigating us out of the ruins. My limp grows worse as we walk up the stairs of Mount Pravitia, the blood still gushing out of my thigh now squelching in my shoe. "It would appear that what is done, is done."

32

MERCY

Wolfgang drags me by the wrist all the way down to the secret quarters which are specially designed for these types of dire eventualities, located deep under Mount Pravitia.

The attack has left me feeling awry. The dull throb on my forehead reminds me I survived with every heartbeat, but I haven't been able to form a single rational thought since the stage crumbled under my feet. I should have acted quicker—should have deciphered death's plan much earlier than mere seconds before the blast. I was distracted. Unable to distinguish what was important from what was just inane and frivolous emotions toward the man now opening the door to the underground quarters.

As I step inside, my mind lingers on Gemini and how he appears to have vanished after the blast. I can't console myself knowing he's alive since my power doesn't work on him. Even if it *were* his time to die, my god would have kept it from me. I would have never known it was coming.

What if Gemini is dead?

And I am the cause.

"We're damned," I mutter out loud.

I'm not necessarily addressing Wolfgang, I just need the words to live outside of me before they slowly asphyxiate me. But since he's the only one here, he turns to study me, concern darkening his face, the silence just as dire as the words I've spoken.

I quickly glance around the receiving room. I take in my surroundings for the first time, having only taken a few steps inside. Aside from the air being musty, it appears clean and well-kept, the servants keeping it spotless for times like these— no matter the improbability. The room is a dark shade of purple, with two large divans facing each other atop a sprawling rectangular rug.

The quarters are smaller than what we're accustomed to but designed to be self-sufficient. Aside from the cramped receiving room, the shelter includes a bedroom, bathroom, and kitchen which is fully stocked with food to last us at least a year.

Not that we'll need to stay anywhere close to that long. I'm sure only a few hours will suffice. The assumption lingers like dead weight in my chest. Maybe the threat is much bigger than I'm letting on.

What if it's longer?

My attention wearily returns to Wolfgang while his gaze lingers on the cut near my temple. It smarts under his quiet appraisal, and I lift my hand to idly touch the drying blood.

"It needs to be cleaned," he says softly, nodding his chin toward my face.

There's a note of concern attached to his words that stings more than the wound itself.

He takes a step closer and my first reflex is to take a step back.

"I can do it myself," I snap defensively.

Wolfgang's expression morphs into something a lot more

irritated, his lips pressing into a thin line, but says nothing. He glares, and I glare back. There's safety in this dynamic.

A loaded stare later, he shifts his weight from one leg to the other but can't conceal the wince fast enough. My eyes drop to his thigh.

"You're bleeding," I state as if he wasn't already aware.

I ignore the pinch in my heart at the sight of Wolfgang injured.

His short laugh is dry and cutting. "Quite astute, Crèvecoeur." He steps further into the receiving room, resting gingerly on the edge of the back of the divan, facing me. "Maybe next time, you can give me a fair warning."

My eyes narrow, my heartbeat spiking. "Fair warning?"

Crossing his arms, he gives me a look he typically reserves for dimwitted plebeians. His mouth slowly curls into a snarl. "Or maybe you hoped my time had come along with all the rest."

I stare at him while his words settle into my psyche like feathers on tar. "Foolish gnat," I spit, charging toward him. "Do you think the gods are *favoring* me at a moment like this? Do you not think I'm just as blind to our gods' plans as you are after what we did?"

He pushes himself off the edge of the divan to stand at his full height, his tongue smoothing over his teeth.

"After what *we* did?" he repeats with a growl. Now face to face, Wolfgang slowly crowds me inch by creeping inch. I need to lift my chin ever so slightly to hold his gaze but continue to stand firmly in place, my chest heaving with every rapid breath. His eyes are crazed, a raised vein pulsing in his neck. "None of this would have happened if you weren't such a selfish cunt."

He says the words slowly and intentionally, and they cut deeper than I would have ever expected. My palm connects with his cheek, his head swiveling to the side with the impact.

There's a pregnant pause as he begins to laugh coldly, head

still slanted. He wipes the corner of his mouth, his fingers stained red by a split lip. I don't bother moving. I'm stuck here with him either way.

But then his icy blue eyes lift to mine, and the threat I find in his stare has my survival instincts uncharacteristically kicking in. Without a conscious thought, I turn away and try to run but only make it a few steps before his large palm grabs me by the neck.

He swivels me around to face him while I struggle to break free and do the first thing that comes to mind, and slam my fist into his injured thigh.

He groans out in pain but doesn't let go.

Instead, my move backfires.

While Wolfgang is momentarily destabilized, he transfers all his weight onto me, and we pitch backward, slamming down onto the hard floor. I get the wind knocked out of me, but I try to fight back knowing he'll most likely go for my dagger. But even with his injured leg, he's still stronger than me.

Pinning my hands to the ground with one hand, he climbs on top of me, his legs bracketing my body as he holds me down. Even with me fighting against it, his free hand bunches up my dress and grabs my dagger in seconds.

Expecting him to threaten me with it, I'm taken aback when he throws it across the room in one swift move of his arm. I hear it clang against the stone wall, and I stop struggling just long enough to shoot him a distrustful look. "Why would you —" I begin to say but Wolfgang cuts me off and grips the side of my face with his palm.

"If we're already damned like you claim we are," he says low and dark, fingers digging into my cheeks. His face is serious but the corner of his mouth curls into a bitter smile. "Then killing you is not how I want to meet my death."

His mouth slams into mine. The kiss is unforgiving, feverish and I can taste the sweet tang of his blood from his split lip.

The taste of him has me dropping all pretense, relieved that Wolfgang has cracked his mask open so I can do the same with mine.

I kiss him back just as hungrily.

He frees me from under his hard grip, both hands now cradling my face while his cock digs into my hip, his entire body now weighing me down. Our tongues interlace, and the more I devour his kiss, the more I starve for all of him.

If this is what it tastes like to die, then there is a reason why I worship the god of death.

Pulling away, Wolfgang sits on his knees, concealing a flinch from what is still a bleeding wound on his thigh. I move to touch it, compelled by some uncontrollable tenderness, but he slaps my hand away.

"Don't," he growls while he tugs his suit jacket off, revealing a tattered white shirt underneath. "Not now."

Out of spite, I push a thumb into the gash and Wolfgang hisses loudly before his hand wraps around my throat, slamming me back down onto the cold marble, the rings from my chainmail corset digging into my skin. "Hateful little thing," he seethes, ripping my thong off with his other hand, his face inches from mine. "You deserve nothing but misery."

"You make me sick," I spit, my nails digging into his hand. But the more he squeezes the air out of my lungs, his fingers wrapped tightly around my neck, the more my legs open for his forceful touch, my thighs wet with arousal. Keeping me pinned down, his arm fully extended, he unbuttons his pants and shoves them down just enough to free his cock.

"If I am your sickness, my ruin," he groans through clenched teeth, looming darkly over me, his disheveled hair falling over his wild eyes while the head of his cock notches against my slick entrance, "Then you are mine."

He slams into me in one powerful thrust, my head hitting the floor beneath me as a long keening moan escapes my lips.

"*Fuck*," Wolfgang says under his breath, his head falling into the crook of my neck as he stills inside of me for a few shaky exhales. "*Fuck*," he repeats, this time much more harshly. When he begins to piston into me with hard, punishing strokes, I feel myself drench around him, soaking his cock with the gut-wrenching pleasure of finally having him inside of me.

He releases my neck and pushes himself up on one elbow, his dark gaze now scorching before he captures my mouth with his again. Bending one of my legs upward, he opens me wider, deepening the angle of his thrusts while the heel of my stiletto digs into his ass. My whimper is brimming with need as I bite his bottom lip until the taste of his blood is back on my tongue where it belongs. We both seem to have lost all manner of speaking, victims of the one thing we swore we'd never desire.

Each other.

With every mind-melting glide of his cock, I turn more desperate, ripping open his buttoned shirt just so my fingertips can find purchase over his heated skin. Just so I can feel the bite of my nails into his flesh.

Somewhere between life, death, and Wolfgang's undeniable effect on me, I begin to bargain with whichever god dares to listen. I plead and beg, and implore.

Let us have this without any consequences.

Let us indulge in the forbidden until we've had our fill.

The gods have their own laws. Why can't we?

Breaking our embrace, Wolfgang peers into my eyes, his thumb stroking my burning cheek and I can suddenly see all the same desperate demands reflected back at me.

"May the gods have mercy on me," he says quietly.

The squeeze in my chest threatens to become the one thing that actually kills me, so I shove Wolfgang off, making him flip onto his back so I can straddle him, now desperate for some semblance of control. My hands land flat on his chest while his fingers clutch onto my hips. My head falls backward, and I close my eyes, effectively shutting out Wolfgang and his maddening, seeking gaze. I grind myself on him, his grunts long and deep as I fuck his cock until I begin to feel myself unravel.

"Wolfgang," I moan almost in shock, my eyes snapping open to find his dumbfounded gaze locked on mine, mouth slightly parted. I'm unable to find any other words to utter before my orgasm rips through me with uncontrollable desire. But Wolfgang doesn't give me the time to experience it all the way through before flipping me back onto the floor and fucking me with renewed passion.

"My terrible demise," Wolfgang says into the shell of my ear. "My ruinous mistake." He kisses me one last time, his hot, searching tongue just as intoxicating as before, and my orgasm crests once more, my pussy squeezing again and again around his cock.

I feel Wolfgang shudder, groaning into my mouth as he comes deep inside of me.

And it takes me every last bit of my sanity not to cry out for this moment to last forever.

Because now that it has ended, we've certainly condemned our fate.

33

WOLFGANG

The silence hanging over us like a thunderous black cloud heralds an insufferable sense of rationality. It squeezes my lungs with an unfamiliar sense of regret. Surely, we've just co-signed our death—or at the very least our mutual downfall. But the selfish part of my nature would do it again if it meant reliving the same bliss I just experienced.

I've known pleasure before but this was ... euphoric.

I expect Mercy to push me off immediately but she does nothing of the sort, letting me slowly pull out and roll onto my back beside her. I catch my breath as she does hers, the closeness of her body next to mine radiating an undeniable heat that dares me to find her hand and lace my fingers with hers.

Instead, I push myself off the floor and gingerly stand on my two feet. When my thigh throbs with renewed vehemence, I lose my balance but right myself quickly. Mercy, still on the floor and now resting on her elbows, fixes her intense gaze on mine but says nothing.

I offer my hand. "Our wounds need to be tended to."

A shadow crosses over her eyes, letting a loaded moment pass between us before slipping her palm in mine. I pull her up, but as soon as she stands, she withdraws her hand and my instinct is to clutch her hand tightly and keep her palm in mine.

I do nothing of that sort.

There's a darkened hallway behind us and I turn to it, sensing Mercy following from behind. The underground quarters are small, and there's no need for an extensive survey of the space to ascertain where everything is located. At the very end of the hallway is the small kitchen with the bedroom situated closest to the receiving room.

Opening the plain door of the bedroom, I turn on the lights, illuminating the large bed that is pushed against the wall and flanked by two small bedside tables. To our left are large wardrobes which I assume now hold clothing to suit both our needs.

Heading for the ensuite, I push the door open. It creaks on its hinges, Mercy following me without a sound except for the soft clicks of her heels.

There's no bath in sight, instead, we find a large open shower area, black tiles covering the entire space. A rainfall showerhead hangs from the ceiling and a half-wall with the same black tiles offers a rather feeble attempt at privacy.

But privacy is not something I currently crave when having Mercy here alone with me.

I don't bother asking if she wants to be left alone. I don't *want* to leave her alone. To my relief, she doesn't request it, her emerald eyes steadfast and penetrating before she slowly steps out of her heels. Dropping a few inches in height, her gaze lifts to remain fixed on mine before she turns around wordlessly. She doesn't ask for help, and I'm sure I'd be standing here for centuries if I waited for her to use her words.

I approach her silently and start on the small leather straps on her back holding the chainmail tight around her chest. It falls with a ripple of clinks next to our feet. My fingers drag over

A Dance Macabre

her hips and then her waist before reaching the zipper of her gold dress.

Slowly sliding it down until it reaches the small of her back, I then drag a knuckle up her spine. I witness her skin break out into goosebumps before I smooth my hands under the silk and push it off her shoulders so it can pool around her feet.

Now naked, she steps out of the dress and turns to face me. Her expression is so serious that I can barely make out if this is affecting her as much as it is me. She approaches me, her eyes never leaving mine. I hide a hard swallow as her fingers trail over my shoulders, sliding what's left of my shirt off. But even with my trousers still unbuttoned from before, I grip her wrists, my face barely concealing the pain.

"Careful," I whisper harshly.

Her mouth is faintly agape, chin slightly lifted while her eyes continue to pierce through me like a well-sharpened blade. She says nothing, yet it doesn't unnerve me, not when her actions say more than her words ever could.

Her gaze drops to my thigh. Her touch is soft and tender as she peels the trousers off of the drying blood stuck to my skin before finally pushing them all the way down. She's about to start on my briefs, but I stop her. An itch of vulnerability is beginning to dig inside my chest, and my first instinct is to avoid the feeling.

"You can start on the shower, I'll be right there," I mutter.

Taking a step back, I turn to face the mirrors. I track Mercy even here. Although it's just her reflection, I can't look away, watching her step under the spray while she unpins her hair, dark strands falling down her shoulders one by one, her family sigil tattoo brazenly visible on her back. It's only when I manage to tear my gaze away from her and find myself staring back in the mirror that I realize the implications of what I just did.

I sought her reflection before even thinking to seek mine.

My heart squeezes in my chest as my throat goes dry.

The significance of what this could mean feels too weighty for me to explore. Especially at a time like this, when everything feels too dire and the exhaustion is slowly engulfing my sanity.

I sigh deeply and undress fully. No need to linger on any of this now.

I step into the shower, the steam rising from below. Mercy's eyes are closed, her head fallen back as she lets the water wash away the blood from her face. I notice a few bruises that are beginning to appear on her skin, as I'm sure similar bruises are appearing on mine.

I don't think I can use the word luck while speaking of today's events, but our injuries could have been much worse.

Mercy senses my presence and straightens up. Her eyes open through the water and her soulful gaze meets mine. The blood turns the water red as it trickles down her face, and I am struck by a vivid memory of her.

Of Mercy covered in blood, bathed in moonlight inside the maze on the night of the Feast of Fools. She was mystifying then, and she is mystifying now.

It's hard to believe that was only a month ago.

So much has happened since then. So much has happened between *us*.

And here we are now. At the very crescendo of our forbidden dance.

A dance macabre, where even the threat of our own deaths did not stop us.

And all I wish to do now as I watch her stand here under the water, naked, bloody, and fucking glorious, is to dig our graves even deeper.

To revel in the fatality of our choices.

To dig and dig and dig until I reach our gods and demand to keep her, mind, body and soul.

The collision of our bodies is as brutal and intense as before. Wet lips and silky skin. Clawing fingertips and teeth sinking into soft flesh.

Her sigh turns into a long, needy moan and all I want to do is lift her up so that her legs wrap themselves around my waist, her back slamming against the wall behind us. But my injury smarts at just the thought and I groan in protest, my hand tilting her chin up so I can deepen the kiss.

While her lips never leave mine, Mercy pushes me until it's my back that is shoved against the half-wall, the edge digging into my hips. Before I can piece together what's happening, Mercy pulls away, her eyes blackened with desire as she falls to her knees before me.

I am breathless.

Never could I have envisioned such a thing as Mercy on her knees, her fingers curled around my hardening shaft as her lips wrap themselves around my cock.

"*Mercy*," I say, her name turning into a low hiss when she swallows me deep into her hot mouth. I barely manage to stay upright, leaning against the edge of the wall, my palms digging into the tiles while my head falls backward in rapt pleasure.

Her free hand cradles my balls and she squeezes them, over and over, the sensation almost too intense when paired with the head of my cock hitting the back of her throat. She chokes and gags but never stops, her cheeks hollowing around my hard shaft and the sound of her is as divine as any melody I could ever play on the violin.

As I find the back of her head with my palm, I grip her hair and pitch my hips forward to feel even more of her around me, I realize she has become *my ruin* in every sense of the word.

Because nothing will ever compare to having Mercy like this.

Peering upward, she slides her mouth off my cock and licks her lips.

Then she speaks, and I am undone.

"I've tasted your blood before," she says breathlessly, "Now let me consume even more of you." Her hand strokes my cock, her eyes burning with wild flames. "Show me what ruinous desire tastes like."

I chuckle darkly, thrusting her head toward me. "Your mouth is just as greedy as your pretty little cunt, I see," I drawl, trying to pretend her words didn't send me halfway into orbit already.

She opens her mouth for me again, and I shove my cock deep into her throat, her hands now digging into the sides of my hips as I begin to fuck her throat with every morsel of possessiveness I have left in me. She watches from under her eyelashes, her gaze severe but aflame. And it only takes a few more thrusts and the feel of the wet glide of her tongue for me to come down her throat with a strangled groan. The pleasure shooting through my limbs is once again incomparable to anything I've experienced before. It almost feels ... undeserved.

And maybe it's because it is.

It's Mercy cloaked in the forbidden.

It's having what I can't have.

A wave of righteous indignation pummels through me, and I lift Mercy by the neck and shove her backward until she hits the wall on the opposite side. Her lips curl into a small snarl, her eyes cutting with irritation, but I kiss her all the same.

I kiss her with such desperation that it's almost as if her breath, her very air, is what I need to survive. I kiss her like this might be our last.

THE HOURS PASS, AND STILL, NO ONE HAS COME TO RETRIEVE US. The realization that maybe we'll be stuck here for the night has somehow managed to wrangle our volcanic feelings into something more dormant. What is left is pointed silence. After the shower, Mercy found a first aid kit and forced me—with quite an effective glare—to let her stitch me up. I'm convinced she took pleasure in repeatedly digging a needle into my skin. Her wound, however, was less deep than mine and only required a few butterfly bandages.

"Are you hungry?" I ask, now having changed into whatever clothes we found in the bedroom wardrobes. Mercy has chosen a black satin set of shorts and tank top, while I slipped into a relaxed pair of loungewear.

"No I'm just ..." she pauses, her eyes lingering on the bed, "Tired."

"Rest it is then," I say, pulling the covers back and climbing into bed.

Mercy stands awkwardly on the other side of the bed, her face painted with a faint layer of vulnerability. "What are we—" she begins to say but I cut her off, uninterested in having any type of discussion about any of it. Not now.

"Pretend," I plead.

The word lingers between us as I extend my hand, wordlessly inviting her to bed. She tries to conceal a small sigh, toying with her lips, but eventually, she turns off the lights and climbs in.

I pull her into me before she has time to shrink away. Her head falls to rest on my chest while my arm wraps tight around her waist. I fall asleep with Mercy in my arms, knowing full well that by morning this will all be over.

34

MERCY

"*Gods be damned,*" Wolfgang says harshly under his breath. His voice is rough and it wakes me from a deep sleep. "Mercy," he adds, pulling at my arm. "Wake up."

My first instinct is to knock the wind out of him, but I'm immediately distracted by yesterday's events tumbling back into my awareness, demanding I replay every little thing in excruciating detail.

I ignore it, just as I ignore the aches throughout my body when I sit upright in bed with a huff. My heart falls into my stomach and I let out a small—but embarrassing—squeak when I realize who is standing at the foot of the bed.

"I thought I made myself clear last time we spoke," the Oracle says with severity. Her white hair cascades to her hips, stark against her black robe. "I did not wish to visit again."

Both Wolfgang and I scramble out of the covers, awkwardly standing on either side of the bed wringing our hands as if we're two teenagers caught sneaking around.

"This isn't what it looks like," Wolfgang blurts out.

I shoot him a searing glare but say nothing, my attention quickly returning to the Oracle.

Her pointed gaze slides slowly from me to Wolfgang, her eyes narrowing as if trying to read our minds. I find solace knowing she can't—as far as I know—do such a thing.

"Yesterday's attack could have been avoided. The gods are not pleased," she states, carefully clasping her hands together. "If the co-rulers of Pravitia could cease their navel-gazing, maybe they'd discern what is happening right under their noses."

I ignore the offense throbbing in my chest and ask, "Which is?"

"I do not care to repeat myself," she answers gruffly. "Handle this, or our gods will handle it for you." She turns to walk out of the bedroom and from over her shoulder, she adds, "It is safe to leave, the others will be waiting upstairs."

Silence falls, her footsteps quietly receding into nothing.

"Unsettling creature that one," Wolfgang mutters, heading for the wardrobes, a slight limp to his gait. I watch him riffle through the clothes hanging inside and let my bitterness build into an angry pulsating thing before I pierce the silence with sharp words.

"This isn't what it looks like?" I spit out, "Seeking absolution are we, Vainglory?"

Wolfgang swivels around, eyebrows raised in surprise but he quickly fixes his expression, his eyes colored by the taunt in his tone. "We are too far gone for absolution, I'm afraid," he answers with a wary lilt. "Besides, she is not the one we should fear, Crèvecoeur."

"And who should we most fear then? The gods?" I ask irritatingly as I cross my arms.

The question is rhetorical.

Wolfgang's face turns serious, allowing the tension to coil dangerously around us before he speaks. "Each other."

The meeting takes place in the same room as the Conclave. There's a chill in the air when I walk in, Wolfgang by my side. It skitters across my skin like a cold shiver. It's as if the memory of Alina, Aleksandr's mother, lingers here. Like a ghost she haunts us. A reminder that we have failed her. Wolfgang and I have failed everyone in this room.

My gaze lands on Belladonna first, sitting at the table opposite the entrance. She sends me a small reassuring smile before my attention is stolen by the presence of the one I was worried about the most.

"Gemini," I say, breathing out a sigh of relief as I hurry over to him. "You're alive."

His eyes twinkle with humor before he stands, and I pull him into an embrace. "Of course I am, love," he says reassuringly into my hair, his arms squeezing my waist tightly. "A hug, Mercy? My, my ... how a threat to our lives has changed you."

I blink back the unwanted moisture in my eyes and try to shake off my show of weakness while giving him a small slap on the arm. "I thought you were dead, you snake."

He hums, dropping back into his seat. "Need not worry about me, love." He shoots me a wink. "I'm an indomitable force."

A giggle coming from the corridor has me turning toward the door. Constantine appears, back in her usual pink garb, sitting in a wheelchair with her left leg propped up in a bright pink cast while Aleksandr pushes from behind.

"Tinny," Wolfgang says, worry etched across his face, "You should be resting."

"And miss out on having the whole gang together?" she says without an ounce of seriousness in her tone. "I'm fine." She shrugs, looking slightly miffed. "I'd be walking if it wasn't for Sasha."

"You're badly injured, Tinny," Aleksandr responds with exasperation as if this is not the first time he's reminded her of that fact.

"I don't *feel* hurt," Constantine replies, a small pout on her lips. Aleksandr groans, a hand raking over his face and mustache while he continues to push her wheelchair up to the table with the other. When she's settled, he sits beside her, and all attention suddenly shifts to me and Wolfgang.

I'm aware that the six of us know the realities behind our co-rule. There's no need to keep up the charade of our united front behind closed doors, but my first instinct is still to stand beside Wolfgang so the image of us together solidifies as a known accepted truth.

However, I hide my surprise when Wolfgang pulls a chair out for me, and I wordlessly sit as I give him a small nod as a thank you. I wait for him to settle next to me before speaking.

"Who would even *dare* to do this?" I ask no one in particular.

"It must have something to do with those pamphlets," Wolfgang answers, seemingly lost in thought.

"What pamphlets?" Belladonna and Aleksandr ask at the same time.

I press two fingers to my temple, before waving my hand dismissively. "A few weeks ago, we were informed of pamphlets circulating—" I pause, quickly glancing over to Wolfgang before continuing, "Calling for an uprising."

"Against *us*?" Constantine chirps, her bewildered look telling me she might very well believe that we've done nothing to merit this kind of hostility.

Belladonna's green eyes narrow. "And you didn't think to warn us?" she asks, her tone harder than I'm usually accustomed to hearing from her.

"We didn't think ..." Wolfgang trails off, his gaze landing on Aleksandr, whose eyes flash with quiet grief. His voice is softer when he finishes his sentence. "That anything would come of it."

"Well," Aleksandr mutters softly, looking away. "It certainly has."

Offering my condolences is at the tip of my tongue, but I can't seem to find the words. I've never been the one to care about someone's feelings toward the death of a loved one.

Clasping my hands on the quartz table in front of me, I sweep my gaze to the four sets of eyes staring back at me.

"The executions," I say with less authority than I expected. I clear my throat and start over. "The real reason for them was because of a play, Wolfgang and I stumbled across it by chance. It was a reenactment of this year's Lottery—"

Wolfgang cuts me off. "I'm afraid, there's a rat in our midst," he says with a prim jut of his chin. I discern by his haughty air that he wishes not to linger on the details of the Lottery, and I concede with zero resistance. "I've had Dizzy and my people look into it but they've found nothing yet."

"Who says it's not *Ditzy* herself," Gemini drawls, his eyes glossed with suspicion.

Wolfgang's lip twitches, his fist slamming on the table. "Who says it's not the two-faced trickster sitting in front of me?" he volleys back, his disdain for my friend fueling his defensive words.

"*Me*?" Gemini says, elongating the word in mock outrage. He laughs, holding out his hand in front of him as if admiring his black-painted nails. "Don't flatter me, Wolfie."

Knowing this will only end with Wolfgang launching himself across the table to tackle Gemini to the floor, my hand lands on his thigh. The effect of my touch is instantaneous, his body visibly relaxes. I almost recoil from the weight of my influence on him.

"We need everyone's people looking into this. The sooner

we find who's behind this, the sooner we can eliminate the threat," I say.

Heads nod in agreement but Aleksandr interjects, "What about Tithe Season?"

"That's not for another—" I begin to answer.

"It's next week."

I fall silent, embarrassment washing over me. As the ruler of Pravitia, I should be on top of these things—*not* Aleksandr. Time is slipping through my fingers like blood from a fresh wound.

So many moving pieces; so many things to think about ... I suddenly need some time alone with my thoughts before I do anything rash like needing someone to talk to.

"Tithe Season is a sacred part of Pravitia's history," Wolfgang declares. "We can't show weakness — especially now. It will go on as planned. The bombing was clearly an attempt to hit us all at once. As long as we stay in our respective neighborhoods during it and reinforce security, I believe we'll be safe."

"Gods be willing," Belladonna mutters, avoiding our gazes.

There's a small beat of silence before Constantine speaks.

"I need your blood," she says, seemingly out of the blue.

"What?" I ask, my eyebrows dipping in confusion.

She sighs as if I'm being deliberately dense. "The ritual?" she presses. "The vials were broken in the bombing. I need to collect again."

"But what about the eclipse?" Wolfgang asks, shifting in his seat. "The ritual demands it."

Constantine waves us off. "Your blood was still spilled during the eclipse, I'm sure the gods will understand. This is for my personal collection." Her smile is fiendish. "It's tradition."

We fall silent, and I give her a nod.

The meeting adjourns not long after. The reality of us having broken a divine law and perhaps being the cursed force

behind these events hangs above Wolfgang and me like a guillotine threatening to sever both our heads.
    But we speak nothing of it.
    A secret we must harbor alone.

35

MERCY

*I*t's only back in the ruler's quarters that I gather exactly how much time has passed since yesterday's attack. There were no clocks underground as if witnessing time's passage meant nothing if we had nowhere to go.

Wolfgang and I separated as soon as we made our way back up to the living quarters. It was a confusing kind of relief, one doused with a heavy dose of yearning.

Never quite felt such a thing.

The sun hangs low in the Pravitia skyline, the orange glow glimmering against the buildings and windows. It's been over twenty-four hours since the bombing occurred and the remnants of its wreckage have been almost all cleared away.

I can hear the noises of the clean-up crew through the open French doors of the balcony even from way up here. I usually keep them closed, especially with all the heavy rain we've had lately. But I'm craving the fresh air like a prisoner craving freedom.

All three of my dogs are crowding me as I stand listless next to the open doors. Lost in thought. Lost in feeling. Éclair bumps my hand, and I scratch her head mindlessly.

I should shower.

Flashes of me on my knees, Wolfgang looking down at me with insatiable hunger has me physically jolting in place.

Maybe not a shower.

I should change into something from my own closet at the very least.

A knock at the door pulls me out of my errant, useless thoughts.

"Miss?" I hear Jeremial say.

"Yes?"

"Mr. Vainglory needs you in the drawing room."

I let out a small impatient groan. *What now?*

I stalk to the bedchamber door and open it. "Did he say what for?" I bite out, not even certain who or what I'm irritated with—just that I *am*.

"You have a visitor from the Agonis House."

I glance at him questioningly. "You mean Constantine?"

He shakes his head, his back against the hallway wall, hands clasped tight in front of him. "No miss, Albert."

"Her lackey?" I respond rhetorically as I begin to walk through the enfilade, leaving him behind. "Why would he want to see us both," I add under my breath.

Entering the drawing room, I find Wolfgang sitting on one of the velvet divans, a tumbler full of amber liquid held loosely in his grip. He's changed into black trousers and a dark mauve shirt, the collar left unbuttoned. Albert stands near the door. Waiting.

"What is it?" I say as a form of greeting, and both men's gazes snap to mine.

Albert stands up straighter, his large physique taking up most of the doorframe.

"I have a message from Miss Agonis," he says with an unusually deep voice.

My gaze bounces to Wolfgang and finds the same questioning confusion.

"Why didn't she just call us herself?" Wolfgang asks.

"I am to escort you," Albert answers solemnly.

"To where?" I snap, impatience bubbling under my skin.

"The ritual needs to be finalized tonight." He shrugs. "The moon must be in the same sign."

Wolfgang lets out a long annoyed breath, his hand dragging through his short beard, and I have half a mind to storm out to protest Constantine's facetious demand. I cross my arms in protest but don't move from where I'm standing because there's a small voice beseeching me not to defy the gods when all I've been doing in the past month is exactly that.

I share a wordless exchange with Wolfgang, something behind his eyes tells me a similar thought is rattling through his mind.

"We can do it here," I say while not breaking eye contact.

Albert interjects. "Miss Agonis demands the ritual be performed in her sanguinary cellar."

Still glaring at Wolfgang, my heart beating widely, I rasp, "*Fine.*"

NEARLY TWO HOURS LATER, WE ARRIVE AT THE VERY LIMITS OF Constantine's property. I had the men wait while I took a long shower and changed into a black sheath dress and fishnets. There's a chill in the air, and I hug my mink coat closer to my body; Wolfgang does the same with the wool collars of his overcoat.

There's barely a sliver of moon in the night sky while we approach the nondescript door hidden inside a small copse of trees. I'm surprised it's not painted bright pink for how

Constantine likes to go about things. Pulling a skeleton key out from his pocket, Albert unlocks the door and waves us inside.

Wolfgang nods, signaling me to go first, and I pass him, the scent of vanilla and bourbon tickling my nose as he follows me inside.

The creak of door hinges has me looking over my shoulder.

"What are you doing?" I bark when I find Albert closing the door with him still outside.

He stops in his tracks, his expression unperturbed. "Just following Miss Agonis' orders." He points his thumb behind him. "I'm to wait here."

"Will *Miss Agonis* be joining us?" Wolfgang asks, his voice dripping with condescension.

Albert shakes his head. "You will find everything you'll need down those steps." And with that, he closes the door leaving us once again—trapped and alone.

I can taste the tension between us like sugared poison on my tongue.

Wolfgang clears his throat. "Well then," he says, walking around me to get to the stairs. "Let's get this over with."

There's a chill coating every word he speaks, and my logical self can't fault him for it. What happened in the underground quarters was foolish and downright dangerous. However, the pinch in my heart is anything but logical.

I muffle a small sigh and start down the stairs, my stilettos counting the dozen or so steps until I reach the bottom. The long corridor is dark and damp, the earthy smell reminding me of the flambeau-lit underground tunnel leading to Pandaemonium.

A large steel door greets us at the very end. Wolfgang glances at me from over his shoulder, a curious look etched on his face before pulling on the thick metal latch. The room inside resembles a cavernous cellar, the space dimly lit with cold artificial lighting. Countless rows of shelves built to accommodate the uneven walls house thousands upon thousands of small labeled vials stacked together like sardines in a tin can. Different shapes and sizes for the different centuries, some with yellowing labels half-peeled and some with the labels missing entirely. I don't need to peer any closer to know they all contain blood.

A large wooden table sits in the middle of the room, and atop it is the same paraphernalia used at the inauguration: A velvet cushion, a ceremonial dagger, and two empty vials. We approach it without exchanging a single word. I idly wonder if the dagger is the same one as yesterday, somehow retrieved and salvaged from the wreckage.

The silence shifts. Like death's call, it whispers in my ears about the immaterial and the unseen. Wolfgang's eyes lift up, his gaze simmering with everything we have refused to speak aloud, and I watch him as he slowly slides his coat off his svelte shoulders.

I mirror his action, goosebumps breaking out all over my arms as the frigid air hits my skin. We both unceremoniously let our coats drop to our feet, our eyes still tensely locked together. The small lift of his lip is enticing as he rolls up his left sleeve with deliberate movements, revealing the day-old cut on his wrist.

My clit throbs, and I bite my inner cheek in retaliation for my body's reaction to simply *observing* Wolfgang. The sharp cut of his jaw. The perfect curves of his lips. The lean muscles of his forearm. The snaking veins over the top of his hands.

The memory of his naked body under the hot spray of water.

I lick my lips and break eye contact, feeling like I'm sinking into quicksand.

My attention travels to his hand reaching for the dagger instead, and my heart skips a beat in response to the anticipation washing over me. Picking it up by the blade, Wolfgang holds the dagger toward me, coaxing me to take it.

"After you," Wolfgang says slowly, a hint of sensuality in his tone. The timbre of his voice sends chills through my body.

I curl my fingers around the handle as I approach him, my other hand searing under the touch of his wrist. I hold his gaze, my thumb smoothing over the broken skin while his throat works around a hard swallow.

I can't quite tell what compels me to do it; maybe I need some kind of reaction from Wolfgang, or maybe it has something to do with the confusing ache I now carry in the pit of my stomach. Whatever it is, the outcome is the same: I press my sharp nail hard into his flesh, effectively reopening the cut.

His hand flies to my neck, and I suddenly feel enlivened. I almost smile.

"Impish little scourge," he growls, his arrogant grin revealing his two gold teeth, eyes wild and zealous.

"Apologies," I say lazily with mock innocence, "did that hurt?"

His fingers tighten around my throat, and I am engulfed once again by the flame of wretched desire. "If it's a grapple you crave, my ruin." His tongue smooths over his teeth. "It's simultaneously menacing and enticing. "Then a grapple I can give you."

The uncertainty of what I *do* want has me drowning in a vat of muddled words. I take the dagger to his wrist instead. He curses when the blade slices into his skin anew, and I use his momentary distraction to free myself from his grasp. Taking a few steps back, I try as best I can to gulp down air that doesn't carry the heady scent that is distinctly his.

Wolfgang stays motionless for a long tense beat, his gaze blazing with unspoken desire, his chest swelling with ragged breaths while blood slowly drips down his hand and fingers.

He pounces on an exhale, lunging at me, arms raised. My reaction lags, almost as if my subconscious held me on a leash knowing full well I have no intention of running from Wolfgang.

His bloody hand splays wide over my chin and cheek as he swings me around, walking me backward into the wooden table. My pulse races, exhilaration burning up my chest and cheeks. My reflexes finally catch up to me, and I press the dagger's blade to his throat, but Wolfgang is unfazed. Even I know my threat is half-hearted. Swiping the cushion and vials off the table, he pins my back to the hard surface.

The sound of glass breaking barely pierces my awareness. Not when Wolfgang forcibly hikes my dress up over my hips, his eyes spiteful but drenched in pulverizing hunger. His leering tut, paired with his fingers roving over my dagger's harness has my breath hitching with a burning ache. His touch is demanding, rough, and impatient, ripping through some of the holes in my fishnets.

"So predictable, Crèvecoeur," he drawls as he unsheathes my weapon. "Never without her special little dagger."

"With the number of times you bring it up, Vainglory," I spit back, a taunting tug lifting the corner of my mouth. "I'm starting to think you've developed an obsession."

He hums in agreement, his thumb slowly dragging his blood over my lips. "I certainly have."

The implications of his reply pound behind my ribcage, my own maddening obsession seeking solace in his words. It claims this moment for itself. Silently, almost daringly, I let my arm drop down beside me, the ceremonial dagger clanging to the floor. Wolfgang's glare flits to the ground, then quickly back up to me.

In a flurry of rapid moments, he lets go of my face and bites down on the blade of my dagger between his teeth before ripping my fishnets open at the hips with both hands. His hand swiftly wraps around my neck before I even have time to think of lifting myself up. Besides, my rational mind has never been the driving force behind this crazed waltz Wolfgang and I have fallen victim to. I'm naked under the fishnets, and my pussy throbs in erratic anticipation. I slowly lick my lips, and Wolfgang's blood pulses on my tongue as if I'm tasting his very heartbeat.

Taking the dagger out of his mouth, his expression turns slightly thoughtful as he drags the blade over the small tattoo in the space between my hip and thigh. His dark gaze pins me even harder to the table.

"I once asked you if this blade had ever tasted the life force of a cold-blooded Crèvecoeur," he muses.

He doesn't bother waiting for an answer, the dagger slicing into my skin as a small gasp falls out of my mouth. He chuckles darkly, his eyes turning manic and obsessive as he presses his thumb into the fresh cut with his free hand, the pain making my hips buck upward.

I've always enjoyed blurring the lines between pleasure and pain, but feeling Wolfgang circle the cut with his thumb, spreading my blood over my unmarked skin is unrivaled. The lines aren't blurred, they are simply nonexistent, and without those useless boundaries, I'm ushered into mind-bending arousal.

A low mewl rises out from my throat when Wolfgang moves downward to my clit, his thumb still stained red with my blood. He circles it lazily, his gaze fixed on my open legs, and his breath turns ragged as he slides his thumb downward, the blood mixing with my wanton arousal.

I find myself blindly grasping at the edges of the table, mouth agape and eyes burrowing into his blown-out pupils. Dragging his palm roughly down my dress, he gropes my breast over my dress, and groans deeply, his focus slicing back to between my legs. Then with one large palm, he pins me to the table.

I feel the cold, hard edge before I realize what it is: The

dagger's handle sliding between my slit, my wet arousal making it glide effortlessly up and down.

There's an arrogant kind of victory to his expression when he slowly pushes the tip of the handle into my entrance, my back arching with the sensation.

I'm rooted in place as I watch him pull the dagger out from between my legs and bring it to his mouth, his eyes a sea of black waves while he flattens his tongue over the handle and gives it a long, slow lick. My pussy squeezes around nothing but air at the sight, a flood of desire dragging me under the surf.

"You even *taste* like obsession," he muses, his voice full of grit. His eyes turn wistful for only a second before hardening and turning the handle over to me, tapping it to my lips. "Open."

My mind is much too ablaze with passion to deny him, my body just as eager. My mouth drops open, my gaze fixed on his as he slowly slides it in, my lips wrapping around the hard pommel. His eyes dip to my mouth, watching in rapt attention as the dagger glides in and out. In and out. His hips pitch into the table with the movement, his hard cock digging into my leg.

Finally, he pulls the handle out and drags it over the fresh cut, my fingers gripping the table harder at the delicious sting before sinking it deep into my pussy with one thrust of the hand. My long moan echoes around the cold cellar, my stomach straining against his palm.

His dark chuckle vibrates all over my heated skin as he fucks me, slowly, deliberately. "What a *delight*," he says, his lip tugging into a harsh grin. "To have your own dagger turn you into my whore."

His words should incense me, instead, my pussy pulses, squeezing around the ridged handle. I try to reach his collar, but he evades me, sliding the dagger out and throwing it to the ground before crouching down to the floor. His tongue is hot and probing, sucking on my open cut before growling into my skin, his lips trailing over my hips, his short beard leaving a pleasurable prick in its wake.

Grabbing my leg, he throws it over his shoulder, widening my thighs apart. With both hands, he rips up more of my fishnets and then spreads my pussy wide with his fingers. He hums greedily before slipping two fingers inside.

My back arches, Wolfgang's name sinful and heavy on my tongue as his hot breath dances over my clit before his lips wrap around it.

I feel crazed.

I never want it to stop.

Never want *us* to stop.

I claw at his hair, pulling, tugging, digging his face harder into me while he continues to pump into me, his fingers drenched and squelching with my heady arousal.

My climax builds and builds like a powerful current until I have nowhere to go but to freefall.

Wolfgang chooses that exact moment to pull away and stand up. My whines have never sounded more desperate, and I am too far gone to care.

Hastily, he unbuttons his trousers, his blacked-out gaze burrowing a hole into me, and pushes them down his legs. He strokes his cock in his large palm with graceful desperation, his neck straining, teeth gnashing, and cheek stained with my blood.

"If I can't have you," he says, his jaw clenching and unclenching, "then let me mark you in all the ways I know how."

Slamming his hand on the table beside me, his moan turns into a long groan as he comes all over my pussy, the hot ropes of his cum coating my skin.

My clit throbs with aching arousal, the vision of him looking so undone just as enticing as his release dripping down my wet slit. Wolfgang barely takes a breath to recover, his fingers sliding back into where they belong, dragging his cum into my cunt as he begins to fuck me with it.

Grabbing my dress into a fist, he forcibly tugs me up to him, his lips crashing into mine while his thumb toys with my swollen clit. I can taste my blood on his tongue and can hardly fight the need to bite down so I too can revel in the taste of him.

The sound of my arousal mixed with his fills the room, our anguished moans rising up and up and up until my climax crashes into me like a fatal collision. Wolfgang fucks me through it, his kiss turning me into ashes.

It must be only seconds, but eventually we both settle back into our bodies, and with it, reality returns. Wolfgang pulls away first and avoids my gaze, the sudden disunion stinging alongside my fresh cut as we both fix ourselves as best we can. I can feel the itch of dry blood on my cheek but don't bother trying to wipe it off.

What does it matter?

Let them see what it looks like to crave a Vainglory.

36

MERCY

I'm crawling out of my skin.

If I could zip out of my flesh and slither away somewhere dark, empty, and void of feelings, I would. Instead, I'm walking down the large domed corridor leading to the boardroom, Wolfgang flanking me. The echoes of our clipped footsteps fill the silent chasm between us.

It's been four days since the attack at the inauguration—two since we last surrendered to our *absurd* carnal desires.

When our lust-laden thoughts finally cleared, deep in Constantine's blood cellar, we realized we hadn't even completed the ritual. With debilitating tension, we replaced the broken vials, now shattered on the floor and filled them with our blood. We left shortly after.

We've kept to our separate quarters since, only circling each other like two sharks in bloody waters when it has been absolutely necessary. Like this afternoon, called down for a meeting to discuss any leads about who's behind this unrest.

Walking into the boardroom, we find two of the four already arrived. Black marker in hand, Gemini is doodling on

Constantine's bright pink cast. She's still in a wheelchair, her leg propped up, soft pink painted toenails peeking out from the cast.

They both look up when they hear us walk in, bright smiles on their faces.

"Their magnificences have arrived," Gemini says in a jovial tone, returning to his derivative drawing.

Wolfgang doesn't respond, his expression somewhat impassive while he unbuttons his silk suit jacket before sitting down to face the two with a muffled sigh. I can't bring myself to sit, pacing at the head of the table instead.

"What's wrong?" Constantine says slowly, but I can't look her in the eye, let alone Gemini.

I focus on Wolfgang, who shoots me a cautious glare.

"What was *that*?" Gemini presses, capping the marker before throwing it on the table.

"Nothing," Wolfgang answers firmly, smoothing his hand over his perfectly coiffed hair in a feeble attempt to seem unbothered.

I stop in my tracks, chewing on my lip, making the mistake of finding Gemini's inquiring gaze. His power might not work on me, but my resolve is nothing but a house of cards right now.

"Mercy," I hear Wolfgang say in warning, but I can't look away from Gemini.

I feel fissured, like a cracked dam ready to burst.

"We've broken a divine law," I blurt out.

Wolfgang curses. Constantine's mouth opens in surprise, muttering under her breath, "The flowers worked." While Gemini leans back in his chair, crossing his arms and grinning like he just heard the best piece of gossip.

There's a long beat of silence, and I sit down in defeat beside Wolfgang before Gemini speaks. "Considering you both aren't currently being wiped from the history records, I take it you heathens have been fornicating." His tone is mocking but somehow coated with just enough sweetness to make his words bearable to swallow.

I peer over to Wolfgang for the first time since I divulged our secret, the broad strokes of his face tense but resolute. "Yes," he answers solemnly, and sudden relief washes over me hearing him admit it.

I expect both Gemini and Constantine to express concern, instead, they share a conspiratorial look, and Constantine bursts into giggles, hiding half her face with her hands.

"Tinny," Wolfgang says carefully, a muscle feathering in his jaw. "I don't care if you can't feel pain, I'll break your other leg just to spite you."

This somehow just makes her laugh even more, her eyes crinkling while Gemini barely contains his mirth beside her.

"We have most certainly co-signed our downfall, and you both find it *amusing*?" I ask incredulously.

"Please, Mercy," Gemini responds placatingly. "Is that really what you think?"

I glance over to Wolfgang, his expression similar to how I feel: Confused.

"What are you implying, Foley," Wolfgang asks, his words dripping with icy contempt.

"What he *means*," Constantine answers for Gemini as she twirls her finger around a strand of blonde hair. "Do you not surmise this was the purpose all along?"

My breathing turns shallow, her implication slowly washing over me.

"Did you really presume," Gemini starts again, leaning his elbows on the table between us, "that the gods chose for you two to co-rule *platonically*?"

He says the last word with such disgust that I almost begin to maniacally laugh.

"Obviously," Constantine adds with a small roll of her eyes, "this was the plan all along."

Wolfgang stands up, knocking his chair over as if incapable of managing his reaction to what our friends are hypothesizing. Quickly, he leans down to pick it up and slams the chair back on its legs, sitting back down without saying a word.

"But—" My voice cracks, and I swallow the hard lump in my throat before continuing, "I did this. It wasn't our gods' decision, this only happened because of what *I* did."

Gemini stays silent as he studies me, his expression thoughtful. Then he pushes out a dry chuckle. "*Sunt superis sua iura*," he says slowly, deliberately pronouncing every syllable.

The gods have their own laws.

He points a ringed finger at me then at Wolfgang. "If you think your *illusioned* free will has not already been preordained, love, then you're not as cunning as I thought you were."

I'm frozen in my seat, any sort of reply lost inside the bubbling heat of affront deep in the pit of my stomach.

"I—" Wolfgang begins to speak but quickly snaps his mouth shut when the sound of footsteps approaches the door.

Seconds later, Belladonna appears in a cloud of seductive perfume and white lace.

She stutters to a stop, seemingly picking up on the tense silence. Her gaze slides to mine. "Did I miss something?"

Still unable to speak, painstakingly trying to suppress the outrage clamoring to get out from inside of me, I shake my head. She studies my expression for a second too long but eventually seems to find answers to some of her questions.

She shrugs and sits. Gemini returns to his doodling while Wolfgang repeatedly taps his finger on the arm of his chair. Aleksandr arrives a few minutes later, looking worse for wear with heavy bags under his eyes. He takes the time to press a kiss on Constantine's forehead before sitting down. Luckily, Wolfgang seems to pick up on the fact that I'm too rattled to hold a meeting and takes the lead.

I spend the next hour, locked in my head replaying Gemini's last words.

37

WOLFGANG

Mercy and I return to our living quarters, an insufferable silence tailing us. The crackles and pops of the roaring fire inside the drawing room's fireplace remind me that the world itself has not gone silent. I'm simply co-ruling with a brute who retreats into silence whenever a problem arises, and today the problem happens to be us.

Upon hearing our friends' theory, I was just as rattled as Mercy, but someone had to save face for the meeting. No legitimate leads about the rebellion yet. The lack of information tickled my suspicion, but my wariness didn't make it very far, caught in a sticky web woven by Mercy herself, my mind *dense* with the thought of her.

Still, I made a mental note to have Dizzy add more men to the job. Gemini convinced us he would no doubt collect some valuable intel during Tithe Season, commencing in a few days.

Noticing that Mercy is trying to head towards her wing, I catch her arm with my hand. She stops mid-step, her shoulders jumping to her neck. Slowly, she swivels around, her eyes downcast to where my fingers connect with her wrist before lifting them to meet mine.

"What?" she says. Her voice isn't as grave as the curves of her mouth; no, there's a wistfulness to her tone that has me squeezing her wrist a little harder.

"This ... *thing* ... between us, Mercy," I respond tentatively, "It needs to be discussed."

She tries to shake her arm out of my grasp, but I don't budge. "I'm tired, Wolfgang."

"The sun has barely set," I counter through clenched teeth. Her arm turns limp, her expression fading into something I can't quite put my finger on. "I know you'd rather ignore it, but we can't evade this forever. The gods won't let us."

Sensing she won't run away now, I let her go, and she crosses her arms immediately.

"Do you really believe those two?" she says with a dry scoff. "Gemini thrives on chaos, and Constantine is just as enamored with mayhem as he is."

"Agreed," I say slowly, rubbing a hand over my beard. "But ..." Mercy tenses, her eyes focusing on a spot somewhere behind me, mouth pressed into a thin line. "You can't deny that —" I shift from one foot to the other. "Well ... that there might be truth in what they hypothesized."

Her gaze focuses back on me. "Truth?" she says, her tone carrying a hint of bewilderment. "That the gods' plan is for us to—" She stumbles over her words, her arms tightening over her chest. "To be ..." Her eyes widen but she never finishes her sentence.

I let the silence fill in the gaps for her. I shrug. The action is just as unsure as I am.

My heart is in my throat. "I claim to hate you, Mercy." My sigh is heavy with memories of our last few weeks spent together. I take a step toward her, my fingers grazing the hem of her short black skirt. Her gaze is just as intense as mine. I lean close to her ear. "And yet," I whisper before biting her earlobe. Her breath hitches as her body relaxes against me, shoulders falling. "The sound of your throaty moans haunts my every waking moment."

Her hands grip my lapels, her forehead falling softly to my shoulder like a leaf drifting slowly to the ground on a crisp autumn morning. I breathe in her perfume. It leaves me light-headed with need.

Finally, she speaks. Her voice is quiet, as if worried she'll be overheard by the gods themselves. "There's only one person who might have answers for us."

I HAVEN'T STEPPED FOOT INSIDE THE LOTTERY HALL SINCE I pushed Mercy down the sacrificial pit and stormed out of there incensed with justified fury.

That was five weeks ago.

And even with what has recently transpired between us; I still stand by what I did. She deserved a lot more than a mere fall into old bones and an injured arm.

Now here we are. Back where it all began.

And oh, how things have changed.

But—

Something in Gemini's words rings true. Maybe Mercy was just enacting a subconscious desire placed there by our gods. *Maybe* the outcome of the Lottery was just a fateful denouement of something much larger than the two of us. Larger than all of us.

"So we just ... wait?" Mercy mutters, slowly walking onto the obsidian platform.

"It's our best bet," I reply, stuffing my hands into my pockets as I follow her up. "Hopefully, she'll sense our need for an audience."

"Sounds a tad cryptic."

"This, coming from the one who answers death's call," I reply offhandedly.

Mercy turns to face me, regarding me with a hint of amusement.

"What?" I ask. She shrugs, her eyes sweeping around the hall, a minuscule grin fighting to break over her lips. "Recalling your coup, Crèvecoeur?" I ask with surprising levity.

"What is it now?" The Oracle's voice bounces against the walls, and I have the ridiculous urge to duck and hide but refrain from moving at all.

We find her standing near the door, her hands tucked and hidden inside opposite sleeves, her face as unimpressed as ever.

With quick steps, Mercy comes to stand by me. I can't help but wonder if it stems from an unconscious urge for us to appear more united.

"We seek—" Mercy clears her throat, unease written clear across her face. "Consult."

The Oracle takes a few steps toward us but keeps her distance. "If this is about your recent *involvement*," she starts briskly, eyes bouncing between us. "I thought I had made myself clear at the Lottery."

I can't conceal my surprise, my hand finding Mercy's wrist. Still, I feel mildly idiotic to have even entertained the belief that the Oracle wouldn't have already known.

"What do you mean exactly?" I say slowly, my voice tinged with trepidation.

The Oracle huffs out a small breath before she speaks. "You shall rule together."

Mercy barks out a shocked laugh and takes a few steps back as if physically pushed. My heartbeat spikes as I carefully digest her words and what she's implying.

"You don't mean …" I trail off, my mind splintering.

"I've known of your union long before your births. Be wise to remember that the gods make no mistakes."

It's my turn to push an incredulous laugh, my hand raking over my face, my thoughts a burning, flaming mess.

Mercy steps down from the platform, approaching the Oracle as if being closer to her will somehow help the spiraling effect she's most likely experiencing. I know I am. As if invisibly leashed, I follow her down.

"What about the divine law that speaks against it?" Mercy says with urgency. "Was it even real? Did it ever even matter?"

The Oracle's lips are a hard line, her gaze steady. "It was. It is no longer."

Mercy scoffs and throws up her arms in exasperation. "What was the point of any of it then but to keep us under their thumbs?"

The Oracle cocks her head, her eyes narrowing. "Where do you think your thirst for absolute dominion comes from, child?" she says harshly. "Have you forgotten whose image you have been created from?"

Mercy snaps her mouth shut, seemingly taken aback. Her eyes slice to mine, her gaze cloudy with horror-stricken confusion. I fight the need to pull her into my embrace.

My focus returns to the Oracle. "Are we the only ones exempt?"

Oracle gives her head a small shake. "The gods are ushering Pravitia into a new era. This one law has been dissolved." She takes the time to peer at us both. "You and your eventual progenies will be responsible for a smooth passage into this epoch."

Without another word, she turns and walks out of the hall, leaving us speechless and reeling from the enormity of what has just been divulged.

38

WOLFGANG

Tithe Season began three days ago on the winter solstice. It reoccurs every three months, celebrating the passage of the seasons. It's a week-long affair where Pravitians can tithe to the gods. Tithe to us, *their* gods.

The manner in which we collect offerings differs from one god to the next. Most of us have a specific day of the week reserved for such a thing. Mine is Sunday. Only two deviate from this custom. Aleksandr's tithing is a bacchanal that lasts the entire week.

And Mercy? Well. Death's call isn't tethered to something as *rudimentary* as a calendar.

Behind closed eyelids, I listen to the last of the Vainglory followers wax poetic at my altar. And what better altar for the servant of the god of idolatry than his naked, radiant body?

Compliments, flattery, praise; I've heard it all today. Every spoken word breathed into the steam of the bathhouse has left an invisible mark on my skin. They hang in the air, mingling with the scent of vanilla from my oils. I've collected the words with an insatiable hunger, and it has created a buzz so rejuvenating that I've almost forgotten the woes of weeks past.

Almost.

When the faceless Pravitian has finally finished enumerating all the ways they idolize me, I wave them away without opening my eyes. Leaning against the edge of the bath, with my arms splayed wide on either side of me, I listen to the receding footsteps turn into weightless silence. Only the low melody of classical music remains.

The warmth of the water surrounding me soothes the aches of my body, dulling the thoughts that ache even worse. I could have observed Tithe Season in Mount Pravitia's bathhouse, but the melancholic perfumes of my old life called me back to the Vainglory Tower, homesick for the last time I've felt ... grandiose. A pleased sigh rumbles through my chest.

The sound of heels pierces the silence.

A cadence I now know all too well.

My skin prickles with awareness before I even open my eyes. There's a foreign giddiness bubbling through my veins, and I can almost feel the invisible string grow lax between us as she approaches me. Mercy stands at the opposite end of the bathhouse, near the stone steps leading into the water. The warm lighting of the candles atop the chandeliers illuminates her face, smooth like marble, devoid of any real emotion.

A charged silence crackles in the vast space between us.

I haven't seen much of her since we last spoke to the Oracle almost a week ago. Part of it was circumstantial, Alina's funeral kept me occupied. Then Tithe Season began, but those were mere paltry opportunities to escape the echoes of the Oracle's declaration.

To avoid the sheer pressure of what was revealed to us that day. Now that fate is involved, it certainly has snapped us out of our feverish state. We've been walking on eggshells around each other ever since.

But this, in no way, has sobered my irrefutable attraction to Mercy.

I have simply repressed it. Until now.

Like the image of death itself, she's cloaked in all black. Fur coat and a simple shift dress. I don't know if receiving tithe has loosened my sensibilities, but I begin to salivate like one of her dogs eyeing a bone.

Without taking my eyes off of her, I address my assistant standing at attention behind me. "That will be all for today, Bartholemew. Leave us."

He mutters a shaky *Yes, sir* and trots the length of the room, passing Mercy with a respectful nod before disappearing out the exit.

Crossing her arms, she circles the edge of the bath and begins to walk the length toward me. There's a hesitant arrogance to the sway of her hips, my eyes lifting upward the closer her steps bring her to me.

Finally, she stops a hair's width from my outstretched arm, my fingers almost managing to graze the tip of her stiletto. My heart pings with yearning, my fingers reaching for her foot of their own accord.

After a lengthy beat, she breaks the silence. "Last time I was here I threw a severed finger at your face."

I resist the urge to smile. "I recall," I say slowly, smoothing one of my hands through my wet hair. "No gaudy fringed hat this time?" I quip.

She clicks her tongue at the small jab, the tiniest of smiles on her red lips, eyes raised skyward before returning to mine. "I am the face of Pravitia now after all."

"*One* of the faces," I can't help but volley back.

Her smile fades, gaze intensifying—studying. I wonder if she's thinking the same thing I am, my mind never lingers far from it these days.

You shall rule together.

Tension rumbles between us like thunder after lightning.

I straighten up from my relaxed position, facing Mercy head-on. When I speak again, my voice has deepened, the words tainted with such complexity that even I'm not sure what all the layers mean. "Have you come all this way to tithe to me, Crèvecoeur?"

She doesn't react, as if she's lost in a maze of her own thoughts. And, *gods be damned*, do I know the feeling intimately. Her stony mask feels unbreakable today, her face calm while vulnerability crackles inside my lungs.

Finally, she breaks eye contact as she begins to take one small step after the next. She circles the edge of the bath until she's standing directly behind me. Slowly, I drop my head backward, resting it on the stones under me, my gaze finding hers.

Lifting her heel, she presses the length of her sole over my shoulder and collarbone. From my angle, I watch her legs widen, revealing the thong under her dress. "Maybe I should be the one to drown you this time." Her words smolder like red coals over my heated skin, and I groan as her heel digs into my flesh.

My eyes still fixed on her, I curl my hand around her ankle, smoothing my wet palm up her calf and then up her thigh. "Tithe to me, Mercy," I repeat with renewed hunger.

Her eyes shudder. Her mask cracks. And the vulnerability I craved to see mirrored in her gaze appears.

"I ... I can't," she answers softly.

I'm not crest-fallen, I knew she wouldn't do it, but I still sought to goad her. To feel her falter under my touch. Because it takes intimacy to compliment someone with devotion. And what is true intimacy but vulnerability stripped naked?

Her eyes burn, and I breathe in the ache drifting down from her like a perfume. "Then show me in all the ways you can't tell me, my ruin."

Her mouth parts open, her eyebrows cinching as if trying to

make out a particularly evasive problem. The silence counts our breaths for us. Until Mercy finally moves.

She steps away, unraveling out from under my touch, and storms out of the room, the click of her heels just as fast as the thrums of my beating heart.

39

WOLFGANG

I charge into the drawing room and find the first servant I can get my hands on. Grabbing them by the collar with both hands, I pull them close to my face.

"Where is she?"

The menacing hiss attached to my words has them gulp audibly, eyes wide, before stuttering out a response.

"In — In the atrium, sir."

I shove them away and head for the East Wing. I've been stewing ever since Mercy stormed out of the bathhouse earlier this evening—her leaving grates me more than I wish to admit.

I feel cracked. Like porcelain hurled carelessly on the ground. I know I've been avoiding her just as much, but something about watching her leave in such haste as if she couldn't get away from me fast enough, has me incensed.

What was the meaning of her visit then, if it ended with her running away?

A coward.

That's what she is. Terrified of any feeling that isn't tethered to apathy or death.

She can't run from me forever. I will chase her into the very depths of our terrible demise if I need to.

I will always catch her.

I will always find her.

And I will possess her like she possesses me. Like a parasite burrowing itself into my soul. She consumes me. And I shall devour every last drop of her in return.

The atrium slumbers within the shadows of the evening sky, candles flickering atop the long oak table, the rain battering against the floor-to-ceiling windows.

I spot the silhouette of Mercy's lithe body against the dark Pravitian cityscape. She stands by the window, the same shift dress as earlier hugging her curves, her shoulders bare, long black hair tumbling down her back.

Mercy turns when she hears my stalking footsteps approaching. There's not even a lift in her brow or a widening of her eyes. It's as if she was expecting me all along.

There's not a single word exchanged. Instead, we let the crackling tension between us speak for itself. Grabbing her by the nape, I weave my fingers through her loose strands and pull her head upward.

I shove her backward into the window just as my lips slam into hers with urgent haste. Our moans merge into one another while the taste of her throws fuel onto an already burning flame. Slapping my hand against the window near our heads, I deepen the kiss while Mercy's long nails rake down my neck.

The cold pane under my palm does nothing to quell the roaring fire under my skin. Letting go of her nape, I trace her curves with my hand, fingers digging into the flesh of her breasts, her stomach, her hips. She presses herself against me, her breath erratic as I swallow every single whimpering moan escaping her mouth.

Our tongues clash, her lips so plump I want nothing more but to devour her whole. I impatiently knock her legs open with my foot as my hand slips under her dress. The heel of my palm pushes against her clit as my fingers rove over the wetness of her lace thong.

"You're soaking, my ruin," I breathe harshly against her lips. "All of this, just from one kiss?" My erection pushes against the seam of my trousers, aching, and I press myself even harder into Mercy. "Or is it that even just the thought of me has you this wet?"

Mercy's hands are now feverish, slipping under my suit jacket, her fingers tightening around my shirt. "Silly little wolf," she says darkly, a jeering taunt curled around her words. "Who says I was thinking of you?"

I know better than to believe her. I know better than to allow her words to slice through me like the dagger strapped to her thigh. But just the simple thought of Mercy fantasizing about someone else has me letting out a low, menacing growl. I give her cunt a sharp, merciless slap. The shocked moan she pushes into my mouth tastes like the finest of wines. Like the sweetest of nectars.

Taking a step back, I forcibly flip her around, bending her just enough that her palms flatten against the window so she can uphold her footing.

"What do you think you're doing?" she asks harshly, her head turning to find my hard, but heated, glare from over her shoulder.

Unbuckling my belt, I chuckle arrogantly, my smile dark and menacing. "Surrendering to our gods."

She could fight me—she certainly has before. Instead, she's malleable under my touch, her legs widening as if daring me to continue. She can no longer fool me; her cold exterior is just an act. I've seen her true self, *felt* her true self when we're alone together, when my cock is sheathed deep inside of her.

Her eyes narrow. "I am not your fate, Vainglory."

Unzipping my trousers, I pull my cock out, my thumb

smoothing over the head before shoving her thong to the side. "Haven't you heard, Crèvecoeur?" I chuckle darkly while dragging the tip against her wet slit. "You've always been mine." I push inside of her, just enough for her cunt to wrap itself deliciously around the head of my cock. "And you'll be mine even when your god has claimed us both."

Snapping my hips forward, I bury my cock to the hilt. The eroticism of experiencing Mercy this way barrels through me, and I lean over her, my hand landing next to hers on the glass window pane. The curves of her body lock perfectly into place beneath mine.

I fuck her with a vengeance. I fuck her with all the hate I still have left for her. I fuck her like she's been my birthright all along. Until there is nothing left but our gazes being reflected back at us. The city lights twinkling. The rain battering.

"Look at her," I whisper raggedly into Mercy's ear. "Behold her beauty, her depravity, her darkness." My palm slips over Mercy's hand, our fingers interlocking in a heated grip against the window while my other hand digs into her hip. I might be speaking of the city of Pravitia, but my words resonate with everything Mercy embodies. "She is ours. We have laid claim to all of it, my ruin."

"Ours ..." she repeats, her breathy whimpers fogging the glass, her cunt fluttering around my throbbing shaft, and I know I have her. Her mask slips. The ice thaws as she moans a series of *yes, yes, yes* as her ass pushes against me with every brutal thrust I give her.

"Touch yourself, Mercy," I groan as I squeeze one of her breasts over her dress, the silk smooth, her nipple hard and pebbled under my touch. "I want you to make yourself come as the city watches."

Surprisingly, she listens, moving her hand down her body. A wicked desire shivers down my spine at the thought of her following my orders. Unclasping my hand from hers, I straighten back up, gripping both my palms on either side of her hips. Her cunt *squeezes* around me, and it's as if I can feel her arousal beside my own. Like two pieces of a whole. They beat to the same sinful cadence.

"I want my name on your lips when you come, Mercy," I demand as I thrust myself deep inside of her again and again, every slide of my shaft into her cunt feeling like the very first fucking time. "Say my name when the pleasure overtakes you. Let me possess you. Let me be the reason your heart beats wildly in your chest."

"No," she spits, the word contradicting the aching desire dripping in her tone.

My jaw clenches, nostrils flaring. I slap her ass, the sting of my palm almost as satisfying as Mercy's sharp moan.

I feel her orgasm build, her cunt choking my cock. I make my demand again. "Say it," I growl.

I'm convinced she will deny me again. Instead, her forehead falls against the window, every muscle in her body contracting as she comes... my name on her lips.

"*Wolfgang.*"

I am possessed.

My thrusts turn desperate, erratic.

Her name becomes the only thing I want on my tongue.

I say it over and over again as I find her reflection in the window pane, blissful and mindless. My climax is violent, an ego death splintering me into a million little pieces as I come deep inside of Mercy, filling her full of my cum—filling her full of me.

Possessed.

40

MERCY

olfgang's weight is still heavy against my back, my clammy palms sticking to the window. Breathless. I feel the slow glide, the wonderful ache of his cock sliding out of me. His release trickles down my thigh, my skin still humming with palpable desire.

He carefully tugs my dress down. Something about the tenderness of his fingers has my heart squeezing woefully. I linger on the feeling, my usual instinct to plunge it back into the depths of myself seemingly absent tonight.

"Wait here," Wolfgang mutters softly.

Straightening to my full height, I turn to watch him. Brown hair disheveled, strands falling over his forehead, his trousers still unbuckled as he walks over to the long dining table. The image of him like this, unkempt, wild—it humanizes him. His wolfish face revealed under the Vainglory mask.

I felt my own mask dissolve tonight. Yet, the fear of Wolfgang seeing me like this does not consume me. Instead, I feel alive. Real.

Picking up a white cloth from the table, he dunks it into a

silver carafe full of ice water. He returns to the window with a sly grin and an arrogant strut.

His steely gaze remains glued to mine as he slowly lowers himself to his knees in front of me. The same painful squeeze wraps itself cruelly around my heart. His smile turns heady. Strong hands smooth up my thighs, pushing my dress back up to my hips.

"Let me wash away any proof of me," he says with the heat of a thousand suns. There's light-heartedness in his tone. I hate it. Somehow loathing the thought of washing him off of me. Let him linger. Let him seep into me and sink into my bones.

But I say nothing.

I suck in a small breath when the cloth touches my burning skin, still cold from the ice water. Wolfgang's other hand grips me tightly on the thigh, his thumb digging into the tender flesh just under my harness.

His gaze is now trained on his slow, meticulous movements. Over my thighs. Across my sensitive slit.

It's then I feel it.

Between the hot breaths of his lips near my skin, his touch echoing the pleasure of how it felt to have him sink into me, knowing we were no longer dooming our fates, but sealing it instead.

Death summons me. Beckoning.

Wolfgang must feel my energy shift. His touch stutters, watchful eyes lifting. "What is it?"

I fix my dress, stepping away from the window as Wolfgang stands close by, flicking the wet cloth on the floor without a care.

Death drifts over and through my senses, and my skin breaks into goosebumps. "I need to go," I say quietly.

Wolfgang's hand snaps out as soon as my words are pushed out from my lips. Fingers curling around my wrist, they create familiar divots, his hand always finding my wrist lately.

"You're not leaving my side, Mercy," he says sternly, his eyebrows furrowing with concern. "Especially now, with the threat to our lives at its highest."

"It's calling me." My voice should sound like a steel rod, unbreakable; instead, it sounds weak like a handful of straw.

I feel pulled apart. As if Wolfgang is holding my life force between his fingers. If he wanted to be cruel, he could ball his hand into a fist and turn me into dust.

I look out the window evading his questioning gaze. The rain streaks the window, blurring Pravitia and its shimmering, glittering lights.

"Is your god speaking to you?"

I shift my attention back to Wolfgang, his hand still holding me. Keeping me close.

"Yes."

Letting go of my arm, he fixes himself with righteous resolve. The tug of his shirt into his trousers. The buckle of his belt. The smoothing of his lapels. It's all done with such aristocratic grace that I realize then that Wolfgang has always been destined to rule. Has always been destined for such grandeur and worship.

I've always hungered for power, but I wonder if I'll ever revel in it like Wolfgang.

There's a melancholy attached to the feeling.

When he's finished, his hair coiffed back to perfection, he offers me his hand. "Shall we?"

My stomach swoops in surprise. "You can't come with me," I say, my tone just as taken aback.

His laugh is dismissive. "And why is that?"

"Because ..." I trail off unsure, after a long beat I shake off the feeling. "Because this is an intimate act, I worship alone. It's how it has always been."

His offered palm is still between us. He reaches for me.

Gently takes my hand in his and lifts it to his mouth, his lips still swollen from our kiss and warm against the thin skin of my hand. His gaze sparkles with levity, gold winking when his smile turns wide.

"Well, my ruin, it's the dawn of a new day."

THE RAIN IS STILL COMING DOWN IN SHEETS.

As usual, I've left Jeremial to sit in the idling town car a few streets down.

I kill. He collects.

I've been pulled to the harbor this time.

Wolfgang's shoulder presses against mine under the wide umbrella as we stay tucked into a small alleyway, biding our time. I can barely make out the tent-like curves of Pandaemonium in the distance. We should be keeping to our respective neighborhoods as instructed, but death knows no boundaries.

I go where it calls.

I pull the collar of my long leather jacket closer to my chin while the sound of the deluge hits the umbrella with angry drumming. He must have noticed my discomfort, the cold chill of the rainy winter night seeping into my muscles. Without a word, eyes trained outward, he slips his arm around my waist and pulls me into him.

I don't resist it, my feet shuffling closer to him as we wait in silence. The streets are quiet, smelling of damp earth and cold wind. Most of the citizens have been called to Aleksandr's side of the city, his bacchanal still ongoing for the next three days.

A prickle at the base of my nape has my head swiveling to the left. I feel Wolfgang's fingers curl into the leather of my coat, almost as if sensing the thrumming of my heart like a melody drifting in the wind.

There he is.

The one destined for death's fate tonight.

His shoulders hunch up to his ears, his pace fast, head down as he tries to weather the storm with no umbrella. Another block and he'll be passing right in front of us. Like an insect walking into a spider's web, all I need is to wait and they come.

A few more strides.

Beside me, Wolfgang turns restless, as if fighting off a bloodthirsty urge to pounce. A similar urge buzzes through me as I count down the man's steps.

It's addictive in its nature.

The flavor of it electric.

Now.

I step into the rain and reach for him like the hand of death itself. I don't bother covering his mouth. Let him scream. Let the stars above hear his plea like a requiem.

I hook my elbow around his neck, my dagger unsheathed and pressing hard against his ribs as I pull him into the shadows where Wolfgang is waiting.

He's thrown the umbrella to the ground as if needing to unfurl, to open himself to the skies while witnessing me. To let the rain drip over his face while I kill. To feel the wet chill of nature while I permit him to share in my worship.

What he doesn't expect is for me to push him into the brick wall, the unsuspecting man pinned between us. Wolfgang's mouth falls agape. The pelt of the rain, the screams of our victim; it silences his shocked puff of breath.

But Wolfgang's eyes speak volumes, and I yearn to read every page of his book. The one I see now imprinted in his irises. His arms move naturally as if we've performed this dance before. They coil under the man's arms, a deadly snake rattling its tail, keeping him from struggling away, his hands rising to his chin, opening his throat for me.

I'm quick. Impatient.

My sharp blade runs over the expanse of the man's throat. His howls turn into something a lot more primal until my dagger slits his vocal cords, and then all that is left is the gurgling choke of spilled blood. His heart beats feebly, just enough for me to feel the warm spray of blood on my face. Wolfgang growls. Drops the man to the ground and spins me around so I'm now the one pinned to the bricks.

The man dies at our feet.

But there's only death to witness his timely passage.

I'd rather witness Wolfgang's glory instead.

How his eyes have turned black. His rain-soaked lips eager to reach mine. His hands repose on either side of my face, fingers dragging through my hair as he takes the breath right out of me. Let him have it. Let him be the reason I breathe.

I moan into his mouth, tongues hot and wet as his hips pin me even harder to the wall. My hands grip his jacket, pulling, pulling, pulling.

Closer.

Closer.

Closer.

Until we are nothing more but two halves of the same body. And that's not close enough yet.

His palm shifts on my cheek, I feel the cold press of his signet ring against my skin. I'm not quite sure what compels me. But I break away from our kiss, the desire of having something of his to wear just as heady as the burning heat low in my stomach.

His eyes smolder. One eyebrow lifts as I take his left hand and slowly wrap my lips around his pinky finger. I suck it into my mouth, listening to Wolfgang's low throaty groan as I drag my teeth over his ring, slowly pulling it off.

The thumb from his other hand smooths over my skin.

Close to my nose, then below my eye. "What are you doing?" Wolfgang asks. His voice is hungry. Demanding.

I smile. Arrogant like him. And I don't miss the surprise flitting through his gaze.

I slip his ring on my index finger, the gold now unexpectedly warm.

"Sealing our fates."

41

MERCY

Standing directly under the spray of the shower, the water runs down the back of my head as I smooth my wet hair away from my face. The steam appeases my aching muscles. It's a satisfying ache, in the way that everything I set out to do has been done.

I've just returned to Mount Pravitia. After collecting death's tithe, Wolfgang pressed for me to let him come with me and watch while I completed my ritual.

A carefully staged photograph. Then the lick of flames.

I declined his request and told him I needed to finish this alone. I looked away when disappointment flashed across his face. But he said nothing, kissing my forehead instead as his thumb smoothed over my chin before leaving me standing in the alleyway alone.

The rain still cold and seeping.

I couldn't tell him it was because I can hardly manage a coherent thought when around him. Answering death's call has always helped to quiet my mind, a meditative act that allows me to center back into myself.

I don't regret refusing Wolfgang to come tonight, I needed

space to breathe before returning to Mount Pravitia. Space to breathe before I returned and sought him in the silence of the halls, the echoes of steps on marble floors.

Turning off the steaming water, I step out onto the plush rug under my toes. I feel anew. Not bothering with a towel, I let the air kiss my warm skin as it slowly dries.

I stand in front of the large bathroom mirrors and brush my wet hair in a mindless daydream until the glint of Wolfgang's ring catches the light.

I stop.

My arms drop to my sides.

I stare at my reflection.

Bringing my hand to my lips, I smooth the hard metal of his ring back and forth, a tingle of heat igniting low in my stomach as I recall our time together earlier tonight.

It would be so much easier to continue to hate him.

To have his presence irritate me like lice itching my scalp.

But I can't deny the past weeks. The slow but inevitable fall into madness.

Because what is this if not madness?

He's burrowed himself into my mind, my heart ... my soul.

While my fingers still hover close to my mouth, my eyes peer deeply into the mirror, remembering the Oracle's words.

The joining of our two fates.

Something in me yearns to accept this, to fall even deeper into folly—with Wolfgang by my side. But that would take an insurmountable amount of trust that I don't believe I even carry inside of me.

Since my unfortunate birth, I have trusted no one but myself.

And now? I'm asked to trust the man who I've already betrayed.

How could he ever trust *me*?

We appear to have doomed ourselves from the very beginning. And yet ... the intoxicating vision of our union as the symbol of a new epoch for our city is as heady and alluring as Wolfgang himself.

AFTER SLIPPING INTO A SHORT NIGHTGOWN AND ROBE, I LEAVE THE bedchamber in search of my dogs. Their absence guides me toward the West Wing. The halls are dark this time of night, small flickers of warm light emanate from the sconces near the ceiling. While approaching Wolfgang's door, I recall the last time I stood at this very spot—when I caught him in a lewd act, and when my hatred for him fueled my spellbinding attraction to him.

I can no longer find solace behind that kind of armor.

And what's left is ... me.

Unlike last time, I do not linger in the shadows, instead pushing the door open, and walking in. Although I was expecting it, seeing my dogs sleeping snuggly around Wolfgang in bed has my breath dying somewhere in my lungs, a small swoop tugging on my stomach.

Wolfgang is shirtless and in a pair of black silk pants, lying over the covers, his back resting against the headboard. Sundae has her chin resting on his thigh, Éclair is curled at the foot of the bed while Truffles snores on the ground curled into the rug.

His eyes lift from the book he's reading, peering from behind his reading glasses, his gaze nearly knocking me over as if I've become as light as a feather.

"You're back," he states, his eyes dropping back to his book.

"I thought you hated my dogs," I reply.

A subtle grin appears on his mouth, and he tries to hide it with a quick rub of his thumb over his lips. "I thought I hated their mother, too."

My cheeks heat, and I almost run out of the room from the sheer embarrassment of my reaction to Wolfgang's loaded words.

The silence percolates between us. I haven't taken another step inside.

With a sigh, Wolfgang takes off his glasses and places the leather-bound book face-down on the bedside table, pinning me with his stare once again.

He says nothing. I say nothing back.

Canting his head, he pats the bed beside him.

With the movement, Sundae perks up her head, now realizing I'm in the room.

I tell myself it's because of the dogs. Not Wolfgang with his bare chest and silk pants low around his hips. As I tentatively approach, his eyes turn a darker shade of blue. I step out of my feathered slippers and take off my robe, draping it over the chair near the vanity.

"I'm not staying the night," I mutter, feeling foolish even saying that out loud.

"As you wish, Crèvecoeur," Wolfgang replies roguishly.

I slip under the heavy quilted duvet while he does the same, the satin sheets cool against my skin. Resting my back against the pillows and headboard, Sundae shifts position, her nose nudging my hand to ask for some affection.

"You know," Wolfgang starts, stretching his arms wide before shifting his body toward me. "Although the circumstances were quite dire." His smile turns cocksure. "I have never slept as well as when we were in the underground quarters fearing for our lives."

I pick at my nail nervously while I maintain his gaze, listening to the words he did not speak.

When we slept in the same bed.

"It was the drop in adrenaline," I say limply.

Wolfgang chuckles. "Right." He waves his hand in front of

him in a lazy flourish. "The adrenaline." His eyes turn serious. "And nothing to do with you."

I study him for a beat, my hand stroking Sundae's soft fur to help me feel less astray. "How are you so unperturbed about all of this?" I finally ask.

His eyebrows crease. "About what? Us?"

My heart pinches at the word *us*.

"Yes." My voice is meek, and I suddenly wish my dear god of death could come and claim me instead of letting me suffer through feelings I'd rather not admit.

"Mercy," Wolfgang says, his hand slowly finding my knee over the duvet. "Why fight it?"

"Because you've wanted my demise for as long as I've wished for yours?"

He drags his hand over his jaw as if in thought. Then a small dismissive wave of his fingers. "And yet, the gods had a plan for us all along."

"So that's the only reason?" I grit out, "The gods?"

Wolfgang's gaze hardens into a glare, one eyebrow quirking up questioningly. "Are we not their servants? Do we not owe them our fate?"

I stare into his eyes but say nothing, chewing on my words. They feel like sand on my tongue and down my throat. Gritty and rough.

"Fate," I repeat. A small mutter, barely a response.

How can I tell him that my feelings toward him are larger than fate?

If that's even possible.

The word fate sounds like chains, it rattles and shakes and moans against its shackles reminding me that no matter what, he did not *choose* me. The gods did.

How can fate be the sole reason why I dismissed the warning bells and bent the rules just for a taste of him? Is this what obsession feels like? Is *that* what I'm feeling? Certainly not *fate*.

Wolfgang reaches for me, through the stony barrier I've managed to slither behind, and I don't pull away when his fingers caress my cheek, tucking a loose strand of hair behind my ear.

"What did I say, my ruin?"

His gaze is soft—too soft—the color of his eyes not steely blue but the color of the morning sky. I look away.

"Nothing," I murmur after a long silence.

Taking my hand in his, he presses his mouth to the cut still healing on my wrist from the blood ritual a week ago. There's a coy smile on his lips as he looks up through his eyelashes.

"Then stay the night."

My throat tightens, and my heart skips like a smooth rock over the water.

"But the dogs," I say weakly, trying to find any excuses other than my teetering vulnerability.

"What *about* the dogs," Wolfgang replies with an exasperated breath. "They seem a lot less skittish than their mother." My gaze sweeps over the bed, the dogs sound asleep. "Stop resisting what already is." He rests our hands over Sundae still between us. "You might actually enjoy yourself for once."

My gaze lifts to his, the words tumbling out.

"I've enjoyed myself before."

"Ah yes, I'm sure answering your god's call is quite the entertainment," he says mockingly, but his usual sting is replaced with something a lot warmer, almost like ... affection.

The words keep clambering out without me wanting them to. "It's not the first thing that came to mind."

"What then?" he asks, tilting his head.

I chew on my lips, not comprehending why I'd have the urge to divulge this. "The day you came to watch me burn the body. When you asked about the photographs."

A Dance Macabre

Wolfgang's smile turns wide as if recalling a similar emotion attached to that day. "Is that so, Crèvecoeur?"

"Before it was ruined," I reply with a minuscule laugh, referring to the troupe of actors and the Lottery reenactment.

He shakes his head, his chuckle sounding almost thoughtful. His hand squeezes my palm. His eyes slide upward, serious. "Watching you," he starts, his voice dropping an octave. "I don't think *enjoy* is quite the word I would use to explain how I felt that day."

Gently pushing Sundae's head off my lap, I order her to the foot of the bed. She follows my instructions with a small whine, curling herself beside Éclair.

I slip closer to Wolfgang. His free hand circles my hip, pulling me closer. "What then?" I ask, my long nail trailing down his stomach. "What word would you use?"

His palm slides up to my face, fingers raking through my hair as his thumb smooths over my cheek, a smile pulling at the corner of his lips. It almost looks like pride glinting deep in his irises. "Mesmerizing."

The word is like warm honey down my throat, spreading into a tame fire inside my chest.

Again, the words escape, and I let them.

"It was my birthday that day."

Surprise dances over Wolfgang's face. "Was it?"

I nod.

His smile turns even balmier. "And you spent it with me?"

I nod again.

"My, my, my," he says with mirth. He pulls me even closer, my head now resting on his bare chest as he leans into the pillows. "What a pleasant thought that is."

I fall asleep in his arms, his hand caressing my hair, his heartbeat against my ear.

42

MERCY

*C*urled up on the leather couch in the library, I try to coax myself to pick up a book and read. Instead, I stare at the stained glass window, my thoughts one long trail of winding roads leading nowhere.

It's the final day of Tithe Season. Gemini's day. Typically, I'd visit him while he collects secrets like handfuls of dirt from his worshippers. Not today. The threat against us is still looming and so here I am, collecting my own kind of secrets in the form of my emotions running wild and amok.

Wolfgang and I have slept in the same bed for the past three days. For the last two nights, he came and slept in the ruler's bedchamber with me. *"Where I belong,"* he said haughtily with a raised chin and pursed lips.

The dogs love him.

So I agreed.

It's becoming too easy to have Wolfgang around. As if behind all that animosity there's an effortlessness between us. I don't think either of us expected it, but somehow it feels like it's always been there. Waiting.

A Dance Macabre

"There you are," Wolfgang declares, and I jump at the sound of his voice.

He circles the couch to stand in front of me. His face is beaming, stance wide and hands tucked into his pockets. His suit is black today, a deep velour waistcoat, with a textured shirt underneath. A fleeting thought dances across my mind.

I wonder if he chose black to match me.

It's silly. And I barely pause to entertain it.

"What is it?" I say with joviality as I wait for him to reveal why he appears so bashful.

"I need you to come with me," he answers while offering his hand.

"What for?" I say tentatively, but still my hand slides into his, his skin warm and inviting.

He pulls me into his arms, and with my heels, we're practically eye to eye. He gives my nose a quick peck. "It's a surprise."

"I don't like surprises." I hardly recognize myself when I follow my statement with a nearly-there giggle.

"Well," he starts with a wink as he leads me out the door, "You've never been surprised by Wolfgang Vainglory."

I say nothing as I follow him out, but I can't help to think that his words ring true even in a deeper sense. Nothing about Wolfgang has been like it seemed.

"Are you taking me to the bathhouse?"

Wolfgang shoots me a droll look. His palm is a comforting weight against mine as we walk down the vacant corridor, our footsteps bouncing against the stone walls. "How could that possibly be a surprise?"

I shrug, barely able to contain the shy smile tugging on my lips. The levity of our shared moment is as delicious as his cologne tickling my senses. The same ease that's been growing in strength in the past week, wrapping around us like a soothing cloak.

"Here we are," he says with excitement as he stops beside a closed door only a few steps away from the entrance of the bathhouse.

"The surprise is inside?" I ask, my gaze sweeping over Wolfgang's face as if expecting to find an answer.

"Open the door," he presses, his eyes shining.

There's a knot in my throat. Maybe from nerves. Or perhaps, it's from the slow realization that the surprise is a gift from Wolfgang.

I bite my inner lip, my hand curling over the large doorknob, timidly pushing the door open.

At first, my eyes can't quite decipher what I'm staring at. It's as if by walking through the threshold, I've somehow appeared back at the Grounds.

"Oh my gods ..."

I peer around the room. My words evaporate into a stutter of indecipherable sounds as I try to absorb what I'm seeing.

It's a near replica of my crematorium.

The stone dome overtop the stainless steel machinery. The sleek look of black obsidian and silk. I don't miss the subtle additions of dark red and velvet, as if Wolfgang couldn't help but need a reflection of himself inside this room as well.

"Now you can stay close," he says softly beside me. His voice is meek as if waiting for me to say I hate it.

"You planned this?" I ask in awe. But of course he did, who else? He nods, smiling. "When? How?"

His expression turns boyish, his hand rubbing the back of his neck. "It's been ... a few weeks."

The knot in my throat grows in size. A rock. A boulder. A brick wall I can barely climb. I hold Wolfgang's piercing gaze.

"But—" I swallow, hoping I can speak through the obstruction, "a few weeks ago, we were still at each other's throats."

He looks down, hands stuffed into his pockets. Peering around the room, his eyes finally return to me. "The gods made me do it." Obviously downplaying his intentions. He cracks a smile, and my heart skips a beat as he lets the silence linger. "Besides, Mount Pravitia should have had one already. Your family ruled the city once before too, didn't they?"

"They used to burn the bodies publicly," I state, my mind still running in circles unable to fully comprehend how Wolfgang planned to have a crematorium built for me.

Before we were even ... this.

"They did?" Wolfgang replies, his eyebrows pulling upward in surprise.

I nod. "Crèvecoeurs were less private a hundred years ago, it seems," I reply with a small grin.

Taking his hand out of his pocket, he steps closer, his fingers curling around my upper arm. He gives it a little squeeze. His gaze is seeking, open, and vulnerable. "Do you like it?"

The tentative intonation of his question finally snaps me out of my daze. My arms wrap around his neck. "Yes," I say, my lips close to his. "Of course. I love it."

His hands slip over my hips, clasping them together behind my back while he kisses me softly. "There's a studio room behind that door for your pictures," he says, tilting his head toward a door to our right.

I laugh warmly and return his kiss. "You've thought of everything."

He smiles, his arms squeezing even tighter around me. "Anything to keep you close."

WE SPEND THE NEXT FEW HOURS TOGETHER, MOST OF IT IN THE bathhouse as I sit in a plush chair next to the water, listening to

Wolfgang play the violin near the large windows, the sun's rays bouncing off his instrument.

It's the first time I can bask in the vision of him like this, without having to hide from view or taunt him into paying attention to me. Sleeves rolled up his forearms, hair slightly messy. He's a masterpiece at play. An animate carving of a god himself. He is beauty in material form.

Abruptly, Wolfgang ends the song he was playing, pulling me out of my reverie. Checking his watch, he curses under his breath while hurriedly putting the violin back into its case.

"Something wrong?" I ask.

His smile is warm and inviting as he looks over to where I'm sitting.

"Nothing, I'm just late for a meeting at Vainglory Tower. I'd usually let Dizzy attend in my place, but she's busy with a lead."

"A lead about the bombing?"

He nods as he shrugs his jacket back on. Walking up to where I'm sitting, he leans over to rest his palms on the arms of the chair. His grin turns seductive as he peers into my eyes, nudging my nose with his before kissing me softly on the lips.

"Will you miss me?" he asks smoothly when he pulls away but still stays close, his voice like a pleasant trickle down my spine. His lips graze mine as he waits for me to answer.

"Perhaps," I say, acting coy.

He chuckles darkly, leaning into a deeper kiss before pulling away. "Are you okay with walking back upstairs alone? I need to leave now," he says as he fixes his tie.

I press my lips into a mocking pout. "I think I'll manage."

He smiles warmly, then sends me a kiss with a quick press of his hand to his lips before walking out of the bathhouse. I stare at the spot where he disappeared, my chest full of strange affection, our kiss still tickling my lips.

A Dance Macabre

STEPPING INTO THE DRAWING ROOM, I HIDE THE SMALL JOLT OF surprise at unexpectedly seeing Dizzy standing near the fireplace.

"Dizzy," I mutter, eyebrows pulling together in irritation. "Wolfgang isn't here."

Upon hearing my voice, she turns to face me, her expression cold while her eyes sweep over my body, then back up. "I know."

The hairs at the back of my nape rise, my senses suddenly on high alert.

Something here is wrong.

"If you know that he isn't here then you should also know you aren't welcome in our private quarters," I say, squaring my shoulders, my fingers instinctively brushing my dagger under my skirt.

Dizzy's dark brown eyes dip to my thigh before flashing me a forced, thin-lipped smile.

"Don't you want to know why I'm here?" Her voice is sickly sweet, and the urge to dismiss her strengthens the more I pin her with my stare.

"I don't care," I reply with a small sneer.

Her laugh is dry as she approaches the two settees facing each other. "Oh, I think you *will* care."

She smooths her ruffled blouse before sitting down, inviting me to do the same with a quick wave of her manicured hand.

The chilly bite to the air around us whispers that I won't like what she has to say but something prevents me from kicking her out. My curiosity wins. I step up to the settee but stay standing.

After a tense beat, Dizzy speaks. "Congratulations on your win, it was well deserved."

I flash her a distrustful look, eyes narrowing as I try to decipher the meaning behind her words. I know she's been Wolfgang's right hand for years now, but she's not related to any of the six families and therefore wasn't in attendance on the day of the Lottery.

Then why does it sound like she knows what truly happened on that day?

"Enough," I spit. "Tell me why you're here or get out."

"Fine then." Her face flattens into something a lot more menacing, her dark eyes souring in distaste. She crosses her legs, her hands folding over her knee. "What if I could help you become the sole ruler of Pravitia?"

43

MERCY

Dizzy's words hang between us like rotting entrails dripping rancid blood onto the rug beneath our feet. It takes me a few racing heartbeats to realize the weight behind her words.

"Vile tactless snail," I snap. "I could crush you with just the tip of my heel. What makes you think I need your help?"

She lets the silence linger as if trying to intimidate me. I should kill her just for the audacity alone. Her smile grows into a demonic slit. "I could kill him for you."

She doesn't need to say his name for me to know who she's referring to.

Wolfgang.

My heartbeat triples in rate as indignant shock washes over me like a harsh, cold wave.

"Do you have a death wish, Dizzy?" I grit through my teeth, the muscles in my jaw tensing painfully. "How dare you mock the gods like this?"

She cocks her head, her long bob falling off her shoulder. "Like what? For saying the one thing out loud that you've wished all along? I know what you did at the Lottery, Mercy."

She leans forward, elbows on her knees. "I don't think *co-ruling* was exactly what you had in mind, was it?"

I narrow my eyes, cold sweat prickling my forehead. "How would you know that?"

She scoffs, resting her back against the settee and crossing her arms. "People talk." She tucks her hair behind her ear. "Not everyone is as tied to traditions as you lot."

My stomach is in knots, anger like rusty nails digging into flesh. "I should eviscerate you for just *thinking* about killing one of us."

Her laugh is cold. "Don't tell me you've grown fond of a Vainglory." She pins me with a hard stare. "Trust me, he would betray you in a heartbeat if given the chance."

"He wouldn't," I retort. But my words evoke a doubt in my own heart. Like acid, they chew through my walls much faster than I would ever expect. I'm stunned by how fast she's able to slither doubt into my head.

"Did you forget I've worked under him for nearly half of my life?" Her red-stained lips curl into another sneer. "Wolfgang will never be capable of loving anyone but himself. So self-absorbed he didn't even realize the threat was right under his nose all along."

"So it was you then," I state, taking a step forward as I pull my dress up my thigh to reveal my dagger. "You were behind all of it."

"Yes," she answers simply; her haughty attitude is begging me to kill her. Yet something keeps me from doing it.

She's planted a seed, and I am now frozen in place, watching the seed grow and grow and grow. Reckless. Damaging. Like invasive vines creeping into every crack of my rationality.

"Would a secret placate you?" she asks, staring me down, elbows back on her knees. "I admit it. Our initial plan was to kill you all — make way for a new era. But we've come to our senses. You six are much too powerful. So we've changed course, decided on the next best thing."

I let the silence thicken, smoothing my tongue over my teeth as I study her. She's a demented weasel if she thinks I believe a word she says. "And killing *one* of us is your solution? You must think I'm just as self-absorbed as your boss."

Her arrogance is unwavering. "Would you prefer taking your chances with Wolfgang?" Her laugh is villainous and my fingers tighten over the dagger still sheathed to my thigh. "Is your life worth the gamble?"

I press my lips into a thin line, my glare turning vicious. "Silly girl. I'm not afraid of death," I snarl.

She holds my stare, quirking an eyebrow. "What about a betrayal, then?"

Betrayal.

The word is like the sharpest of blades, flaying my chest to shreds, cracking my ribs open one by one until the only thing left is my heart, unprotected, bloody, and weak.

My throat tightens, and I take a second before speaking, needing to make sure my voice won't crack.

My dry laugh is full of condescension. "How do you know I won't go to Wolfgang with this?"

There's a pompous air to Dizzy, and I can't help but wonder if she's learned such arrogance from Wolfgang himself.

"Just a hunch," she answers with a shrug.

Finally having enough of her grating attitude, I dismiss her. "Get out of my sight," I bark.

The threat in my tone has the same effect as a dagger to her throat, and she winces. Her fear soothes my nerves somewhat.

She stands, and I don't give her the courtesy of a single look.

"You know where to reach me. Just know I won't wait forever," she says solemnly.

Without another glance, she leaves.

I CAN'T TELL HOW MUCH TIME HAS PASSED, BUT THE LONGER I SIT here in silence, the more it feels like the walls are closing in on me. I stand up abruptly and storm out of the drawing room.

Our conversation should not have rattled me like this. Moronic low-class *peasant* thinking I would fall for her threats. She must think me a fool if she thinks I believe that she'll stop at just Wolfgang.

The walls pulse around me as if sentient while I storm through the long corridor. I feel trapped. Deceived in my own house.

By the time I end up in the atrium, I'm breathing heavily through the nose like a raging bull, so worked up that I can barely think.

"Get out!" I yell at the few servants in the room setting up for dinner. It's almost a shriek and I can barely recognize the sound of my own voice.

They all jolt in fear and then quickly scamper. I don't wait for them to file out of the room before heading for the table and swiping my hands through fine china and crystal.

It all crashes to the floor, and the sound spurs me further into my spiral. By the time I'm done, the table is empty, and I'm standing amidst the shattered aftermath.

Broken pieces. Shards of glass.

My breathing is shallow. And I don't feel remotely better.

Betrayal.

The word pulses over and over, slowly seeping into the blood in my veins, taking more and more space inside of me.

I can't let it go.

Her offer.

It's a loophole on a silver platter.

If I don't take it—take *advantage* of it, Wolfgang surely will.

I would be naive to think I can trust anyone but myself.

Wolfgang has said it before: The only reason he's had a change of heart is because the gods *decreed it.*

And now this.

Is this not a divine invitation?

Is this not fate calling my name?

I know that if I give Dizzy the go-ahead, Wolfgang's death will not satiate her. She'll come after me next, but I'll deal with that pest later. As if she could ever touch me.

Pushing my hair off of my face, I straighten my dress and take a deep breath before stepping up to the large windows. The sun is setting over Pravitia, and I watch the dying rays refract against the tinted windows of skyscrapers, the water of the harbor twinkling orange in the distance.

Wolfgang will never be capable of loving anyone but himself.

I feel sick. The idea of Wolfgang betraying me slithers through every single insecurity I've held on to so tightly during all these weeks with him.

Maybe it meant nothing.

Maybe our fate was our demise all along.

The echo of Dizzy's words continues to ring shrilly in my ears. And maybe a Crèvecoeur will never be capable of trusting anyone else but themself.

By the time the city has donned its nightly cloak, I know what must be done.

44

WOLFGANG

There's something about the sounds of Mount Pravitia in the dead of night that are distinctly different from the whispers of Vainglory Tower when darkness descends. The silence howls like the restless wind outside the window. It groans as if alive with a bellyful of memories from every ruler who came before me.

If the walls could talk ...

The tales would be thick with blood, murder, and betrayal.

I wonder then, if the sounds currently keeping me awake are sounds of betrayal too.

The lights are off in the ruler's bedchamber, Mercy's side cold and vacant. No sign of the dogs either. It's raining again. It batters against the windows adding to the ghostly melodies of the oldest building in Pravitia.

I pretend to sleep.

If I can even call it that.

My eyes are closed but I'm wide awake.

Listening. Seeking. *Feeling*.

Does she know I feel her when she's close?

But she's not the one opening the door right now. There's

barely a sound. I wouldn't have discerned it if I were asleep—if I wasn't seeking the tell-tales of deceit.

My breathing slows, and I try my hardest to keep myself relaxed. A slumbering body under a heavy velvet duvet. My adrenaline spikes, and the subtle sounds in the room amplify.

Soft steps on thick carpet.

The rustle of clothing against skin.

A long, slow inhale followed by an even slower exhale.

Soon, I'll need to reveal my hand. But for now, I lie in wait, like a predator masquerading as prey. I will strike when the time is just right.

But the time never comes.

Instead, the walls of Mount Pravitia hear a series of different sounds.

Ones of surprise.

And of treachery turned into blinding vengeance.

The lights are flicked on, and I am momentarily blinded.

My eyes crash into Dizzy who is standing at the foot of the bed. She looks just as shocked as I feel, but our reasons for the feeling are worlds apart.

Because I knew Dizzy was coming.

It's Mercy standing in the doorway that makes me freeze.

I don't want to believe that she's the one behind this breach in security.

Did she really let Dizzy into our private quarters?

Mercy's glare burns red. Her movements are hastened, tense, and violent as she charges for a frazzled Dizzy but not before reaching for the heavy bust of a long-dead ancestor.

She swings at her head, the marble statue hitting Dizzy straight across the jaw. Her face swivels hard to the side, her body twisting and falling over the bed.

Letting out a feral snarl, Mercy jumps atop Dizzy, pinning her between her legs as she pummels Dizzy's face with the statue.

She never stood a chance.

And I'm unable to move from next to the headboard as I behold Mercy's unleashed fury, not an arm's length away on the bed.

Dizzy's eyes roll backward, blood gushing out of her mouth and from the thick gashes to her head. But Mercy doesn't stop. And Dizzy turns unrecognizable.

Macerated flesh. Broken teeth. Limp limbs soaking in a pool of blood.

A pool reeking of betrayal.

Mercy is more red than black, gore covering her hands, arms, and face as she screams in rage. I should command her to stop.

Dizzy's dead.

Instead, I let her avenge Dizzy's treason. But my anger is a complex, ever-morphing thing.

And Mercy is not unscathed from it.

The note she left tonight before she disappeared. It preceded a peculiar call from Gemini. Her absence became an oozing abscess. And Dizzy's reaction to seeing Mercy storming in confirmed my suspicions.

Mercy was involved. Mercy tried to have me killed.

Nausea roils in my stomach. I feel sick at the thought.

Dizzy's face is now a flattened mess of sinew and bones, the gurgling sounds of death gruesome even to a seasoned ear like mine.

This is crazed repentance.

This is pleading for forgiveness.

"Mercy," I finally say, pulling off the covers and stepping out of bed.

It's a soft order, and I'm not sure she'll even hear me through her murderous daze. But her arm stops mid-air, her other hand still pinning the mess that is left of Dizzy to the bed.

A Dance Macabre

Her crazed eyes fly to mine.

I think even Mount Pravitia has stopped breathing.

Through the blood dripping down her face, her gaze widens as she takes in my enigmatic face. My feelings are a bloodied mess, like the corpse underneath her.

She drops the bust on the ground as if it's suddenly burning her and scrambles off the bed. I take quick steps to reach her before she even considers running away. I grab her by a handful of her hair, my other hand slamming against her throat. Her eyes are wild, and for the first time since I've known her intimately, I find fear splashed against her face.

She doesn't fight me. Doesn't even try to pull her hair out of my harsh grip.

I sneer while we stare at each other nose to nose, letting the tension turn deadly around us. Letting go of her throat, I roughly wipe some of the blood off her face, and I don't miss the small wince she makes whenever my palm smooths over her skin.

I still have her hair gripped in my fist, I don't let go while I study her.

"What do you fear, Mercy?"

There's a hardness to my tone, but it's also seeking. I ache for her. Whether she conspired to have me killed or not, I ache for her. And my heart beats hoping it's beating is in cadence with hers.

Her gaze is still racked with fear, black pupils blown wide. Her breathing is ragged, mouth open as her eyes bounce from side to side.

She swallows hard.

Her shoulders fall.

"A life without you," she says so quietly I could almost convince myself I made it up.

My heart pitches out of my chest and into hers. I let out a harsh breath, and by the time I've let go of her hair, our lips slam together, her hands flying to my face, nails digging into my nape.

"Forgive me," she says with such desperation that I nearly crumble to my knees. "Forgive me," she repeats over and over as she kisses my lips, my face, my neck.

Letting go of Mercy, I reach for Dizzy's corpse, shoving her body off the bed. The duvet and mattress are soaked with blood but I'm too far gone to care, throwing Mercy onto her back. I push her dress up to her hips and tug my pants down my thighs before falling over her. I drag her thong to the side while her hands continue to feverishly claw at me as if she fears I'll disappear from under her touch. She's as desperate as I am.

I need to feel her.

I need to *fuck* her.

I need to remind myself that she is capable of more than just death and betrayal.

I drag the head of my cock over her wet slit, and her moan sounds closer to a sob.

"Forgive you?" I say harshly as I rip her dress down her chest, freeing her breasts and groping one hungrily. Her eyes are deep with regret, and it somehow gets me even harder. I thrust inside her cunt with force, groaning loudly when she tightens around me. "Tell me why I should forgive a treacherous snake like you?" I ask between clenched teeth, my hips slapping violently against her.

The urge to claim her becomes a thrashing, growling need clawing through my skin. Her legs curl around my hips, her pointed heels digging into my ass, and I'm undone, unleashed, and anguished. She traps me in her imploring gaze, her mouth agape in pleasure, eyebrows creased in painful rapture.

"Let me beg for forgiveness for the rest of our lives," she pleads breathlessly. "*Please.* Let me tell you every day that I choose you and only you."

My cock throbs with the promise of a lifetime spent with

Mercy. But my soul seeks an even deeper promise. A merging of our flesh where I become her and she becomes me.

"A lifetime isn't enough, Mercy." I punch every word with a savage thrust, my cock so achingly deep. "A lifetime is still much too short."

Her body seizes under me, swept into a powerful climax. Her back arches pressing her chest to mine, and I steal another kiss, needing to feel her pleasured breath against my lips more than I need to feel her clench around my cock. I fuck her deeply through her orgasm while her moans turn into sobs, and my skin pebbles with goosebumps at the sound.

"When will I ever get enough of you?"

My voice is strained with anger, yet streaked with defeat.

Defeat of ever trying to deny her.

"Let it be never," she says beseechingly, her nails creating divots into my neck. Her eyes shimmer with regret. A vulnerable shade paints her blood-stained skin. "Let it be never," she repeats softly.

Pulling out, I climb to my knees and kneel over her flushed face. I pump my cock into my fist, her arousal coating my shaft, my palm gliding smoothly against it.

"Open your mouth and claim me then," I demand, my voice a low gravel timbre. The head of my cock smooths over her lips, and she opens wide, raising her chin to open her throat. "Drink from the well of the gods and take all of me."

And as I coat her throat with the thick ropes of my cum, her green eyes crashing into mine, I realize the gods blessed me when they created Mercy.

Because she is everything I've ever dared to love.

45

MERCY

The bathhouse is the darkest I've ever seen it. Only a few lit candles are scheming with the nighttime shadows. The moon is only a sliver hanging low in the obsidian sky.

Wolfgang's lithe and muscled naked body cuts through the water as he swims laps, his family sigil sprawled across his back shimmering against the light.

I'm sitting on one of the submerged steps, my back to the edge of the bath—watching. We haven't said much to one another since I intercepted Dizzy mid-assassination.

After cleaning ourselves off, we both called our assistants to help remove the body from the bedchamber and told them to keep it in the morgue. We'll deal with Dizzy's corpse later.

We came down to the bathhouse not long after. I think Wolfgang needed to be somewhere he felt safe. And I can't blame him.

I almost had him killed.

Almost ...

Is that word enough for him to forgive me?

His actions right now are confusing me. He's barely spoken

a word now that the adrenaline has been washed away along with the dried blood sticking to our skins.

But he doesn't seem to want me gone either.

He held my hand as we walked the corridors. Watched me undress near the edge of the bath, and held my hand again when we stepped into the warm waters.

But his actions contradict his demeanor.

Cold. Distant. Impassive.

And my heart aches knowing I'll have to live with the effects of my betrayal.

What kind of evil possessed me to allow Dizzy to break the bond of trust Wolfgang and I were carefully building?

Wolfgang reaches the far side of the bath and pops his head out of the water. Wet hair slicked back, the bottom of his face still submerged. I can barely discern his expression with how dark it is in here. But I know his eyes are trained on me.

I can almost feel the water ripple with the tremor of his inner turmoil. My heart batters against my chest, and if I was one to cry, I believe I'd be wiping my cheeks from all the tears streaking my face right now.

What is this feeling?

It hurts. Uncomfortable. It's a grating, throbbing thing.

Is this what it feels like to experience regret?

Deep and soul-churning regret.

I hate it. I need it to stop.

Slowly, Wolfgang glides through the water to reach me. The angles of his face are sharper here while the shadows dance over his body. He sits on the same step as me, droplets trickling over his tanned muscled stomach, the hair near his lower stomach disappearing into the water. He keeps his distance and leans into his outstretched arms behind him.

I wonder if showing off his toned glistening body is a punishment in itself. What I no longer have the right to freely touch.

His voice bursts the bubble I've been cowardly hiding inside of. "Planning on telling me why you wanted me dead, Crèvecoeur?"

The way he asks the question. It's so casual. So devoid of emotion. But my gaze tracks the clench of his jaw and the strain in his shoulders. It's an act.

My words feel like paste, too thick to mold into a sentence.

How can I ever explain myself?

I listen to the trickle of water as he reaches up and smooths his hand over his slicked hair before leaning his weight back onto his palm, his attention trained on the vaulted ceiling above us.

Waiting.

I can't sit still. My skin is crawling with unwelcomed emotions—regret, guilt, shame. So I stand up and tread down deeper into the water, facing him.

"I was foolish," I finally say.

Wolfgang keeps his posture but quirks an eyebrow.

"Foolish?" he says quietly, but there's a bite to his tone. "Not strong enough a word for what you did."

"So what then?" I ask, my fist splashing the surface of the water with irritation. "Why are you not angrier? Yell at me! Shove me against a wall, get your revenge, make me pay, something! Just not this." My chest heaves in frustration as I say the three last words in quiet defeat. His rage I can handle. Heated insults. Furious glares. But his pointed silence is a fate much more agonizing.

I don't know how to face the disappointment burning in his hard gaze when his eyes finally drop to mine.

"I'm not interested in making *you* feel more at ease." His expression softens into something even more painful to witness. Hurt. "Why, Mercy?" he asks softly.

I would rather be drowned than endure this.

My throat tightens, my eyes stinging with tears I swore I would never shed. "It was either you, or me."

The answer feels flat. Weak. Devoid of any real meaning.

His gaze lingers. Needing to feel closer to him, I approach him and kneel on the steps in front of him. He tracks my movements, leaning his elbows on his thighs to better look at me from above.

"Is that what Dizzy told you?" His tone is gentle, his gaze searching.

I nod, my chin raised up to hold his gaze. I can't control the single tear from falling down my cheek, and I don't move to wipe it away.

His sigh is full of defeat. "She would have never come to me."

My eyebrows dip skeptically. "Why are you so sure?"

His expression turns a shade darker. His hand reaches out, softly collecting my fallen tear on his finger. He brings it to his lips. I'm not even sure he realizes he's done it, his expression looking thoughtful before returning his full attention to me.

"Why didn't you just kill her then?"

Taken aback, I stutter over my response. "I — I ..."

Why didn't I just kill her then?

The answer is simple, but I struggle to say it out loud, ashamed that Dizzy could have such an effect on me. I avoid eye contact, staring at the water.

"She somehow got in my head," I answer with a subdued shrug. "I was then too caught up on the toxic idea of you eventually betraying me."

"So you decided to betray me instead." Wolfgang's voice is hard, and a twinge of anger filters through. But I can still hear the hurt through the cracks.

My heart tumbles deeper into a dark hole of remorse.

I lift my eyes to meet his gaze. "She caught me when I was at my weakest."

His eyes narrow. "Your weakest?" he repeats slowly with derision. "What could have possibly made *Mercy Crèvecoeur* weak?"

Telling him the truth feels like another cruel punishment. I inch my body a little closer before speaking, my hand finding his foot in the water. My lip trembles. I bite down hard to make it stop.

"You."

"Me?" Wolfgang says, his shoulders straightening, almost like an accusation. "*I'm* the one making you weak?"

"Yes," I reply.

Wolfgang scoffs and starts to stand up, but I stop him, grabbing his hands in mine, now kneeling between his feet.

"I've never felt like this before, Wolfgang. You — you madden me. You've left me unguarded and have made me ... *care* for someone outside of myself. To trust you, Wolfgang," I press, my voice cracking, "I must place my heart into your hands and believe you will not damage it — trust that you won't strangle it with your fists and bleed me to death." Another tear falls. "I could not bear the thought. I could not bear the threat of this kind of agony."

Wolfgang stays silent. My hands still wrapped around his.

"And what made you change your mind, my ruin?" he asks softly, his gaze searching mine.

I choke on a sob. "You." I swallow the tears down. "I realized that it was too late—that my heart was already beating outside of my chest. You had already claimed it."

Wolfgang gives me a weak smile, his fingers caressing over my cheeks and lips.

"Do you trust me, Mercy?" he asks solemnly.

"Should I not ask you the same?" I can't help but say.

He lets the silence linger. His blue-gray eyes piercing. "Not today."

My stomach drops, fear snaking tightly around my throat.

"What can I do, then? To prove to you my loyalty? My devotion? Tell me and I'll do it."

He lets my question hang between us for a beat before his morose smile slowly turns into a cocksure grin as if my question has brought him solace. As if whatever answer he's come up with has restored him to his typical arrogant demeanor.

"The servant of death on her knees is a good start."

46

WOLFGANG

Mercy stands next to me while we are transported down the streets of Pravitia on a large gold palanquin, half-enclosed and high enough for us to stand in. Ten bearers carry us, large poles resting on their shoulders as they rock gently from side to side. They take one heavy step after another while the crowd cheers boisterously from the side.

The weather is particularly mild for early January. The cloudless skies are crystal blue, and the sun's rays are warm and inviting.

Mercy's expression is a masterpiece of power and authority, the curves of her face enforcing the very image of a Crèvecoeur as a Pravitian ruler. The collar of her dress undulates up the length of her neck, a large diamond necklace resting overtop the fabric. She is a regal vision, and I match her energy perfectly with my long velvet coat of a deep burgundy with gold stitching.

Although the threat of Dizzy had vanished, we had no way to tell if the threat of the insurrection was over. But the unexpected visit from the Oracle in our bedchamber early morning

A Dance Macabre

after Dizzy's death did soothe some of our anxious ruminations. She told us that the gods were pleased and to not disappoint them again. She left shortly after.

It only took a few days to organize the parade.

Advertised and broadcasted through every medium Vainglory Media controls.

Which is every single one of them.

However, celebrating the two rulers of Pravitia isn't why we're parading down the streets of Pravitia today. No, this is a deliberate warning.

A reminder that the fate of a treasonous rat is much worse than merely being ruled by us.

A few feet from our palanquin is an even larger float, this one needing hundreds of bearers to carry it, the poles over twenty feet long. Atop the float is a rectangular table, and around it sit six scarecrows, each created in our likeness.

Because this parade is a traitor's parade.

A Feast of Fools just for Dizzy.

If she craved to overpower us—craved to rule this city in our stead—then let her. If she wanted this so badly then let her have it.

Her body has been dismembered. Six body parts for the six scarecrows representing each of us. The legs, the arms, and hands. All are carefully stitched and attached. And right in the middle of the table, amongst the plethora of large plates of food is the centerpiece.

Dizzy's head on a spike.

Whatever is left of it anyway.

All six scarecrows face the centerpiece while they feast. A mockery of Dizzy's death and her moronic dream of ever stealing the power from our grasp.

Gemini—the real, living Gemini—stands near the end of the table, entertaining the passing masses while the parade carries on down the street. Heavy step by heavy step.

He's dressed especially eccentrically today, most likely reveling in the cruel theater of the entire affair. A black top hat is perched over his bleached hair, paired with a yellow tailcoat and white lace gloves. He prances around, twirling a cane adorned with a silver snake twisting up along the stick.

It was Gemini who warned me about Dizzy. He called me as soon as he found out during his tithing day. He collected secret after secret until eventually it was revealed: Dizzy was the leader of the insurrection. and she had plans to kill me—kill all of us.

Gemini brought in the help of Constantine, and together they tortured the information out of the one who spilled such a valuable secret, throwing a handful of my Vainglory Media employees to the wolves alongside a trickle of followers from each family. Even the random break-in involving Mercy was linked back to the uprising.

I was stunned—outraged. How couldn't I have been? How could someone who claimed to pledge their loyalty to me want my demise? I had let my control over Dizzy slip over the years. Foolishly convinced that she didn't need any more persuasion to follow my orders blindly and willingly.

I should have known never to trust a low-born like her.

Did I know *when* exactly this betrayal would happen?

No.

But Mercy's suspicious disappearance that same night left me on edge. It's as if I had been standing on the tip of a dagger this entire time, and Gemini's call had finally revealed the peril staring me in the face.

Mercy isn't the only one capable of sensing the unseen.

I suspected Mercy could betray me if she had the chance, the knowledge like a splinter I would rather ignore. But it being confirmed right before my eyes hurt more than I ever expected.

But then.

The desperation in her remorse afterward ...

I've been using it like a balm, recalling Mercy pleading for forgiveness at my feet anytime I need solace.

Gemini's booming voice rips me out of my wandering thoughts. "Citizens of Pravitia! Behold your witless queen!" His laugh is chilling as he jumps on top of the table, his speech echoing the little performance he did for us before the maze hunt. Kicking a cluster of grapes, it hits the severed head before landing with a splat into a bowl of gravy. "Feast your eyes!" he bellows, arms out wide while he turns in circles on the spot. "And see what it means to oppose one of us." He picks up an apple and takes a large bite. He chews and swallows before dazzling the crowd with his smile. "Foolish indeed."

I turn to Mercy, her hands on the gold railings of the palanquin while her gaze is fixed on Gemini. There's a subtle twinkle in her eyes, and I smile wide for the both of us, knowing Gemini is the only person in this city able to amuse her in such a way.

I might not have forgiven Mercy ... yet. But her penance has been ever so sweet to taste. I might not be able to persuade her like I can with most, but having her surrender to my whims—out of guilt I'm sure—will do for now.

I let the sound of the crowd cheering wash over us as I wrap my arm around her waist and pull her to my chest. A soft, but shocked, gasp tumbles out of her lips, her hands now pressing against my chest.

"Wolfgang," she says quietly, almost like a warning.

My fingers crawl down her hips and over the swell of her ass.

"Something to say, Crèvecoeur?" I ask with a wide, derisive smile.

Her eyes narrow, clearly unimpressed by such a public show of affection. She knows better than to dispute.

If she wants my trust, she'll need to abide by my rules.

It's a rare instance to have Mercy like this, and I will savor every single second of it.

Careful not to mess with her updo—I know my limits—I slip my fingers around her neck, my index finger tracing the soft skin under her jaw. With my thumb, I lift her chin and softly press my lips to hers. She's wearing a dark shade of red lipstick today and the possibility of it staining is inconsequential.

Because this is the very purpose of it, isn't it? To claim her as mine. To let her lipstick defile my mouth as if I'd drunk a mouthful of blood from her artery. I deepen the kiss, my hand near her hip curling into a fist, pulling her dress along with it.

I can almost make out the crowd roaring even louder than before. Or maybe it's the roaring sound of my heartbeat in my ears. There's a sick sense of pleasure to have Mercy like this.

She's hardly resisting. Her hands snake inside my coat, wrapping around my waist. She can pretend to hate this, she can pretend she would rather keep our affairs private, but the pleased sigh that I nearly miss over the crowd solidifies that she's just as smitten as I am.

Except I didn't have to try to have her killed to realize that.

The thought is a bitter crumb, polluting the moment and seeping into the sweetness of her tongue against mine. I break away from our kiss but keep a cocky smile on my lips so as not to have Mercy question my train of thought. Her lipstick is smudged, and my cock can't help but twitch at the sight.

I drag my thumb under her bottom lip, fixing it, and she does the same to me. From the corner of my eye, I notice my signet ring on her finger catching the sun's rays.

I snatch her hand and keep it near my mouth. Dragging my tongue over the skin next to the ring, I then press my lips to it as I keep my gaze fixed on Mercy.

"You never took it off," I murmur into the ring.

It's not a question.

A Dance Macabre

Her eyes turn glassy as if I've triggered too many conflicting emotions for her to manage all at once.

She shakes her head.

While I study her, I let the sounds of the enlivened city fill the silent space between us.

It makes me think that maybe, there was always a part of her that never believed she would ever go through with it. Never believed she could ever send her god to claim me.

I latch onto that hope for the rest of the afternoon as I keep Mercy as close to me as possible, showcasing my claim on her for every person in Pravitia to witness.

47

WOLFGANG

At the bottom of a short flight of stairs, I open an industrial-looking door and enter The Tea Room. Now that the threat to our lives has been publicly—and privately—handled, we are finally able to traverse the city freely again.

Our victory has brought with it a fresh air of relief. I've been in dire need of stretching my legs and visiting someone who does not currently have my heart in a vice.

I'm looking forward to a night out with Aleksandr. I've been unable to see my best friend since his mother's funeral. I even had to miss his birthday this year, a few days before Tithe Season began, due to the increase in security.

The Tea Room is another one of Aleksandr's many bars around Pravitia. It's a speakeasy known for its elaborate cocktails but much smaller than Vore.

The venue is packed as always. There's nothing more alluring to common folk than the promise of depravity at a bar owned by the servant of excess.

The candles on every table and ornate sconces near the low ceiling create a dark but inviting atmosphere. There's an understated opulence to the place with its large private booths and ceiling dripping with plants hanging from chains and wooden beams.

Nodding to the hostess, I hand her my coat before heading to the far back of the bar. No need to look for Aleksandr here, the corner booth is always reserved for him and his entourage.

I find him in conversation with some vapid leeches, a pink short-sleeved shirt unbuttoned to the middle of his tattooed chest, leaning back into the booth. By the look of the vacant boredom on his face, he's anything but amused.

When he spots me approaching, he only needs a quick flick of his fingers for the gaggle of sycophants to disperse. While I wait for the table to clear, his hand disappears under the table, and I can only surmise that he's signaling to whoever is under it servicing him to stay put.

Which reminds me ...

"I forgot to mention," I say while I slide into the booth. "The law against us six fornicating has been nullified."

Aleksandr's face slips from bored to shocked as he straightens abruptly. "What?"

"By the divine word of the Oracle," I say with a smooth lift of an eyebrow.

This time, both of his hands disappear under the table, shoving whoever is down there away from him. The helpless rube lands on his side on the floor, body fully sprawled out. Quickly gathering himself, he doesn't even glance back to Aleksandr before scurrying away.

"What do you *mean* the Oracle said so?" Aleksandr says while he zips himself up, hazel eyes questioning.

I let out a small sigh as if his interrogation is taxing me. I signal for a drink before answering. "Allegedly Mercy and I were always meant to ... become an item."

His shoulders fall. "Just you two, then."

"Any of us. The law has been dissolved. Something about our generation ushering in a new era for Pravitia."

"A new era?" Aleksandr mutters. He smooths a hand over his mustache while he takes in the news. "So that means ..." He doesn't need to finish his sentence for me to know what he's insinuating.

I grin and nod.

He falls back into the booth, crossing his arms while his expression turns hopeful. Looking up at the ceiling, he appears to lose himself in the possibilities of what this means for him.

His gaze snaps back, a stern crease between his eyebrows. "And you *forgot* to tell me? How long have you been sitting on this information?"

I purse my lips, avoiding eye contact for a few breaths. A bourbon on ice appears in front of me, I take a slow slip before answering.

"Two weeks."

Aleksandr's palms flatten on the table while the upper half of his body leans in. "*Two weeks?*"

I shrug, but there's a small twinge of guilt tickling my throat. "I've had a lot on my mind."

"Was that before or after my mother's funeral," he presses.

Heavy silence. "A few days before."

Aleksandr huffs and returns to leaning his back against the booth, arms crossed.

"Well now you know," I reply a little dismissively while straightening my cuffs, feeling slightly attacked. I shoot him one of my most dazzling smiles. "Consider this a belated birthday gift."

I take another sip of my drink, the bourbon warms my throat as it goes down smoothly. Aleksandr continues to glare at me.

"So you and Mercy," he finally mumbles.

I nod. "So it seems," I drawl. Falling silent, I consider not telling him the recent turn of events and keeping Mercy's betrayal to myself. Even after all of this, I feel protective of her.

In spite of this, I relent.

"She tried to have me killed," I say nonchalantly. I pick at an invisible piece of lint on my sleeve. "We've resolved it now."

Unfortunately, his confusion signals that he won't be dropping the subject like I hoped. "How did she even manage that? Hiring someone to kill you would go against *damnatio memoriae*."

"Dizzy offered."

Surprising me, Aleksandr bursts out laughing. Grabbing the bottle of vodka chilling on ice, he pours himself a fresh drink while still chuckling to himself.

"What's so droll?" I hiss through my teeth.

His eyes lift to mine, full of mirth. "Beloved servant of idolatry betrayed twice over. Must sting."

I suck on my teeth and look away. Aleksandr's right, it does sting. Discovering that a handful of my followers were colluding against me was a hard blow to the ego.

And then to have Mercy involved.

I've had better days.

"That's behind me," I say dismissively.

Aleksandr slowly stops laughing, his face falling serious as he studies me over his glass while he takes a slow sip of vodka. "Why would you continue to trust her after this?"

I let the electronic beat of the music wash over us as I chew on my inner lip. I play with the condensation of my glass. Avoid his interrogating stare. Take a sip.

Finally, I slide my avoiding gaze to his.

"I don't," I say. Sighing deeply, I tap a finger on the table and look away. Eventually, I focus back on Aleksandr. "But does it matter? When now even our gods would fail to keep me away from her."

48

MERCY

"*And* agreeing to Dizzy's half-baked plan is what you went for?" Gemini asks, a small smirk lifting his upper lip up as he hands me one of the two dirty martinis he made for us.

I huff loudly but accept the drink and take a sip. When Wolfgang told me he was off to see Aleksandr, I thought it would be best for me to venture out.

The walls of Mount Pravitia are beginning to feel narrow and suffocating when everywhere I look there's somehow a memory of Wolfgang attached to it. However, now there's a giant smear over all of it, like toxic paint carrying the perfume of my betrayal.

So I showed up to Gemini's house unannounced.

"I wasn't in the right state of mind," I answer primly, setting the martini glass atop a coaster on the large glass coffee table.

I settle into the red leather couch, leaning on my left side, and cross a leg over the other while I rest my temple against my index and thumb. Falling silent, I gaze out of the floor-to-ceiling windows that make up his living room. Gemini's property faces the harbor and his casino, spanning the entire cliff, and is the only house for miles on either side.

"And this was *after* the Oracle confirmed what Tinny and I already suspected?" he asks with a laugh. He takes a long drink of his martini before setting it on the coffee table and plopping beside me dramatically.

"I don't know what I was thinking," I mutter, my eyes still trained on the shimmering lights of Pandaemonium, having no idea how to respond to Gemini's probing questions.

Now looking back, it all feels like a feverish nightmare. Surreal and immaterial.

Wolfgang hadn't given me any reason not to trust him. Quite the opposite if I'm honest, and instead of sitting with my unguarded feelings, I chose the worst possible solution to my problem.

Was there even a problem to begin with?

"Ruthless little thing," Gemini sing-songs.

Begrudgingly, I look back over to him. He faces me, mirroring my posture, his head leaning against his palm, an idiotic grin slicing across his face. His hair is a light yellow today. It matches the knitted tank top tucked into his wide-leg tweed pants.

"He doesn't trust me," I mutter as I sit up straighter, wringing my hands.

"Can you blame him?"

"Gemini!" I exclaim in exasperation, "You're not helping."

His brows lift in surprise. I'm sure it's due to my uncharacteristic outburst. His hand falls to the couch while he cants his head, eyes narrowing. "Gods be damned," he says slowly before pointing a finger at me. "You care."

I sigh loudly, leaning over to take a large gulp of my drink. "Of course, I *care*."

"Never thought I'd see the day," he muses, looking out the window.

Feeling restless, I stand up and start to pace. "I *am* capable of caring."

Gemini falls serious, his eyes tracking my nervous movements. "Not like this."

I stop my pacing. Find his gaze. Swallow hard.

"What can I do?" The tremor in my voice makes me want to open the sliding doors to the balcony and throw myself off the cliff and into the harbor.

"Have you tried apologizing?"

I feel like screeching. I start pacing again.

"I *did* apologize, I told you this already."

Gemini lets out a derisive puff of air, reaching for his drink. After a sip, he pins me with his mismatched eyes. "Have you tried apologizing when there isn't the disfigured corpse of his former employee at your feet?"

My arms flail, fists tight. "Why does that matter?" My cheeks are burning, chest heaving with offense.

Gemini chuckles, stretching himself across the couch, his arms behind his head as if our conversation is as casual as an afternoon picnic. "Oh Mercy, you know nothing about life but the affairs of the dead, don't you?"

"Gem ... I *will* maim you," I say through clenched teeth. "Speak plainly."

His eyes twinkle. "I'm too pretty to maim, love." My hand reaches for my dagger, and Gemini barks a laugh, sitting back up straight and holding out his palms as a sign of surrender. "Fine, fine." He taps the couch beside him. "Sit, you're making me nervous."

My shoulders fall in defeat, and I do as he says.

As I sit, a muffled sound coming from the hallway behind me catches my attention. Turning around, I see nothing but Gemini's eclectic decor, his walls full of mismatched frames and trinkets.

"What was that sound?" I ask quizzically.

A Dance Macabre

Gemini gives me a bewildered look. "Sound? Must be the wind," he mumbles as he jumps to his feet. "Let's put on some music, shall we? Something to offset your glum mood." He flashes me a grin from over his shoulders, shimmying his hips as he puts on a record and delicately places the needle on top of it.

When the music begins to fill the room, he lets out a satisfied sigh. "There, much better."

Sitting back down, his attention is again back on me, and I shrink in my seat.

He picks up the conversation right where we left off.

"What Wolfgang needs from you is sincerity," he says much too seriously.

"I've been sincere," I snap back.

Gemini gives me a quick eye roll. "If you're going to rebuke any advice I give you, love, then I'd rather save my breath."

My heart sinks. Is this a feeling of regret again?

"Please," I press, taking his hand in mine.

Gemini pauses and looks down at our joined hands as if he's never seen me purposely make physical contact before. When his gaze slides back up, his smile is smug. "Wolfie sure did a number on you."

I shove his hand away and cross my arms in protest but say nothing.

Gemini's laughter slowly wanes into silence, his expression turning thoughtful.

"I could tell you the same thing six million ways, love — but the meaning will always stay the same." He pins me with his stare. "Your apology needs to come from the heart."

MARCHING THROUGH THE ENFILADE, SHOULDERS STRAIGHT, HEAD held high, I head for the library where I know I'll find Wolfgang. I left Gemini's house with the conviction that this apology needed to happen now, or I would lose the courage to follow through.

I burst through the door. Wolfgang sits near the crackling fireplace, a book on his lap, and Truffles curled up at his feet. He seems surprised but says nothing as I stomp up to his chair.

"You would have done it if I didn't do it first, I just know it," I blurt out. "If anyone could understand the motivations behind my actions, it's you." I start to pace. "Isn't it good enough for you to know that I *regret* what I did?" I furtively sneak a peek at Wolfgang. The corners of his lips are curling up in amusement as he slowly takes his reading glasses off and closes the book on his lap but seems in no hurry to interrupt. "If our gods could turn back time, I would beseech for them to do just that. I was possessed, Wolfgang. Possessed!"

I fall silent. Turn my entire body toward Wolfgang. Try to control my heavy breathing and pumping heart.

I seek reassurance in his steely gaze but find nothing but levity.

He lets my speech fill every crack in the library before speaking, his grin growing wider. "Was that an attempt at an apology, Crèvecoeur?"

I feel struck. "It — it *was* an apology," I stutter out.

He tries to hide a chuckle behind the hand holding his glasses. His gaze slides up the length of my body, gradually turning serious. "Try again, my ruin."

The sound that comes out of my mouth can most likely be defined as a shriek, I can't tell—I've never acted this way before.

But I do the only thing that feels appropriate—and stomp right out of the library.

49

WOLFGANG

*A*djusting my gold cufflinks, I give myself one final survey in the full-length mirror.

Perfection. As usual.

I exit the family quarters and head toward the drawing room. I haven't slept in the same bed as Mercy since Dizzy's blood seeped into the mattress.

I'm not necessarily trying to punish Mercy—who's yet to give me a proper apology—but I'm trying to keep the temptation as far away as possible until she finally gives me what I've been asking for.

And what is that exactly?

All of her. Cracked open and vulnerable.

But keeping her at arm's length is not quite far enough. I practically need to chain myself to the bed so I don't end up crawling to her at night.

However, in public?

We are the carefree rulers of Pravitia.

A celebrated union.

And tonight, as we spend an evening at the opera, our charade is nothing different.

I enter the drawing room first, and not wanting to crease my suit, I stay standing near the fireplace as I wait for Mercy to appear.

I listen to the tick of the clock on the mantel to pass the time until I hear the sound of Mercy's heels approaching—then I listen to those ticks instead.

When Mercy finally enters the room, I'm dumbstruck. My throat goes dry, my stomach twisting in shock.

Mercy is a vision in *red*.

I am nearly brought to my knees.

I've never seen her wear anything but black. But tonight she chose to match her dress to my herringbone tweed suit.

She looks exquisite. Her long black hair pulled up in an elegant updo, her dress a dark shade of red, like spilled blood running down her body. There are flounces of taffeta gathered around her hips, the material tumbling to the floor, with a long slit up her left thigh, revealing her harnessed dagger.

My palm slowly drags down my face as I take her in, ravaged by her lethal beauty.

She quietly adjusts her red lace gloves near the elbow, keeping her face impassive.

"Something wrong?" she asks all too innocently as if her wearing red is an ordinary affair.

My primal reaction aside, I know Mercy well enough by now to know that this is her way of trying to apologize—again.

It's been half a week since she stormed out of the library. She didn't have the words then, and she certainly doesn't have the words now.

I can't deny my heart warms at the effort.

But gods be damned, I will have her use her words and apologize if it's the last thing I do on this cursed earth.

Quickly hiding my surprise, I flash her one of my charismatic smiles. I can tell she knows it's fake. But I'd rather play the cocksure Wolfgang than admit she has me by the throat.

I ignore her question and say with an upbeat tone, "Shall we?"

Her expression shutters, but she's fast to right herself, like she expected a much bigger reaction from me.

She'll wait all night if that's the case.

I take a few steps closer and offer her my elbow.

Her sparkling eyes darken as she studies me. Finally, she nods and curls her gloved hand around my arm.

"We shall."

Stepping out from the town car first, I help Mercy climb out after me. The loud shouts of the paparazzi heighten behind us as soon as they realize who we are.

My gaze dips to Mercy's uncovered leg as she steps out, and my throat tightens, longing to sink my teeth into her skin once again. Luckily, I can indulge *some* of my lustful yearnings now that we have the cameras in front of us.

But Mercy surprises me. Before even walking up to the sidewalk, she pulls me against her. Her laced fingers caress my cheek as she presses a lingering kiss against my lips, the paparazzi roaring in excitement. My arm immediately wraps around her hips, pulling her up against me as I groan against her mouth.

"My, my," I drawl when she finally pulls away. "What was that for?"

She daintily lifts a shoulder and purses her lips, giving me a teasing pout. She doesn't answer. Instead, she wraps her arm around the crook of my elbow and waits for me to lead us inside.

Mercy doesn't need to tell me. I know why she's being more than accommodating. And if I were a gambling man, I'd bet my entire fortune that she knows that I know.

She'll do everything not to use her words.

THE OPERA HOUSE IS A HISTORIC PRAVITIAN LANDMARK IN THE heart of the Vorovsky neighborhood. It's one of the oldest buildings in the city alongside Mount Pravitia and has just as many ghosts haunting the halls.

Inside, we're escorted upstairs to a private balcony. Since we arrived fashionably late, the first act has already begun, and we silently find our seats behind a heavy-drawn curtain.

I love the opera.

The music, the costumes, the drama.

But tonight, nothing is as breathtaking as my own muse sitting beside me. I have trouble concentrating, carefully studying every move Mercy makes instead.

She peers down to the stage from behind small gold binoculars. Her back is straight, puffs of red taffeta surrounding her as she leans her torso toward the railing, her breasts pushed up and spilling out of her corset.

What I would do to take a large bite? I would chew slowly, savoring every flavor of Mercy I could taste.

Eventually, I cave to the impulse of needing her near and pull her closer to me with a forceful tug on the front leg of her chair. Her eyebrow lifts, shooting me a curious glance from the corner of her eye, but keeps the binoculars raised.

Slowly, I trail a finger down her left arm, the texture of the lace soft under my fingertips. I take her hand and bring it to my lap. Interlocking our fingers together, I drag her palm over my trousers, pressing our hands over my hardening cock.

I audibly groan, my head falling backward for half a second before focusing back on the stage below.

I ache for her.

Two weeks feels like a lifetime, and if I didn't have any more self-control left, I'd drop to my knees and bury my head between her thighs.

Who am I truly punishing at this very moment?

I'm cracking alongside Mercy.

I need her.

I'm desperate for her.

Making her squeeze the length of my cock, I lean closer so that my lips whisper across the sensitive skin of her neck. I run my nose behind her ear. Tug her earlobe with my teeth. I feel her shiver and smile against her skin.

"You look ravishing tonight, my ruin," I finally rasp, "But if you can't use your words to apologize." I press her palm even harder against my cock. "Then I might have just the thing for you."

50

WOLFGANG

After the opera, I take Mercy to Vainglory Tower. She doesn't say much as I lead her up to my private quarters. It's as if her unspoken apology is taking so much space inside her mouth that she doesn't have room for anything else.

Her gaze sweeps the rooms we walk past, furtive glances here and there. She's visited the Tower before, but never my private quarters. Finally, we enter the Hall of Mirrors.

The hall is full of candles. I had my servants light them before we arrived, the countless flames flickering and bouncing from one reflecting glass to the other, while still leaving some corners cast in shadows.

"A room full of mirrors," Mercy muses softly, "I should have known."

I smile. "It's my favorite place to play the violin," I answer while I pick up a black box from the bench where my instrument is kept. I had my assistant leave it here for me earlier today just for this.

Mercy, still donned in glorious red, turns to meet my gaze.

"Don't you miss it?" she asks with genuine concern.

Warmth spills across my chest and I nod. "I do ... sometimes." My steps echo as I approach her. "I've had more pressing matters on my mind as of late — here," I say, offering her the box.

At first, she stays poised, fingers clasped near her waist, looking down at it. "What is it?" Her eyes lift up, watching me through her long eyelashes.

"A gift," I answer plainly, giving the box a small rattle signaling her to take it.

"But—"

"Just open it."

She bites her bottom lip but finally takes it. Carefully removing the lid, her face falls when she peers inside.

I chuckle darkly at her expression, feeling quite smug.

"If you don't want to waste both of our time, I suggest you don't protest and put it on," I say with a wide arrogant grin.

Her eyes narrow in defiance. "Why?"

I casually shrug as if there's anything *casual* about this. "Since you won't use your words—" I puff out a small chuckle. "I'm offering you a way to make it up to me."

Her stony face shouldn't look so adorable while a storm brews behind her eyes. "And the other item?"

I fall serious. "To give me full control, my ruin, is to trust me."

She stays silent as if deliberating her options, her throat working around a hard swallow.

Then, without saying a word, she turns around, and my heart sinks thinking she's about to walk away from me. Instead, she doesn't move, and giddiness bubbles up through my body and limbs when I realize she's waiting for me.

I begin to unpin her hair, letting her long black strands cascade down her back and shoulders. When I'm done, I circle to face her and pick the first item from the box that Mercy is still clutching to her chest. My heart is slamming against my ribcage, the implications of what I'm holding in my hands sending me down into the very depths of my carnal need for Mercy.

"Open your mouth," I order.

She hesitates, her gaze darkening.

But finally, her mouth falls open.

Carefully, I place the ball gag between her teeth, two gold chains attaching it to leather straps, clasping them tightly at the base of her neck.

I can't help the lecherous grin forming on my lips when I step back to look at Mercy. Her mouth is wide around the silicone ball, the chains digging slightly into her cheeks. A satisfied shiver skates down my spine.

My grin widens, and she huffs loudly through her nose. Ignoring her miffed complaints, I take the box out of her hands and place it on the floor next to us.

I snap my fingers as I straighten back up. "Gloves off."

She rolls her eyes but does as I say, petulantly pulling them off with a dainty index finger and thumb before dropping them at her feet. My grin is now glued to my face and, with a teasing lift of the eyebrow, I signal her to spin back around with a twirl of my finger.

When she's facing away, I delicately sweep her hair off her shoulder and press a lingering kiss to her nape near the leather strap while I tug on the zipper of her dress, slowly revealing the Crèvecoeur sigil tattoo. When the dress gathers at her feet, she steps out, now standing in only a thong and her black stilettos.

I watch her gaze dip as I crouch on one knee, pulling her thong down and over the dagger on her thigh. Then, I slowly take off her heels, one foot at a time as I keep my gaze lifted and locked with hers.

Before standing back up, I remove the final item from the box. Without her heels, Mercy is a few inches shorter than me, and I take full advantage, looking down my nose at her while I let the leather harness hang from my finger.

"Put it on."

I could very well do it for her, but the satisfaction of seeing Mercy willingly put herself into this harness without putting up a fight is a memory I will keep burned into my mind forever.

She takes it from my hand with a forceful tug, stepping into both thigh straps and pulling it up to her hips. Wrapping the other strap around her waist, she ties the small buckle with impatient tugs while she flays me with her glare.

My smile only widens.

I circle her like a wolf stalking a lamb.

Taking her arms, I pull them to her back and slip her wrists into the leather cuffs chained to the harness at the base of her hips. The chains are long enough that she has some mobility, but only a few inches on either side.

"There," I say with a pleased sigh as if I've put the final touches on my masterpiece.

Leading her to the middle of the hall so that the mirrors surround us, I face her.

Drool has started to trickle down her chin, and my cock hardens at the sight. Splaying my palm over her chin, I squeeze her cheeks as I push her down.

"On your knees."

She tries to resist again, her eyes hardening, cheeks flushed, and breathing hard. It gives me a sick thrill, lust burning me from the inside out. She only fights me for a split second, just long enough for me to savor it before she follows my order and drops down to the floor.

The refracted light of the candles dances over her pale skin, and I can't control the dark chuckle that tumbles out of me, having Mercy at my feet like this.

"Eyes on the floor," I command as I begin to circle her again, needing to take her in from all angles. I take off my suit jacket as I coo, "Look how sorry you look now." My voice is wreaked with desire. "Sweet little whore repenting on her knees."

She lets out a gargled noise through the ball gag, and my cock throbs with greed. "What pretty sounds you make when at my mercy," I muse mockingly as I take off my shirt, throwing it in the same general direction as my jacket.

Dropping to my knees behind her, I pull her backward against my chest, my movements anything but delicate. "Watch me through the mirror," I demand harshly.

Her eyes slide up, finding my gaze through the reflecting glass as I grind my hard shaft against her cuffed hands. Her chin is wet and glistening with spit, and I wipe my palm through it before sliding it down her neck and kneading her breasts passionately.

"Are you sorry now?" I ask, lustful disdain dripping from my voice. "Does it keep you awake at night to know you did this to me?" She whimpers as I give her nipple a hard pinch, her lips quivering around the silicone ball. "Sad little Mercy kills men for sport but can't utter a singular meaningful apology."

My cock aches but I ignore it. Shoving her forward without any forewarning, I hold on to her harness while her face settles on the ground, her ass lifted in the air.

Taking two of my fingers, I drag them clinically up her cunt. I tsk when I find her soaking wet.

"Filthy girl," I spit as I slap one of her ass cheeks with the flat of my palm. The sting is almost as delicious as Mercy moaning through the ball gag. I give her another hard spank directly on the same reddening spot. "Is being treated like nothing but a common whore easier than apologizing?" I ask as I salivate at the keening sound she makes.

Smoothing a hand down her spine, I give her a small soothing hush before standing back up to remove the rest of my clothes. I keep my gaze fixed on her weeping cunt as if hypnotized and entranced—I might very well be—while taking my trousers, socks, and shoes off. Kneeling back down, I pull her by the criss-crossed straps over her ass and push my cock into her cuffed hands.

"You feel that, Mercy?" I growl next to her ear.

She moans, her eyes seeking mine through the mirror while her fingers curl around my hard shaft. I shunt my hips up, fucking her tightening grip, and smile like a madman, delirious in my obsession for her.

"You don't even deserve my cock inside your cunt," I push out through gritted teeth. "Maybe I should fuck your fists instead." Curling my arm around her, I yank the strap of the ball gag, her head pulled backward onto my shoulder. My next words come out of a harsh whisper, "Paint my cum all over your perfect ass and leave you aching and sore."

I listen to one more of her lovely, whimpering moans knowing full well I'm but seconds away from fucking her. Her sounds are so breathtaking to listen to that I almost accept her desperate gargled protests as an apology. Almost.

It nearly makes me wonder who has *who* tied up and leashed.

Pulling my cock from her grasp, I drag the head through her arousal, notching myself at her entrance, and then thrust deeply into her. I might as well be the one gagged with the sound I make when her cunt squeezes around me. I fuck her hard but slow, relishing the long drag of my cock and the tortured mewl when I push back deep into her.

I watch her in the mirror, never once glancing at my own reflection, a pink blush crawling over her cheeks and chest.

I study her.

Savor her.

Devour her.

And imagine both our sigils merging into one. Flames burning up the strings. Consuming. Transmuting.

With my free hand, I find her swollen clit and give it a slap, and she moans even louder, my other palm firmly around her chin and jaw. My fingers slip through her soaking arousal as I pleasure her with tight, circular motions, slapping her swollen clit once more. When I feel her climax is close, the flutters of her cunt pulsing around my cock, I release her face from my grip and hurriedly unclasp the ball gag, selfishly needing to hear her cry out without any obstruction.

And oh, is it perfect.

It fills the hall with divine melody and I am taken.

When my orgasm soon follows, and I pump her mindlessly full of me, I'm struck with a mind-splintering realization.

That I love Mercy more than anything in this damned world.

Even myself.

51

MERCY

The small velvet string purse I'm clutching in my fist burns a hole into my palm, the ridges and edges of what's inside reminding me of what I've set off to do tonight.

I hate it.

I'm a nervous wreck.

My gait is stiff as I stalk through the enfilade, hoping to find Wolfgang in our bedchamber.

When we returned from our time at Vainglory Tower two days ago, he promptly had all of his belongings moved into the ruler's quarters without a word of explanation. I must admit that I was relieved that there was at least *some* progress being made.

Something shifted between us after the Hall of Mirrors, especially in Wolfgang's demeanor. Although we have spent time alone since—reading in the library, soaking in the bathhouse—he's kept mostly silent, evidently still waiting for my damned apology.

Entering the bedchamber, I notice the French doors leading out to the balcony are ajar, Wolfgang's silhouette beyond it.

My heart flies into my throat.

I swiftly turn around and take a large step out of the room. I stop myself from going any further. I curse under my breath. Swivel back around. My steps stutter, and I nearly let out a loud shriek at how embarrassing I'm acting.

I squeeze my eyes shut and take a deep inhale. I focus back on the open balcony door on my exhale and straighten my spine.

It's pouring rain outside, the scent of muddy earth rising from the ground and wafting around me even from this high up. Most of the balcony is covered, and Wolfgang sits on one of the large cushioned seats sheltered from the downpour, his back to me.

Smoke lazily curls around his head, a cigarette hanging from his long fingers, his wrist reposing on the armrest.

I've begun to familiarize myself with his habits; he only smokes when he's in a pensive mood.

Thinking the heavy rain is concealing my furtive steps, my stomach flips when Wolfgang's head turns to the side, glancing at me from the corner of his eye.

I stop dead in my tracks as if I've been caught, my fist gripping the string purse even harder into my palm.

When I don't move, Wolfgang reaches for the ashtray and stubs his cigarette out before sitting back in his seat. He keeps his head facing the cityscape, but his arm stretches out to the side, his palm up, slowly uncurling his fingers as if silently beckoning me to him.

He pulls on the invisible string.

I'm tugged forward.

Just a few steps and I'm standing in front of him.

His attention lingers on my tight fist and the small velvet pouch spilling out of it. He says nothing, his eyes sweeping up my body to meet my anxious gaze.

His smile is warm but distant.

Taking my free hand in his, he pulls me into his lap. I don't resist. Not even a little bit. I welcome his embrace as I slide my arms around his neck and rest my head on his shoulder, staring out into the rainy sky. He wraps an arm around my waist and pushes out a pleased sigh, the drum of the rain feeling meditative as he caresses my hair and down my arm.

We stay silent for what feels like an eternity.

It's barely a few minutes.

But every moment feels like a lifetime with Wolfgang.

He's the first to break the silence, his voice hoarse when he speaks. "What's in your hand, my ruin?"

The dread returns like a tight noose around my neck. I almost throw the damned thing over the balcony.

Trying to create distance between us, I pull away, hoping to find a seat of my own—or run away, I'm not quite sure yet—but Wolfgang pins me to him, his arm locking around my body.

I huff loudly and avoid eye contact as a form of protest.

His low chuckle rumbles in his chest. "Is it something for me?" he asks, trying to reach for it but I pull my hand away. "Mercy," he warns, his warm palm squeezing my naked thigh teasingly.

I swallow hard. Find his seeking gaze.

"It's something for us," I finally admit softly.

His brows jump up. "Oh?"

I stare into his eyes, wishing words weren't so important.

"I—" My voice sticks in my throat. Sighing, I look away. He gives me another squeeze as if coaxing me on. I turn back to face him.

"I'm so sorry, Wolfgang," I whisper. His body tightens underneath me ... almost as if he never thought he'd hear those words from me. "I apologize," I continue, my chest feeling heavy, "Please forgive me — I need you to forgive me. I can't take it a second longer."

I feel faint, my heart battering against my ribcage, and I've never despised silence more than I do right now. Wolfgang conceals a small grin as he studies me, his palm smoothing up and down my thigh.

"What's in your hand, Mercy?" he repeats.

I feel outraged. "Did you not hear me?" I say gruffly. I once again try to leave his lap to no avail.

"I heard you," he rasps, "I want to know what's inside that pouch first."

"Why?" I ask petulantly, my heart racing so fast I think I might be having a heart attack.

"Indulge me," he urges.

Unceremoniously, I drop it on my lap between us and give him a quirk of the eyebrow signaling that he can pick it up himself.

He doesn't conceal his victorious grin this time, and I find it especially hard not to smile in return. He takes his arm away from my waist and delicately opens the string purse. His hand disappears inside before reemerging with two necklaces between his fingers.

Both are made of a thin gold chain, a small engraved vial hanging from each of them.

"The vials contain a mixture of our blood," I blurt out nervously.

Wolfgang's fingers curl into a fist, the chains still in his hard grasp, his burning gaze blazing a hole right through me.

I nearly lose my courage all over again.

I somehow find the strength to soldier on.

"I had Tinny make them for us, one has my initials and the other yours. I thought we could—" Everything in me wants to look away. Run. Hide. Anything but this. I can barely manage to push the words out. "I thought we could exchange them at our wedding."

Wolfgang's expression brightens, turning boyish, and a weight suddenly lifts from my shoulders.

"Our wedding?" he says, his voice silky with hope.

"I want you to be my husband," I say, looking into the distance, trying my best to act unbothered. "If you forgive me, that is."

Wolfgang's laugh is dark and deviant as his hand finds my cheek, turning my head back to face him. His thumb smooths over my lips before he presses a soft kiss to them. Pulling away, he gazes deeply into my eyes, his thumb still caressing my cheek in small circles.

"To forgive you is to love you," he finally says.

My breath hitches in my throat.

The silence lingers.

"And do you?" I ask quietly, not sure to which statement I'm asking for an answer.

He smiles wide, revealing the gold of his canine.

"I do."

52

WOLFGANG

Two weeks later ...

"She's ready for you," Jeremial declares with a formal nod.

Giddy anticipation bubbles up my chest, and I nearly tackle him out of the way to get to Mercy. He somehow avoids my lunge and still manages to look stoic while opening the door for me. Eagerly, I enter the spacious waiting room connected to the large hall where our most important ceremonies occur.

Or in this case, the official union of the co-rulers of Pravitia.

The waiting room walls are full of formidable paintings of our ancestors, our likenesses soon to adorn the same walls.

But none of that matters right now.

Not when Mercy is standing near the crackling fireplace in her wedding dress, a long black veil cascading down her back, reaching the floor. Her dress is a blend of a dark red corseted bodice and black lace overtop, long flowing sleeves falling over her hands, and a wide circular train. Her gaze slides to meet mine from across the room.

And she smiles.

It's almost demure as if she's seeking my approval.

My heart explodes at the sight.

I stalk to her, setting down the gift I'm holding on a table nearby before cradling her face between my hands.

"My ruin," I groan deeply, my forehead pressed to hers. "You look divine. A goddess amongst mortals. The entire city is undeserving to even *lay eyes* on you."

The smallest of giggles leaves her lips, the puff of air warm against my skin, and I can't stand the countless seconds separating me from calling Mercy my wife.

"You look dashing yourself," she says breathlessly.

Hearing her voice laced with such levity is intoxicating. Especially momentous, when I know it only happens when it's just us two.

"Did you expect anything less?" I ask amusingly. Pulling away, I preen like a peacock as I show off my outfit; a red velvet tuxedo, with black lapels to compliment her dress.

"Like the very embodiment of the god of idolatry," she says with a twinkle in her eyes. We fall silent for a few bated breaths, Mercy's gaze brimming with affection.

Somehow ripping myself away from her enchantment, I reach for the gift. "I have a surprise for you." I offer it to Mercy. "To my muse," I say with a proud grin.

Her brow lifts in surprise. "For me?"

"Open it," I urge.

Her smile returns, and I am enamored.

She rips the gold wrapping to reveal a thick leather-bound book inside. Letting the crinkle paper fall to the floor, her gaze jumps to mine and then back down as she inspects the simple black cover.

I'm jittery, but bite my tongue, trying not to rush her.

Finally, she opens the book, and her small gasp is the only thing I had hoped for in return.

I don't bother to hide my pride. "Your photographs deserved a better home than a mere shoebox." Referring to the ones she keeps of the dead.

Her green eyes turn glassy. Her smile watery.

"I love it ..." Her gaze is serious and penetrating. She takes a small step toward me. "Thank you, husband" she finally professes, and my entire body feels bathed in light. She swallows hard, setting the book aside before approaching me, her hands slipping into mine, gaze ablaze. "Know that I am yours forever. Not even our gods can keep us apart. I am yours beyond this life, Wolfgang. Beyond death and the shadows of the eternal." She kisses me softly, her arms wrapping around my waist, and whispers, "I love you."

"Mercy," I say, my voice aching and racked with need. "I am chained to you for all of eternity. Take my soul into yours and ruin me evermore."

We stay embracing, hearts pulsing with the beat of our devotion, our interlocking gazes steadfast and yearning.

"Ready?" I finally ask her. She smiles and nods. "Then, let's go my betrothed," I say with a wide grin as I pick her up and twirl her around. Her shocked giggle is effervescent as she slaps my shoulder playfully. "Impish brute! Put me down," she yelps.

My laughter rises from deep inside my chest as I settle her back on her feet. "Who's calling who a brute, Crèvecoeur?" I shoot her a wink, lacing my fingers with hers as I lead her out the door. "Now come, I cannot bear another godsdamned second not calling you my wife."

EPILOGUE
GEMINI

Ten weeks earlier

The smell of fear has a peculiar scent. It coats the night air, sickly sweet like a room full of funereal flowers. My legs and arms are pumping just as hard as my heart as I turn the corner of the maze, and the gleeful anticipation of catching my very own fool has me grinning like one too. The bellows and screams of fate met violently tickle my ear as I try to focus on the frightened sounds closest to me.

Quickening steps.

Harried breath.

Pushing myself against the hedge, the green foliage tickles my neck as I wait.

I can tell she's close, I've been tracking her for the past ten minutes. She'll appear around the corner soon enough. Slowing down my breaths with a few deep inhales, the smile on my lips never falters as I stay pressed against the maze wall.

I hear her stumble, swearing under her breath, the words racked with the same sweet fear permeating the air. Until, *finally*, she appears before me like a naive little gazelle under the moonlight. Her long brown hair is matted to her face, brown eyes wild and terror-stricken. She must have been running ever since the hunt began over half an hour ago.

Stepping out of the shadows, I snatch her by the front of her neck with a firm grip of the hand. She screams and tries to fight me off, twisting the upper half of her body away from me as if trying to bolt in the opposite direction. It only makes her lose her footing, and she pitches backward, making us both slam to the ground, me on top.

My greedy laugh only amplifies as she continues to fight me. I let out a few small tsks followed by a dark chuckle. "Don't think you can escape me now."

"Get off me, you monster!" she shrieks as I finally manage to pin her legs with mine, my hands slamming her wrists over her head.

Her threat is half-hearted.

We both know it.

But something about her words hanging between us makes me pause.

I quirk my head slightly to the side, sniffing the air.

The *absence* of something.

My eyes slice to hers. "Say that again."

Confusion flits across her face, but it's gone just as fast before she renews her vain attempt to fight me off. "Let me go!"

There it is again ...

Or the lack thereof.

I drop my smile as I lift a brow, my grip tightening around her wrists.

"Who are you?" I ask slowly.

She stills under me, her glare burning into me, a small divot forming between her brows. "I–I'm ..." she begins to say but then seems to change her mind and starts to struggle under me again. "Let me go!" she repeats.

A shiver forms near the base of my neck. The air grows thick as a sudden apprehension crawls over my heated skin.

This doesn't feel right.

As I deliberate, I keep her pinned to the dewy grass, the seconds slowly drifting past us like clouds drifting across the pregnant moon.

Finally, I make up my mind. Pushing myself off of her, I jump up to my feet.

She skitters backward on her hands and feet as soon as I release her, frightened but questioning. We stare at each other for a long tense moment before I finally speak. "Two rights, one left, and another right." My voice holds defeat, but I'm resolved in my decision. I lean a little closer, one hand on my hip while I flick the other in her direction. "Run run run little rabbit before I change my mind," I sing-song as I curl my lips into a leery grin.

When my words finally sink in, she scrambles to her feet, chest heaving. She barely gives me a parting glance as she turns to escape her fate.

She rounds the corner and disappears into the dark night.

And I am left breathless, the scent of sacrifice still sticking to my skin.

THE STORY CONTINUES WITH GEMINI FOLEY IN BOOK 2 OF THE Perverse City series!

Stay tuned ...

More from Naomi Loud

a line cook x server romance

MORE FROM NAOMI LOUD

Don't miss out on the bestselling dark romance series "Was I Ever".

Sunny and Byzantine	Was I Ever Here
Lenix and Connor	Was I Ever Real
Lucy and Bastian	Was I Ever Free

If you don't want to miss out on any future book announcements make sure to follow me on Instagram and Tiktok at naomi.loud or subscribe to my newsletter! You can find the link on my website: www.naomiloud.com

You can also join my Patreon to receive exclusive behind the scenes updates, teasers, character art, giveaways and bonus scenes!

And if you loved A Dance Macabre, I'd be forever grateful if you could leave a positive review on Amazon. Your support is why indie authors can continue doing what we love.

Thank you!

ACKNOWLEDGMENTS

This book—no this entire universe—would not exist without the multiple late-night zoomies of my chaos crew: Meghan, Bella & Shani. I know I've told you this already but I will say it again and again: Your friendship, love, and everlasting support fuels me to be the best version of myself. I had a blast writing this book; half of the fun was the crazy ideas we came up with that didn't even make it into the manuscript. This universe is a love letter to you. I love you all so much.

My lovely, funny, unhinged alpha team: Cait, Lotte, Shani, Bella & Meghan, a true dream team!! Thank you for putting up with my daily dramatics and my casual meltdowns over ellipses, you're stuck with me now. Your support means everything to me. Cue me crying.

Thank you to my beta team, Casadi, Jessy, Ada, Janine & Dani, for helping me polish the rough edges and making the story shine!

Thank you to Salma, Lo & Amanda for helping me ensure there weren't any major plot holes, Val for the amazing map and family tree, Rim for those beautiful sigils, and to my sensitivity reader Ruth for ensuring everything was in tip-top shape pre-release.

Thank you to my husband Aldo, for listening to me gush about all my wildest dreams and believing in every single word. My rock, my best friend, my forever person, I love you so much.

Thank you to my editor Louise as always! I can't believe this is our fifth book together!!

And lastly, thank you to my very own book fairy: My graphic designer Cat!! I cannot express how much I love our creative relationship, our little lunch dates, and how you seem to just get me and my creative vision. I'm obsessed with your mind, especially when I give you the liberty to go rogue and come up with covers that genuinely blow my mind. Love you!!!!

ABOUT THE AUTHOR

Naomi Loud is an author of angsty dark romance. While her first love are words—spirituality and magic are the lenses through which she experiences the world and this heavily influences her writing, especially in her debut series "Was I Ever". She lives in Montreal, Canada with her husband and three cats but secretly wishes she could live underwater.

Printed in Great Britain
by Amazon